Praise fo

"*The Late Americans* is Brandon Ta[...] ments and misunderstandings and incompatibilities, [his characters are] all attempting to make peace with the cosmic bêtise of existence, to figure out how to live without compromising everything they value. It's beautiful and wrenching to watch them try."
—*The Boston Globe*

"Exquisitely sensitive . . . with flashes of beauty."
—*The New York Times*

"Erudite, intimate, hilarious, poignant . . . A gorgeously written novel of youth's promise, of the quest to find one's tribe and one's calling."
—*Oprah Daily*

"With *The Late Americans*, Taylor has at once deepened and moved beyond the traditional campus novel. . . . Taylor's empathy for his characters is bone-deep. . . . [A] bruising, brilliant second novel."
—*The Washington Post Book World*

"Brandon Taylor writes with such precision and perception that reading his work is an immersive experience: you inhabit his characters, you share their nerve endings. *The Late Americans* is a brilliant and electrifying symphony of a novel. I loved it."
—Lily King, author of *Writers & Lovers* and *Euphoria*

"This book assures and deepens Taylor's position as one of the most accomplished, important novelists of his generation. He is undoubtedly onto something expansively new in his sense of what the contemporary novel can do."
—*The Guardian*

"Brandon Taylor's third book is the most dazzling example of his sharp pen and keen observations of human nature yet. . . . Taylor develops his characters so precisely, they feel like close friends: recognizable, sometimes infuriating, and always worth following to the book's last page."
—*Harper's Bazaar*

"The best writer on work in America today."
—Garth Greenwell

"Amid financial concerns, artistic frustrations, and the judgments, jealousies, and posturing of their classmates, [Taylor's] characters find solace in moments of shared tenderness. . . . His multifaceted portrayals show each of them to be as innocent and as flawed as any human."
—*The New Yorker*

"Startlingly original."
—*The Wall Street Journal*

"I loved *The Late Americans* and its funny, merciless, brilliant portrayal of the beauty and pointlessness of art, and the absurdity and horror—and occasional transcendence—of being a person. Magnificent."
—Curtis Sittenfeld, author of *Romantic Comedy* and *Prep*

"One of the best contemporary writers on young queer creatives, Taylor continues the theme with this offering about a group of Iowa City friends . . . simultaneously chaotic, messy, and loving." —*Rolling Stone*

"Remarkable. If you're going to write about art, the folly of pursuing it and the irrefutable power of it, you should probably do it well. Taylor does it truthfully and beautifully." —*Financial Times*

"A beautiful writer. His tautly constructed sentences are as concrete and vivid as the poems that the hapless Seamus adores." —Associated Press

"Brandon Taylor has both a classic sensibility, expansive and elegant, and a razor-sharp ability to speak to the contemporary moment. *The Late Americans* is a full expression of his singular talent." —Emma Cline, author of *The Girls*

"*The Late Americans* is a dizzying plunge into the lives of young people making art in America in the era of survival capitalism, grappling over the big questions like they're fighting over a gun. Deep within their ambitions, their pettiness and lust, is the meaning and even grandeur they seek—and whether or not his characters ever find it, Brandon Taylor has. A bravura performance on the edge of a knife." —Alexander Chee, author of *How to Write an Autobiographical Novel*

"*The Late Americans* is a compelling, clever, funny, structurally audacious book of relentless psychological acuity, emotional resonance, and technical control, and reconfirms Brandon Taylor as one of the preeminent American authors of his generation." —*Hazlitt*

"Taylor's elegant works of fiction . . . keep a tight focus on their characters, like a magnifying glass. . . . Taylor's vision is unsparing, but never bleak. . . . He has a Chekhovian generosity that enables him to convey character with something like tenderness." —*Harper's Magazine*

"Taylor deftly explores the myth of youth's unbound possibilities as it plays out in the face of constraints of time, space, class, and wealth disparities. . . . The characters constantly strive to become better versions of themselves by embracing an ideal of passionate empathy that goes beyond pity or kindness, by striving to plumb the dark, even unspeakable parts of themselves." —NPR

"Taylor is a sharp chronicler of the body. In *The Late Americans*, the body is an instrument and an archive, vulnerable to the complicated violence of pleasure and work." —Raven Leilani, author of *Luster*

"Deftly directed by Taylor, characters swim in and out of the story, exploring a lived-in symphony of questions about what it means to make art, love truthfully, and live morally. . . . [His] novels are so big—they contain the world." —*Esquire*

"[An] intense, finely tuned book. Taylor is an inimitable talent."

—*Elle*

"Provocative . . . Through Taylor's signature intimacy, we see casual emotional devastation, prickly social interactions, and wry humor with keen clarity."

—*Vulture*

"Brandon Taylor's characters in *The Late Americans* are obsessed with art, money, integrity, success, survival—and with one another. They can be deliciously catty, but they're also desperate to be loved. And repulsed by that desperation. They are, in a word, human. Taylor realizes each character so fully, with such enviable—and often hilarious—granularity, that it's hard not to feel like I know these people, that I could pick up my phone right now and call any of them. It's the best kind of magic, this book. I'm already rereading it."

—Kaveh Akbar, author of *Calling a Wolf a Wolf* and *Pilgrim Bell*

"Brandon Taylor takes a new spin and reimagines the classic friend getaway with queer characters. . . . Contemporary readers will love this provocative but intimate novel about friendships, ambition, and community."   —*Cosmopolitan*

"Finely rendered."

—*Vanity Fair*

"Taylor sanctifies the earthly via his characters—not by elevating them but by revealing them as painfully human. . . . [A] productive tension between freedom and restriction gleams in Taylor's prose too. The language's force accumulates like prayer beads."

—*BOMB Magazine*

"A stunning work of fiction, with characters that are unforgettable and writing that is frequently breathtaking. I can't shout its praises enough."   —*BuzzFeed*

"Elegant and restrained."

—*Vox*

"Anyone who's ever struggled to find themselves while so many around them are doing the same (hello, everyone's early 20s) will find kinship in this novel."

—*Good Housekeeping*

"Tender and unflinching . . . written with bristling clarity, wicked wit, and audacious assuredness . . . A wonderful book."

—Colin Barrett, author of *Homesickness*

ALSO BY BRANDON TAYLOR

Real Life

Filthy Animals

The Late Americans

BRANDON TAYLOR

RIVERHEAD BOOKS

New York

RIVERHEAD BOOKS

An imprint of Penguin Random House LLC
penguinrandomhouse.com

Grateful acknowledgment is made for permission to reprint lines from the poem "A Top Won't Save You But Neither Will Prayer" by Derrick Austin. First published in *MumberMag* (December 28, 2020).

The Library of Congress has catalogued the Riverhead hardcover edition as follows:

Names: Taylor, Brandon (Brandon L. G.), author.
Title: The late Americans / Brandon Taylor.
Description: New York : Riverhead Books, 2023.
Identifiers: LCCN 2022021915 (print) | LCCN 2022021916 (ebook) |
ISBN 9780593332337 (hardcover) | ISBN 9780593332351 (ebook)
Subjects: LCGFT: Novels.
Classification: LCC PS3620.A93534 L38 2023 (print) |
LCC PS3620.A93534 (ebook) | DDC 813/.6—dc23
LC record available at https://lccn.loc.gov/2022021915
LC ebook record available at https://lccn.loc.gov/2022021916

First Riverhead hardcover edition: May 2023
First Riverhead trade paperback edition: April 2024
Riverhead trade paperback ISBN: 9780593332344

Printed in the United States of America
1st Printing

Book design by Cassandra Garruzzo Mueller

You know how you'd receive a god.
  What if it was
a portion of his flesh? What if you
  were terribly hungry?

DERRICK AUSTIN

The Late
Americans

The Late Americans

I n seminar, grad students on plastic folding chairs: seven women, two men. Naive enough to believe in poetry's transformative force, but cynical enough in their darker moments to consider poetry a pseudo-spiritual calling, something akin to the affliction of televangelists.

Outside, the last blue day in October. Snow in the forecast.

They discuss "Andromeda and Perseus," a poem submitted by Beth, who has reversed the title of the Titian painting in order to center Andromeda's suffering rather than the heroics of Perseus—rapist, killer, destroyer of women.

"The taking is as brutal as the captivity," says this squat girl from Montana.

The poem spans fifteen single-spaced pages, and contains, among other things, a graphic description of period sex in which menstrual blood congeals on a gray comforter. This is designated "the Gorgon's mark," in relation to "the iron stain" left on Medusa's robes following her decapitation by Perseus.

Around they go, taking in the poem's allusive system of images and its narrative density, the emotional heat of its subject matter, its increasing cultural salience re: women, re: trauma, re: bodies, re: life at the end of the world.

"I love the gestural improvisation of it all—so very Joan Mitchell," says Helen, who had once been some kind of Mormon child bride out in a suburb of Denver, and who now lives above a bar in downtown Iowa City, writing poems about dying children and pubic lice.

"I mean, like, so sharp, diamond sharp. Could cut a bitch, you know? God." Noli, nineteen, child prodigy. Disappointing her parents. Poetry instead of, what, medical school, curing cancer?

"Totally. So raw, though. So visceral."

"And heightened—" Mika, twenty-eight, Stevie Nicks impersonator in her bangles and boots and gauzy drapery.

"—charged-up, high-voltage shit—" Noli again, so talkative today. So chatty.

"Voice, voice, voice." Here, Linda, black from Tulsa. Braids. Glossy, perfect skin. She went to UT Austin, did a PhD in physics at MIT. Finished. Or dropped out. Either way, here in Iowa with the rest of them. In some kind of tension with Noli, also black, also brilliant. Not sisters. High-intensity mutual exclusion.

"Finally, something *real*," Noli says. Linda's gaze sharpens. "But totally rigorous. Like, not fake slam-poet shit. Just voice."

"I want this in my veins. Hard," Helen says.

The effluvia of praise washes over Beth, who receives their compliments with a placid glow. The instructor, never quite in contention for the Pulitzer but never quite *out* of it either, nods slowly as he presides over them like a fucking youth minister.

Or so Seamus imagined as he drowsed in half focus. Then, coming back to himself, to the room, becoming present, he really *looked*. Beth's lips were in a thin line, her eyebrows in deep grooves. Miserable despite the praise, when praise seemed so much the point of the poems they wrote. To be clapped on the back. Celebrated. Turned into modern saints and martyrs.

Curiouser and curiouser, thought Seamus, that a person, presented with what they wanted most, could seem so miserable about it.

Along the upper wall of the seminar room, trapezoidal panes of glass. The room was all sleek, dark-wood beams and soaring windows, barnlike in its effect. Early afternoon sunshine pooling on the scuffed floors. Locked cases of books by writing program alumni who had gone on to midlist glory.

The patina of prestige, so much like the corroded wax on the floorboards, had seen better days. That was the thing about prestige, though—the older and more moth eaten, the more valuable. There was a certain kind of poet for whom prestige was the point. The poetry *was* the prestige, and if no one saw you writing a poem, being a poet, then you were *not* a poet. For these poets, seminar was the zenith of their lives as artists. Never again would they have, on a weekly basis, such attention channeled upon their performance of poetry.

"This poem really troubles notions of reliability. Because, like, who is more an authority on an experience than the person doing the experiencing, right? But, like, the inconsistencies in the telling really make you wonder if the truth is really a palimpsest of falsehoods, and—" Helen again, though now interrupted by Garza, half Tunisian, half Quebecois, but raised in Toronto and Oakland.

"Totally. In this very Vicuña way, like in *Spit Temple*—"

"I prefer Moraga's take on personal history, and how we bridge gaps in the archive with—" Noreen, West Virginian with a faint lilt that might have been faked—it was curiously absent when she was drunk—cutting across Garza's response.

"Hartman tells us that archives are constructed in the manner of—" Noli, cutting in, too.

These sundry interruptions and redactions, all the skirmishes and misdirection. Like a dog finally catching its tail and chewing it down to the gristle. Seamus looked to his right at Oliver, who was listening intently with a pleased, receptive expression. How, Seamus wondered, could he take this all so seriously, as they wore on talking about the violence of the archive and Cherríe Moraga and Cecilia Vicuña, whose work was not even remotely on point for the poem at hand. This wasn't poetry. This was the aping of poetry in pursuit of validation. This was another kind of poetry theatric: If you just said enough names, people assumed you knew what you were talking about and tended to attribute the vagueness of the reference to their own ignorance. But Seamus had read both Moraga and Vicuña. He had read the critical essays of Saidiya Hartman—avant the Mac-Arthur, bien sûr—and the critical essays in response to Hartman's work. He knew America to be a war of contradicting archives. Different histories with their own particular turbulences.

It would have been easier for these poets to say that sometimes you lied and sometimes you were mistaken and sometimes the truth changed on you in the course of telling. That sometimes trauma reconfigured your relationship both to the truth and to the very apparatus of telling. But no, they went on signifying. Tethering their bad ideas to recognized names and hoping someone would call them smart, call them sharp, call them radical and right, call them a poet and a thinker and a mind, even if they were just children.

"And the part about the blood on the sheet! I mean!" Noli said. "Stunning. Irrefutable."

Seamus flipped back through the poem until he got to the line about the Gorgon's mark, which had surprised him in its venereal vividness. It had the vibe of a detail you *might* find in a good poem. As if out of O'Hara by way of Kooser.

But reading back over the line, Seamus felt tickled. What kind of person, what kind of poetic organizing intelligence, upon seeing menstrual blood on a bedsheet after not-great sex, thought of Medusa's decapitation? Too funny. Not the blood itself, but the pretentious linkage. *There* was the duress. The transubstantiation of the real thing into something so freighted with meaning that it collapsed in on itself. The whole poem became a joke. This variety of poem often surfaced in seminar: personal history transmuted into a system of vague gestures toward greater works that failed to register genuine understanding of or real feeling for those works. Self-deceptions disguised as confession.

Seamus giggled to himself.

The instructor, low troll of a man with a head of high white hair, looked at him. Paused.

"Something to add, Seamus?" Everyone looked at him then. This was, he knew, a way of marshaling attention to himself. It was the only charismatic trait he possessed, but he had no control over it. True, he could have tried harder. This too was a performance, but he considered it morally acceptable because he *knew* it was a performance. He didn't pretend it was poetry.

He shuffled the papers a moment, but then, breaking out into a little giggle, he said, "So, like, her pussy is a Gorgon head? Is that like a Trump thing?"

A little magic trick: silence, the rolling blackout of their anger. Then, gradually, the lights going back on. Annoyance. Irritation.

Ingrid Lundstrom said, "I think it's more saying that we live in a world that has turned women's bodies into objects of revulsion and pain—and, how our pleasure is not our own? I think we need to honor that."

Ingrid had been in his class at Brown. In their sophomore year, she got published in *The New Yorker* with a nakedly autobiographical poem about her father's conversion to evangelical Christianity and his subsequent self-immolation. She was the kind of poet whose work was chiefly about herself, as if all that had transpired in the existence of humankind was no more consequential than the slightly nervy account of her first use of a tampon. He thought her poems craven and beautiful and utterly dishonest.

"Yes, but, like, her cooter is full of Medusa blood. Am I being obtuse? Am I missing the allusion?"

Oliver tried to intercede, laughing. "Negative capability, right?" he said.

The instructor said, "We are here to witness the poem."

Seamus snorted. Ingrid replied dryly, "I just think it's important to remember that the speaker of the poem is clearly carrying a legacy of violence, and this ambivalence toward desire/body/love/want is valid."

Witness and *legacy of violence* and *valid*: such terms made poetry seminar feel less like a rigorous intellectual and creative exercise and more like a tribunal for war crimes. Seamus hated it very much—

not because he believed that trauma was fake, but because he didn't think it necessarily had anything to do with poetry.

"Are you a poet or a caseworker?" Seamus asked.

"What the fuck did you just say to me?"

Such withering piety, such righteous fury. He delighted in Ingrid's façade cracking.

"It's not a gendered term—unless you think it is. Now that would be sexist."

Ingrid stood and gave Seamus a bored, dismissive glance. Then she went to the sink in the back of the room to fill an electric kettle.

"You're being a child," Helen said, sotto voce.

Seamus made a show of screwing up his face and rubbing his eyes. He pouted.

"We are getting far afield here," the instructor said. He was looking straight up into the exposed beams, as though waiting for a signal from the divine.

"They're the ones calling names. My comments were textual," Seamus said. Through all of this, Beth stared into her notebook and scribbled furiously until she had soaked the corner of a page black with ink. Seamus leaned forward, elbows on his knees, watching her wrist wrench back and forth.

"Inappropriate."

"Asshole."

Such a chorus of opprobrium. Like the witches in *Macbeth*, but less fun. Less ridiculous glee.

"I'm triggered by your insults," Seamus said. "They remind me of my torturous childhood. Please stop."

Ingrid set the kettle on its stand and flicked the switch. It screeched as it came to life.

"The poem," the instructor said. "The poem is everything."

"Maybe you should take a breather, champ," Oliver said. He brought his hand to the back of Seamus's neck.

"You betcha, pal," Seamus said. He showed his teeth. Oliver just shook his head. But Seamus couldn't stop. He tasted the glut of their attention. The sweet iron tang of it. He was thirsty for more. The looks on their faces, the anger, the annoyance. So sure of themselves. Of their positions.

"I think we could all do with some fresh air," the instructor said. "Maybe we table for this week. You are free to go."

Oh, no fun. No fun at all. How unfair. Seamus grunted as he stood. Oliver followed. The rest of them remained in place, composed in various tableaux of waiting. Whispering to one another, exchanging notebooks and pointed looks. Seamus wondered if he and Oliver alone were being dismissed like disruptive children, while the others were all waiting for a second, secret seminar—the real class—to begin. He stood there a few seconds more, but then felt Oliver's hand at the crook of his arm, pulling at him.

Well, fine, he thought. All right.

"Enjoy your yoga," Seamus called over his shoulder, and Noli replied, "Enjoy your bowel impaction."

Them on the bridge, Seamus and Oliver.

Seamus hated, but couldn't resist, the compulsion to relive the harrowing of seminar. Same story, every week, really: so and so said this, so and so said that, can you *believe*? A silly question. Belief had died with the rise of the contemporary, the instant. Belief being one of those hangovers from some other era, a mere shading of history. But then again, they were fags for belief. They were poets, after all.

"I hate when people title their poems after paintings. Ekphrasis is so dead, man. Bleak and needy shit."

"Yeah, I guess that's right. Fatuous intellectual cachet and all."

"It's what you do when you know your art is bad. Is explicitness supposed to be a substitute for depth? I don't know."

"Kidding themselves."

"Totally."

"Abstract nonsense."

"Yep."

Underfoot the swaying bridge, sluggish green water. The bramble and dark mud of the riverbanks, the golden grass. Oliver's ruddy cheeks and the scent of his loose-leaf tobacco. Almost unbearably tender, the look in his eyes.

Not for the first time, Seamus imagined Oliver's face going grotesque with pain. Imagined the slant of his mouth in suffering, beautiful in the way of those early, crude carvings of Christ, the suffering and the beauty one and the same. Seamus turned away from Oliver, took in the industrial park and its long tusks of steam. The cars on the bridge near the library ambling along.

"It's nice we got out early, though," Oliver said.

Seamus nodded, though for him the timing was kind of annoying. Seminar could go until six or end at four. The variability prevented him from working on seminar days. It would have been too embarrassing trying to explain to the shift lead why he needed the flexibility on his start time, so he just kept the day free. Yet now, with class lasting barely an hour, he had almost the whole afternoon free.

"Nice is a word for it. If you don't work for a living."

Oliver laughed.

"What's so funny?"

"Just the way you say that. *Work for a living*. It's almost pretentious. Weren't you just skewering fake piety?"

"It's fake piety to support yourself?" Seamus asked, somewhere between irony and earnestness. Oliver just laughed again. "What's so fucking funny about it? Not all of us have money. Or parents. Some of us really do have to support ourselves."

"The unshackled rage of the working-class white male, how terrifying," Oliver said. He was really cracking up now, and Seamus felt a hard knot at the base of his throat. He wanted to shove Oliver into the river.

"You're first against the wall," Seamus said.

"I've made my peace with it."

"I know you're joking, but it still sounds terrible. Sure, I can be a jerk, whatever, but I do give a fuck about this shit. Like, poetry. It matters to me. And it makes me sick, sitting in that room every week while they fucking braid each other's pussy hair about their trauma or whatever. When I could be doing a shift. Paying my rent. Working. Like normal people. So that I can write poems. That they just *shit* on. Because they're not about being molested. It's such a sham." He grunted.

"Hey, I'm on your side. You know I love your work," Oliver said. Seamus shrugged.

"Group therapy." Seamus bit down at the corner of his thumb, chewed away at a translucent sliver of dead skin. Then, like a penny at the bottom of a well, down and down below the surface of his anger, an idea glinted.

"You know what I should do?"

"Get drunk? That's my plan," Oliver said.

"I should write a poem called 'Gorgon's Head' and watch those uptight assholes lose it."

"Do it," Oliver said, leaning against the rail. The wind, raspy with cold, moved through his hair.

Again, the leading edge of an image as forceful as a premonition: Oliver's face gone lean and taut with agony.

"I should, right?"

"You'd get tossed out. Are you nuts or what?"

"But it's funny, right? Come on!" Seamus slapped Oliver's shoulder with the back of his hand. "It's funny!"

Oliver gazed across the river. Three modernist buildings crouched low on the banks, like a herd of grazing mammals. The bridge was studded with flags from each of the countries represented in the student body. They snapped in the wind. Oliver pushed off the rail. Seamus followed. The bridge pulsed low under them, alive almost.

"You hate the idea? You think it's stupid?"

"I don't," Oliver said. "But is it worth it? Like, why?"

"Because it's funny!" Seamus gripped Oliver's shoulders and shook him hard.

Oliver jerked back and Seamus felt sad, then annoyed.

"You think I'm going to hurt you?"

"Not at all. But people have feelings, Seamus. I think you forget that sometimes. Or you think it's something to make fun of. But people do have feelings, and it's okay that they do."

"So I hurt your feelings? I didn't shake you that hard."

"Not *me*."

On the river trail, they passed the modernist galleries, which housed various exhibits and shows. The previous fall, Seamus and Oliver had gone to a talk on race and the poetry of John Berryman in one of the galleries. Some of their classmates had been there too—Garza, Linda, Ingrid. During the talk, the speaker, who was white, had used the word *nigger* while quoting a source. It seemed to come out without her knowing it, but the room noticed and grew cold then quite hot. Seamus felt a frisson of glee. The talk up to that point had been tedious, mainly because he agreed with it all—racism bad, Berryman good, but also bad re: race. White people talking about racism had the effect of a news report. But here was *theater*. For days after, the incident got retold and reconfigured. Linda ended up on the local news recounting the violence that had befallen her at this talk, and the speaker was put on leave in the lit department, and then asked not to return to her post in the spring. She made the mistake of writing a long article about it for *The Guardian*, which Linda shared on Twitter and mocked. It turned into an ugly mess on culture blogs and Instagram, and now Linda was verified on social media, and the speaker was an occasional guest columnist for *The New York Times* on matters of cancel culture, which was not real except that sometimes it kind of was.

There was a hostility to public life now. Or maybe that hostility had always existed, and what was new was simply the directing of it toward people who had long been exempt. Seamus thought that the whole thing had the absurd drama of a great play. All the Shakespearean misunderstanding and misspeaking, everything doubling in its extremity and consequences until it ruptured into something truly cathartic. Except that there was no catharsis. Just people hardening into the caricatures of their roles.

But Linda was right. The speaker *had* broken the social contract when she said that word aloud, and, as had been the rule since the very beginning of society itself, there was a price for breaking the contract, for saying what you shouldn't say, for going off script.

They walked on in silence, though Seamus could still hear the flapping of the flags on the bridge. The sky was a deep, tranquil blue. The sun warmed his face.

"I just don't want you to get into anything. Distracts from the work," Oliver said.

"But it's funny, though, right? Like, be real, you have to laugh. It's insane not to laugh." Seamus hated the plaintiveness in his own voice, how much he needed Oliver to side with him. But more than that, he hated that Oliver didn't see how objectively hilarious it would be to write a poem that exposed the falseness that dominated their program and their discourse and the whole sham of American art.

Oliver sighed. "Yes, it's funny to title your poem 'Gorgon Head' and then make everyone read it. And yeah, I'd laugh. But her poem was really personal. It was about her life. And that's not funny, right? People's lives?"

"Why don't you just go to nursing school?" Seamus barked.

"Jesus," Oliver said. "Maybe you *do* hate women."

Seamus's neck got hot at the insinuation. This was not about *women*. This was not about *feminism*. This was about a hollow and false ethic in art. Bad art knew no gender.

"Because I hate lazy generalities?"

"Do whatever you want, man. You're determined, I know. But don't be surprised when it blows up in your face," Oliver said. No heat. No malice. But that only made Seamus feel worse. The resignation of it.

The water frothed near the shore under the struts of the bridge. Some plastic bottles had been caught there and filled slowly with river silt. Seamus crouched to scoop up some rocks. He lobbed them into the center of the river, each descent dark and irrevocable.

"I'm not a monster," Seamus said. "Despite your implication."

"I don't think you're a monster. Like I said, you're determined. I just don't get why."

"Some pal." Seamus wiped the grit from the rocks against Oliver's jacket. "Thank you for the support."

"Well, I am your friend. That's why I'm trying to talk you out of being an asshole. For your own sake."

"Sure, I'm the asshole."

"I wish you hadn't gotten that on me."

"And I wish you had a sense of humor!" Seamus gave Oliver a quick, hard punch to the side and took off up the path. He had an easy, smooth stride, but Oliver was taller and his legs ate up the distance between them. Seamus soon had to slow down and jog backward. He tried to tamp down the urge to cough and clear his lungs, but he ended up bent over, hands on his knees, hacking up a yellowish glob onto the concrete. It hitched and burned as it came up and out.

He had to stop smoking.

Oliver struck him hard between the shoulders three times, and each slap made the dark of Seamus's eyelids swim red and blue.

At the last one, the hardest, he felt himself breathe free and opened his eyes.

Penance.

Seamus worked evening and morning shifts in the hospice kitchen—broths and stocks, chop and peel, shit like that. He'd gotten the job when he first came to Iowa City because, unlike Oliver and some of his classmates, he didn't get the *good* fellowship, and the nonfiction goons across the river had taken all the comp/rhet sections for themselves. The director had looked at him with somnolent pity. "Sometimes, our students have had great luck finding jobs in the area," she said in what she must have imagined was a helpful tone. "Little things to supplement."

He knew a lot about that word, *supplement*.

At Brown, among the lesser talented of the very rich, his scholarship had accounted for tuition but just barely that. His other needs multiplied in the dark like some invasive predatory species: textbooks, meal plans, shower gel, shampoo, toothpaste, laundry detergent, his part of the dorm fridge rental, the dorm itself, notebooks and pencils, tech fees, rec fees. How amazing that, at college, even basic amenities were considered luxuries and therefore to be covered at your own expense. It had cost him quite a lot to get up the money for the SAT and ACT, for the AP exams, money he'd gotten by gigging in bakeries and mowing lawns. But that wouldn't do for college. There was simply too much need.

So in undergrad, he supplemented his scholarship not with paper writing or academic scut work in department offices (the faculty did not like him), but with shifts at a bleak hospital kitchen in

Providence. The women took a liking to him, taught him the rhythms of cooking for dozens, for hundreds. He learned the intricacies of scale and mass consumption, and what waste there was—for there was always waste—he took home and stored. When he needed a quick job, he went to hospital kitchens. They were always hiring. People were always quitting, because they had no choice but to hire the desperate, the tired, the needy, people who were already on a carousel of shit jobs that chewed them up. Hospital kitchens were home to junkies, ex-cons, and old women—people who could never afford the hospitals where they worked.

Seamus was suited to that kind of work. He liked the cooking, and he had, in a way that was not dissimilar from writing poetry, an affinity for the long, repetitive hours it took to make anything good and for the tedious preparatory work. He felt best when he was alone in the kitchen at the end of a long day, peeling and chopping vegetables or making stock for the week's soups. The simmering constancy of it. Alone in a kitchen, he was at peace. Not free to wander in his thoughts, exactly, so much as existing in a state of thoughtlessness. Nothing could bother him.

Since there was still so much blue sky left in the day, he thought he'd ride over and see if he could get in a few hours at the hospice kitchen to help take the sting off the month's bills. He wondered how people with families could get by on a grad student's stipend. He thought of one guy he knew in the lit department, Gerard, who had two small children and a wife.

Gerard was studying something useless, something like medieval poetry and form, and his wife was looking after their children. Sometimes, he saw them down at the corner of St. Mary's for the weekly food bank. It was the height of foolishness, academia. You sank down and down in debt, in desperation, in hunger, so that you could feel a little special, a little brilliant in your small, dark corner of the universe, knowing something that no one else knew. Art was worth many things, but was it worth putting your whole family on the brink of extinction? Seamus didn't understand Gerard's calculus. He loved poetry, but he couldn't always square it with the essentials of life.

Like, if he had a family and responsibilities, he wasn't sure that he would pick poetry over them. And in that case, if he could think of a set of circumstances that could justify turning away from poetry, then why bother at all? This kept him up at night, wondering if he lacked the resolve to be the kind of poet he wanted to be. But then he remembered that he was just another white man in the world pondering the extinction of poetry, which had survived the ending of the world innumerable times. It would survive whatever contemporary apocalypse he could dream up. Poetry didn't need him. It certainly didn't need his elegies for its demise. It was a delusion, he knew, the delusion of everyone whose life had been touched by poetry, that somehow poetry needed them to go on existing. But it did not.

Poets. God, fucking poets.

The hospice was a ten-bedroom house on a grassy tract of land out on the edge of town. This had once been the good part of town but was now populated by a strip mall, five pharmacy chains, a dialysis center, a plasma bank, a check-cashing place, and three fast-food restaurants. There was an apartment complex, a row of tan stone buildings set front to back with their edges abutting a road. On the other side, the trees on the soggy, sloping hillsides were dotted with white houses and trailers with gravel driveways. The hospice had once been the home of an old family in Iowa City who had died out sometime after World War II. The heirs, distant cousins in New Hampshire, didn't want the house, which was far away and old and ate up taxes. They got rid of it by selling to a company that was bought by another company that was bought by yet another company. The house pinged around a series of shell corporations, absorbed and spun off until it was purchased by a national organization that turned old homes into nursing facilities and hospice care for the old and infirm. The thought was that people shouldn't have to sit alone in warehouses like bad furniture that no one wanted, that people deserved to die with some semblance of human comfort.

In the hospice, Seamus noticed, the residents liked to talk about animals that had gone extinct. Tortoises and obscure mammals, birds and amphibians, fish. It kept their minds occupied, enumerating all the creatures that had ceased to exist. Some of the nurses tried to fight it, thinking it was too morbid, but the residents would not be moved. Every day at mealtime, when they gathered at the long table in the kitchen or out back in the gardens, the residents ate their soft food or swirled their plastic cups of water and talked about the decline of speciation. It cheered them, like finding a rare piece of hard candy in their pockets or a getting phone call from their children or nieces and nephews. Little bursts of pleasure.

Seamus often skimmed their conversations for odd facts to tell Oliver about later. Did he know, for example, that warm winters meant that tick-borne diseases were on the rise? And that the migration of deer from the East Coast out into the west was causing a migration of Lyme disease, and also the death of ash trees and cedars? It was all connected in a prickly web. Ticks and deer and trees and the warmth of the short days of winter.

In the spring, they planted flowers and vegetables in the back. In the fall, the residents took turns raking leaves. Checking the soil for compost potential. Looking after the small family of deer who lived in the woods. The residents were active here, spent their days in motion. They had a reason to get up in the morning. Even though it was all just a highly orchestrated and carefully managed illusion.

Upstairs, they suffered. In their dark rooms, they lay in their hospital beds while nurses sponged off their sweat and wiped up their vomit and shit. They shivered and groaned as their bones broke down or their muscles atrophied. Everyone was always so optimistic at first, when they arrived at the hospice. See, look at how beautiful it is. See, you will have a view of these trees. It's hardly even like being on the East Side. Oh, look, there are ducks in the pond. There is a knitting circle every day. Once a month, a group of young children comes to read and do crafts. The busy politeness you offered the god of dying in order to pretend for a little while that you were simply on a brief respite from your life, that before long you would get to return. But that wore off. Some came out of it, joined the ongoing projects of hospice life: the garden, the compost, the deer, the bird-watching, the knitting, the crafts. And some did not. They sat by their windows and waited. And then they died.

At the hospice, Seamus propped his bike against the side wall in the garden and hopped up the steps into the mudroom. Eunice's radio was playing Chet Baker while she brushed and inspected a shipment of mushrooms from the local foragers. Seamus knocked his boots against the door jamb.

"You ain't on today," she said.

"Got sprung early."

"You better not be cutting out on that lesson."

Seamus put his hands up in innocence. "Pat me down, sarge. I'm good for it." Eunice waved him on.

"You can help with the bisque."

"How elegant," he said.

"Do it up nice the way you do."

Seamus leaned over Eunice at the table and pretended to be checking her work with the mushrooms. She had gout in her left knee and complained of swollen ankles. She sat at a stool to do this minor but careful work. Passing the brush around the button caps and across the tender gills of the oyster mushrooms. The morels like something out of a fairy tale.

"It'll do," he said.

Eunice swatted at him. "Get."

He found Lena at the counter, cutting aromatics. She was on the other side of forty, but she had skinny arms and the kind of stubby ponytail Seamus associated with girls from his middle school. Her hair was box-dye copper with black roots. She looked up at him, watery green eyes, and gave him a smile, showing the craggy craters of her gums, missing teeth on the right side of her mouth.

"Bisque," he said.

"You know I hate this shit."

Seamus gave his hands a wash and draped a dry cloth over his shoulder. Lena leaned to the side and watched him survey the shit job she'd done dicing the aromatics.

"You got the garlic too early," he said. "It's going to give up the goods before it even has a chance to get hot."

"I just do what that thing tells me to do," she said, waving her phone at him. It was the PDF he had downloaded to both of their phones last year when he had come on, a file of recipes and ideas about how to cook for the dying and the almost dead. Eunice said it hurt her eyes, so he'd printed her a copy with extra-big type. Lena was good with a phone, though she had no sense of a recipe's intrinsic sense of order. She tended to want to get it all done up front, then knock it off one step after another. She could follow, but she could not—or at least did not—understand what any of it meant.

"Don't worry."

With the back of his hand, Seamus moved the slimy, poorly diced garlic along the cutting board and into a metal bowl for compost. There he added the onions and their skins that Lena had butchered. He peeled a fresh pile of onions, and pulled the knife through their bulk with one certain motion. He loved that first bite of the knife through the material wet of the ingredients. He could read, in that very first moment, the final taste of the dish. It was just an onion, but in bisecting it, he felt a little closer to himself.

The partial cuts, first vertically and then horizontally, getting a dice the cheap way. Hot oil in the pot, waiting for it to shimmer. The sizzle of the onions and celery. Tossing them around, letting them settle, sweat. Eunice's radio down in the mudroom, Chet Baker's perfect, clear horn, the sweet sadness of his music rising up to them out of the under dark.

The frustration from seminar fell away from him. In this place, he was free of all that horseshit. It was just him and the sweating onions. The garlic he shucked swiftly of its paper, and then—one hard whack with the back of his knife—turned it to pulp. He ran his knife through it to break it up, keep it from getting too gummy.

That instant allium odor, sweet and pungent. Into the pot with the onions and celery.

He opened a can of whole San Marzano tomatoes and wet his fingertips in the pulpy juice. He liked that metallic aftertaste. He strained and mashed the tomatoes with his wooden spoon. The hiss of the veg in the pot went sharp, so he reached over and poured in mushroom broth that he had made himself last week. It squelched the hiss and got the veg out of contact with the pot bottom. This he simmered. In went the tomatoes then, all mashed like tartare. And, finally, the rice. He ladled in some of the can water. Salt. Just a little sugar.

Lena had been watching him the whole time. "I would have just put all that shit in there and left it to go," she said.

"Yeah, well. You kind of do that. But the order. It's important."

"Your mama teach you that?"

"No."

"She didn't cook for you?"

Seamus set the lid on the pot.

"I'm going to do the dishes."

"I bet she must have liked having you around then. Doing all the cooking."

Seamus stacked the lunch dishes in the sink and scooped up what he'd dirtied with his prep. He ran the water hot into the deep sink and lathered the bowls, the cups. The plates. The pans and pots. Up to his elbows in the biting water.

No, his mother had not cooked for him. His mother, when he thought about her now with the benefit and generosity of adulthood, had suffered from debilitating headaches. She spent her days lying in bed. His father worked in construction, splitting bricks and working the roads in summer, pouring asphalt so that in the winter he could be a bad actor who toured the Midwest in small company productions of *Hamlet* and *Othello*. Most often he played Iago, but sometimes he was also Desdemona's father.

One night, his father came down wrong during a tech rehearsal and broke his foot. It didn't heal right or something, and an infection set up. His father lost the left foot. And some of his fingers. He almost died from sepsis. For some reason, his mother had blamed herself for the injury and the subsequent trouble. She said that they had abandoned him—hadn't been vigilant enough, hadn't checked the wound the way they should have. She blamed herself because she couldn't get out of bed, and blamed Seamus because, well, with her not getting out of bed, it was on him to help his father. And apparently he hadn't done enough.

His mother loved his father more than she loved him. They spent most of their time in the hospital at his father's bedside. He missed two or three weeks of school, had to be held back a year. His father went on disability, and he grew fat and tough.

Seamus thought with a silly kind of meanness that if he were another kind of writer, a tacky writer, he could write about *that*. About the smell of his father's rotting foot. About the simultaneous brightness and dullness of the beige room where his father did rehabilitation at the hospital, watching him fasten himself into plastic limbs that pinched and bit. Or watching him stretch the partial nubs of his fingers as wide as they would go, and the anger in his eyes when he found that he could no longer do this simple task. Outside the window of the rehab room, there had been a small garden with a cedar tree in it. Seamus spent a great deal of time looking at that tree while his father cursed as he was Velcroed into and out of temporary prosthetics. Or he could write about the smell of pills sweating in their plastic cylinder, like sea salt and shit.

Once, his father asked Seamus to put ointment on his leg. Seamus squeezed the oily white cream onto his fingers. He streaked it across the tan, knitted surface of his father's leg. He recoiled, surprised. He'd thought the flesh there would be dead and cold, but instead his father was warm and lightly furred. The thinness of the skin, the loose, fibrous quality of the muscle underneath, and the tingling static of something alive. Vividly, painfully alive. His father hissed.

"You can't do anything," he said.

"I'm sorry," Seamus said, "I'm so sorry."

"Get away from me. Go away."

He might write about that, being sent away to stay with his grandparents for the summer in Pennsylvania. Their dark house in the middle of a field of yellow grass, as if the land were unwilling to believe that spring and then summer had come. Everything about the Pennsylvania house was cold and half eclipsed.

His grandparents were so polite to him that it felt like estrangement. He ate their bitter breakfast and their cold lunch. For dinner, they had strange pies made of offal and other things. The house smelled like vinegar and embalming fluid. They did not speak to him often, and he spent a lot of time reading to himself. When he returned to his parents, he was taller and paler. His parents looked like their anger and their pain and their sadness had burned them through, leaving only the struts of their foundations.

But no one had a happy childhood. No one had a good life. Human pain existed in a vast supply, and people took from it like grain from a barn. There was pain for you and pain for you and pain for you—

agony enough for everyone. The pain of his childhood was of such a common source that it embarrassed him. Perhaps it was this that he resented in the work of his peers. It wasn't that their lives were worse than his or that his life was better than theirs—it was that they all had the same pain, the same hurt, and he didn't think anyone should go around pretending it was something more than it was: the routine operation of the universe. Small, common things—hurt feelings, cruel parents, strange and wearisome troubles.

These were not worth poetry, surely. But he knew, in a way that was more feeling than knowledge, that if he wrote a poem about it, about his life, they would call it brilliant. They would say it was his best work, as if everything he had ever done before had been mere illusion, smokescreen. He knew they would call it *good*, call it *vulnerable*, and what was worse than that?

Seamus hosed down the dishes and hung them on the rack to dry. He took his time arranging them, setting the plates into the slots above the sink. Arranging the forks and spoons at diagonals so the water ran along the grooves of the rack, collected, and fell in a stream down into the drain. He liked a clean kitchen, a regimented kitchen. It was the way he'd been trained in that first hospital. Everything in its place. No slick surfaces. No knives pointing out the wrong way.

Under his T-shirt, his back had gotten sweaty from the kitchen's heat. He squirmed and pulled his shirt free of his shoulders.

"Swamp back," he said to Lena, passing her. "I gotta change."

Down he went into the mudroom. Eunice was still playing Chet Baker. She had gotten somewhere, he saw. In the small bathroom, he shucked his shirt and blotted himself dry, then pulled on a fresh shirt and a sweater. His gums tingled. He patted down his pockets, but his cigarettes must have been in his coat up on the hook in the kitchen.

He peeked through the mudroom door at the top of the stairs.

"Chile, he swear he know everything."

"I just let him go. Hey, better him than me."

"Well, according to him, he is better."

Seamus could hear his own blood pounding in his ears. How fucking embarrassing. But he couldn't go down without risking the steps creaking, and he couldn't go in without them knowing he had heard them. He kind of wanted them to know that he had heard them, but he *liked* Eunice and Lena. That made it worse. He just held his breath and waited for what he thought was five minutes, but which could have been years or just seconds. Into the kitchen he went, smiling at them, wondering if they saw him trying to play off how he felt. He couldn't do or say anything different. That would have made it all worse. That would have been acting. But he *was* acting. He had already been conscripted into acting. They all had their little parts to play in this moment.

"Forgot my coat," he said. He took the chore jacket off the hook and put it on. "Watch the pot for me."

Lena laughed at his bad joke. Eunice smiled at him.

"You bet, boss man."

Seamus flinched. Then descended into the dark of the mudroom.

The inside of his nose burned, and he brought his hand up to check for a nosebleed. The skin was so hot with shame it shocked him.

Seamus smoked out on the garden steps. The cold had deepened as it descended. Out over the tree line, the glinting refractory of the town's edge. The high-output glow of the CVS across the highway blunted into gauzy white by the moisture in the air.

Smoking near the building was technically against regulations, but out in the garden there were allowances. A certain softness to the rule. They were in the business of mercy, after all, and seeing your beloved father or mother or whoever die was enough to drive you to smoking. But it was the evening, and the garden was empty except for Seamus. Turning over his bad feelings about the moment when he'd snapped at those girl poets. Though he did laugh remembering how he'd used the word *cooter*, which he hadn't used in years. It had come on him so suddenly: *cooter*.

That was the closest he'd come to a poem in what felt like a lifetime.

In his first year, Seamus had written three villanelles about a young Jesuit at the end of World War I who receives the news of the armistice just as he has woken from a wet dream. Seamus wanted to write about the profane and the sacred, flesh and spirit, the death of God and the life of man, and the giving way of old things. He wanted to write of the comic circumstances of life and the universe, and the whole dark mystery. He wanted a great many things, and he had boiled it down to those three poems, but when the time came for discussion, no one said a word about his pieces.

It was only after the professor said, "Well, certainly someone has to have felt *something*," that Oliver raised his hand and said, "The second piece does something interesting with form." A shiver went through the room, and someone else said, "Yeah, totally, yeah." The conversation whirred to life, and the discussion broadened to take in the scope of history and what it meant to be writing about World War I in today's world of forced migrations and drone strikes and the famine in Yemen. What it meant to be writing about World War I and Old World suffering at a time when there was so much New World suffering, and Linda said, "I think it's frankly Western European masturbation about the one time in their lives they felt like the prey instead of the predator—like, boohoo." Helen mentioned that another interesting point was the lack of critique of the Jesuits, "and, like, colonialism, what about that?" Garza responded, "What about colonialism, exactly?" And then Helen replied, "Totally!" Garza said, "No, I meant, like, what do you mean by colonialism in this context?" Which prompted an embarrassed shuffle and then a defense, "The Catholics? Latin America? Hello?"

"To me," someone interjected, "the biggest issue here is that the author has substituted formal stricture for emotional rigor, and seems unwilling to engage with the political dimension such a choice entails?"

Seamus had looked up from his scribbled notes to squint at the person who had spoken. It was Ingrid. She'd looked at him with her pale green eyes and bright blond eyebrows fixed in a perfect expression of lucid hatred.

After class, he went home and tore up all his poems and all drafts. Then he flung the bits from his window, and down they had rained like so many white leaves, landing on the top of the porch roof.

That was the first and the last time he had put something up for discussion in seminar.

He started begging off from including his pieces in course packets, telling himself they didn't deserve his work. Then, later, he convinced himself that this was actually humility, an act of humble regard for *the process*. That his lack of submission was really about submitting totally to the nature of writing. That he would turn something in when it was ready, and it wasn't about having his ego assuaged with praise or whatever, he said, chiefly to Oliver.

After that seminar, he and the professor had met for coffee to discuss his work. Seamus brought up obliquely the idea that he wasn't writing for now or to now, for that matter, that he wanted to write for the eternal, for the everlasting, for the hereafter and for yesterday, forever and ever, amen, and the professor, north of sixty-five and weary with gratitude for life and liberty and the American way, who wore Wranglers and smoked American Spirits every morning as the sun came up, looked at him with passive approval.

"It can be difficult," he started to say, and Seamus drew a sharp breath because he felt as though he was on the cusp of being understood for the first time in his whole life, but then the professor shook his head and sipped his black coffee. Seamus felt something roll up and store itself away from him.

"What can?" Seamus asked, but the professor was already fiddling with the edge of his newspaper. He looked startled that Seamus had asked him to continue his thought.

"Oh, I was just thinking that it can be difficult in your first year, but it gets better."

Seamus felt stupid for having expected something more to follow from the phrase *It can be difficult*, as if he'd somehow been tricked into thinking that this person, this professor, cared about him.

It was a problem in the world, he thought, people going around pretending to care about others when they really didn't. Or else, people feeling that they had to go around pretending that they cared about others when in fact they did not, or could not, or were without room in their lives to do so. He could understand that, at least—that sometimes your life was so filled with other things that there was no room for other people and their stuff. But perhaps he was overthinking this whole thing, and perhaps the professor did care about him and his work, and that this was not just a thing people said to make themselves feel better, *It gets better*. Perhaps this was an attempt, a genuine attempt, at an intervention in his life. Perhaps this was the moment he'd look back on and think, Yes, that's when it all changed. But in the cynical part of his mind and his heart, Seamus could not help himself in discounting and discarding the professor's sentiment even as he smiled and nodded and said, "You're right, you're right."

That day in the café, they talked about the three villanelles and the difficulty of writing in old forms, of trying to bend them around to make them say something new, and Seamus hated the professor a little more with every word. He despised the suggestion that he should make his poems say something new, since that posited a progressive view of literature, located the importance of a piece in its being contemporary. The professor's eyes were bright with the effort to connect or reach, and this too was something that Seamus resented. Why couldn't his professor look at him like a peer, like an equal, rather than a riddle of pedagogy? He quietly sipped his coffee, and when he reached the bottom of his mug, he pretended there was more to drink. The professor gestured in loose orbits to poets dead and alive, of this moment and of the last, and Seamus thought, God, this is vulgar. This is so fucking vulgar. Just gross.

When his professor asked at the end of that first term why Seamus had stopped including his work in the packet, Seamus had just said, "Oh, you know. It can be difficult."

Seamus put out his cigarette and breathed smoke. The gate at the edge of the garden opened and he heard someone walk toward him. The grass hissed underfoot. He squinted along the wall, blue-white in the dark.

"You got another one?" came a raspy voice.

The man passed into the light of the kitchen window. He was tall, bullish in a trucker cap and old-fashioned glasses, with a double bar running between the lenses.

"Sure." Seamus flipped open the pack. The man took one of the cigarettes, but instead of lighting up, he looked at it.

"These one of them funny boys?"

"What do you mean?"

The man examined the pack in Seamus's hand and then frowned. "I don't know them kind."

"American Spirits," Seamus said, then feeling embarrassed, "They're just smokes, man. Take it easy."

The man's look of judgment did not soften, but Seamus took it on the chin.

"Thanks," he said, then, lighting up with a red plastic lighter, he inhaled. "This is like smoking potpourri."

Seamus did laugh at that. He had gone almost noseblind to the scent of American Spirits, but early on, the smell had been the thing he liked most about them. His high school English teacher had smoked them. He'd bought Seamus his first pack. Mr. Fulton, a balding man with a wide mouth and watery eyes. Mr. Fulton, whose semen had tasted like damp hay.

In college, American Spirits became shorthand for a certain kind of young person they all wanted to be. Stylishly unkempt in the way of the 1960s Greenwich Village crowd, but in far-flung college towns where all they had was affectation. But that kind of putting-on had gone out with stomp-clap-yeah in the mid-2000s, and marooned them all in a sea of cold, sterile irony. It was now outré to smoke American Spirits, but Seamus couldn't break the habit. His parents smoked Menthol 100s.

"Tobacco's a sweet plant," Seamus said.

"Don't I know it."

The man leaned against the wall by the window, and Seamus watched him. "You work here?"

"Kitchen," Seamus said.

"Must pay decent, you smoking these things."

"It's all right."

"Mmm," the man laughed a little, one eye pinched closed in the smoke.

"What do you do?"

"Oh," the man said. "*What do you do*. You must be in school."

"That obvious?"

The man dumped his ashes against the wall, drew the cigarette back to his lips and shrugged.

"I guess so. Fair enough."

Seamus didn't always know how to talk to townies. If he was supposed to be obeisant or obsequious or haughty, if he was supposed to pretend that grad students weren't parasites. Sometimes, the townies didn't want to do the two-step of pretending to care about higher education, but sometimes they did. Seamus followed. He didn't know how to lead. How to have a real conversation with someone who didn't care about what he cared about.

The man went on smoking. He let his eyes drift closed. The cold cement steps made Seamus's ass numb.

"It's gonna get bitter tonight," the man said.

"Yeah, probably."

"I didn't put up my hens. I better get going. Hey, thanks for the smoke."

"You bet," Seamus said.

The man went back along the wall, bracing himself with his right hand, smoking with the left, but before he was gone he turned back.

"Hey, man. You want to see something?"

Seamus lifted his eyebrows.

"See what?"

The man nodded to the long driveway. Seamus looked back through the kitchen window, where Lena was wiping down surfaces. He stood up slowly, shaking out the numbness in the backs of his thighs, and followed the man into the dark.

They walked a little way down the crunching gravel, along the wooden fence posts that lined the driveway. The man was smoking as they went along, not talking, which made Seamus's throat dry. The anticipatory silence of it. He had a thought about what all this meant. About where it was going and why. They climbed over the fence and stepped onto a shaded path. Seamus kept his eyes on the back of the man's head. The white of his nape. He made his way carefully, but the man moved with such an easy, loping stride that Seamus was a little in awe of it. They reached the top of the hill and then hitched awkwardly down the opposite slope.

They were in what looked to be a dirt roundabout.

The man stood with his hands on his hips, at the center of what had once been a trailer park, and surveyed the long white trailers. The RVs. The campers. A utility pole shone yellow like a sick bruise high up over them. An array of dirt paths led to the ruins of these homes, these lives. It felt like a lonely, sad place.

"My old man owns this shithole," the man said.

"Owns what exactly?"

"This land. He used to lease it out, let people park their trailers here. The bubble—before it went pop, you know."

"The bubble?" Seamus asked.

"You know, with Obama and them. All the people, suddenly, needing a place. We opened up this little lot to them, and they stayed, and paid rent, but then it got a little worse, and with no jobs, because ol' Raghead sent them overseas, people was in a bad way. And we had to close down because nobody was paying the rents on these things."

"Oh," Seamus said. He didn't mention that the recession had started before Obama came into office. Both because there was no point to the argument and because the truth did not change the material reality of what had happened to this place and to these people. The names, really—the names of history—did not matter. The who did what to whom and when. Petty facts and details. But when you were in it. Before the present became the past and before the past became history, when it was your family going hungry or your town losing their jobs, getting wrung out, it didn't matter if you got the blame pinned on the right son of a bitch. It didn't matter if you could recite the tenets, or the lines of descent, of the class traitors. That was just stuff. Republicans. Democrats. Conservatives. Liberals. Libertarians. Communists. Socialists: Whatever made you feel good at night. They were all just kidding themselves. Seamus kept his mouth closed. Looked into the busted windows and the gaps where the metal siding had been taken off.

"Few years ago, some dopeheads came around," the man said. "They took everything. Copper. Siding. Anything they could get their hands on. Like a pack of coyotes. Before that, the old man thought we'd do that cash-for-clunkers shit. You probably don't remember it, but was some good prices for a while. We thought we'd do it. Or have this shit hauled. But we never got around to it. Then the old man got sick. You can see how all that turned out."

Seamus felt some of that old Marxist guilt. The reflexive pity and shame of being a little better off than a person to whom he was speaking. But then it occurred to him that this man probably had more money than he did, and it eased some of the guilt. They occupied simultaneously two systems then. How strange. These networks of human relation.

"This what you wanted me to see?"

"No," the man said. He turned then, and unzipped his pants unceremoniously and took out his dick. "This is."

The nakedness, the blunt end of it, was distantly shocking to Seamus. But then, low, skidding across the surface of his tongue, something like want. Confirmation. He approached the man and reached down. Took the human warmth of his dick into hand and gave it an experimental tug.

"I see," Seamus said.

"Well? You gonna do more than see or what?"

Up close, Seamus could see his scraggly sideburns, the wisp of hair peeking out from under the trucker cap. He smelled like American Spirits, sure enough. The man sucked down the last of the cigarette and flicked it away into the dry, cold grass. It sank into the dark and vanished. Seamus knelt and closed his eyes and pressed his face to the musky surface of the man's pelvis. He smelled powerfully of sweat and all-day living, but there was something powdery and clean under that smell. He opened his mouth and the man's cockhead slid over his lips, the tip damp, tasting a little like urine. He hadn't shaken off good.

The man grunted in pleasure, and Seamus took this to be a sign that he was to continue, and continue he did. Until the man had worked himself into a real rhythm pumping into and out of Seamus's mouth. Seamus liked to be used this way. Sometimes he thought the only things he really needed in life were poetry and to be occasionally held down and fucked like dogmeat. He closed his eyes and braced his hands against the man's hips, but the man swatted his hands away.

"Don't touch me," he said. "You don't get to touch me. Now open that mouth up, I want you to gag on it."

Seamus sank deeper then, let the man's dick stretch the delicate webbing at the back of his throat. The guy wasn't hung. Not impressively. There was nothing impressive about it except that he had malice to the way he fucked Seamus's mouth, and that wasn't *nothing*. Seamus enjoyed that. His mouth grew gooey with phlegm. And there was a persistent burn down in his throat, but he accepted this, too, as one accepts the outer dark of estrangement from grace.

The man squeezed the back of Seamus's head in a way that was almost tender, and Seamus opened his eyes, looked up. For a moment, in the amber light of the utility pole, he saw Mr. Fulton and then his teacher from the poetry seminar. But it was neither above him. It was the man in the trailer park lot, fucking his mouth and mumbling under his breath that Seamus was a good boy, had a good mouth, knew what to do.

The man shoved home. Down, down, down in Seamus's throat, and Seamus did almost choke. But he didn't. He held it down. And the man groaned and finished, and when he pulled out, he rubbed what was left across Seamus's face. Like some kind of anointing, warm and sticky, smelling like spit and the sea.

Seamus stood up. Wiped at his mouth with his arm, and tried to compose himself. His mouth was full. He didn't want to swallow, but the man's eyes were on him. And he felt that if he spat it out, something terrible would happen. The man was up on him, just watching him with hard, close eyes.

Seamus swallowed. The man pulled Seamus close and kissed him. There was no love in it. There never was. But in the kissing, Seamus felt if not close to the man, then at least some acknowledgment that they were together in something, whatever that was. It had been a long time since Seamus had been together with someone in something. Even fleetingly. The kiss wasn't even particularly pleasant. They were just pushing spit around in a gross play-acting of desire and pleasure. Seamus wasn't hard. The man kept groping between his legs, trying to get something going, but down there Seamus felt cold and flaccid. More than anything, it hurt to be gripped that hard and pawed at. The man licked his face clean and Seamus closed his eyes and imagined a smaller, more private darkness in which he was totally alone.

"Give it a rest," Seamus said.

On the way back, the man, smoking another one of Seamus's cigarettes, said, "I needed that."

"Dying people make you hard or what?"

"No," he said, stopping. Then he stuck his fingers hard in Seamus's chest. "Don't make jokes about the dying. Show some fucking respect."

"You're the one who said you needed it."

The slap, when it came, was a surprise. They were standing on the path in the woods. The hospice lights were visible through the trees at a distance. Seamus felt their aloneness acutely. The man caught him around the throat and put the cigarette out on the side of his face. It burned, slowly, down through the skin.

"My dad is in that fucking place dying. He was a giant. And now he's fucking wasting away like some faggot with AIDS. You don't make jokes about what dying does to a person."

Seamus tried to get free, and the man just clenched his throat tighter until he again sank to his knees. The man crouched with him, and they were face-to-face on the cold ground, the man squeezing off his windpipe, looking at him like he was a child.

"You ever have something in this life make you feel small? I didn't think so. What this world does to people. You don't know the first thing about cruelty. I should show you. If it was any fairness in the world, I'd show you. You think just because you like sucking dick, the world showed you the back of its hand. But it ain't. It ain't nothing to what real suffering is."

As he talked, Seamus could see channels of spit foaming around his canines. Pronounced. Yellow. He had the mouth of a predator. Seamus could smell the cigarettes and the come and the drying of the man's spit on his face. They were so close then. As possible as two people could be. Their faces so near. It was like they had joined in communal prayer. The man was gazing into his eyes.

"I ought to split your head open," the man said. "I could. I could take you back down to them trailers and show you something funny. Then see how you laugh. What do you have to say about that, funny man?"

How inadequate he was to this moment. What did he really have in the face of his own extinction? It was funny, almost. He felt so dumb. So dumb and helpless.

"Good night Joe, good night Joe, good night," Seamus rasped.

The man blinked slowly, as if struck.

"I hate faggots like you." But he did let Seamus go. He shoved him away and stood. He spat at Seamus, then relit the cigarette and walked on ahead.

Seamus sat alone on the ground. He gingerly touched the burn on the side of his face. It was small. So small. Already, he could feel how much worse it would hurt later. But he was safe. He was alone and he was safe and he looked up to the tops of the trees and tried to catch his breath. Then he laughed and coughed—how did the rest of that fucking Tate poem go?

In the hospice bathroom, Seamus blotted at his face. The circular burn from the cigarette. The puckered angry ridge. The oozing yellow of the fat and flesh below. In the light of the bathroom, everything a little lurid. A little bit like horror. The water stung. And the antiseptic from the medicine cabinet. Stinging, but the pain also distant from him.

Why had he not done something in retaliation for what was done to him out in the woods? Why had he let it happen? The man was stronger than him, he knew. But he could have done something. Anything. He might have tried to get loose and free himself.

The image of himself on his knees. The man's hands around his throat. Briefly, the cold of the air, the damp musk of the woods. The smell of his own cigarettes breathed back on him. He was okay now. Safe now. But the man lingered. Seamus washed his face and stuck a Band-Aid across his jaw, pulling it so taut that he thought it might snap.

In the kitchen, the air humid. The bisque humming along. Eunice cutting up a crusty baguette. Lena churning salad. They were talking about the weather. Ice on the roads. It had been a long fucking day. Too long.

"You look like hell, boy," Eunice said.

"Feel like it."

"What happened to you?"

"Just a cut. You know. Happens sometimes."

Eunice hummed like she didn't believe a fucking word he said. Stupid shit.

"Was that you and Bert I saw out in the garden?"

Seamus looked down into the shiny, battered work surface. His shadow. The burst of ceiling light radiating out from his head like a bruised halo.

"Is that his name?"

"He must have bummed a cigarette. He's always bumming something."

"That he did."

"His daddy up on three. He a mean one."

"Him or his daddy," Seamus asked, smiling despite himself. What was this goading thing in him.

"You a mess," Eunice said.

"He's the meanest dying man I ever seen," Lena said. "One time, his food beat *me* out the door when I was up there. Nurse come around talking about some, 'He prefers it left outside.' Like, no shit. He almost painted the wall with it."

"Some of them don't know no better," Eunice said. "Some of them just. You know. They making they transition and don't know what else to do. So, they just. Take it out on everybody. I understand. It's a hard thing, giving up this world."

"Is it?" Seamus asked. "I mean. Sometimes. I'd like to just. Give it all up."

"And do what, boy? You ain't seen the world yet. How you know you wanna give it up and you ain't seen nothing?"

Seamus put his chin on his hand and gazed at Eunice.

"They should let you teach the poetry workshop," he said.

Eunice stopped and turned her head to look at him. Her expression closed and her eyes got dark, distant. All you could hear was the sputter of the pot and the rustle of the leaves as Lena turned them over in the bowl.

"I don't know nothing about that particular life," Eunice said. "Wouldn't know the first thing about it."

Seamus had trespassed somehow, he realized. He had said something stupid and naive.

"I didn't mean anything by it," he said.

"That's exactly the problem."

"I don't get it."

"No, you don't," she said, and she cut the last of the bread and put it on the sheet pan. She opened the oven and set it under the broiler. "Check on that soup. Do some work."

Seamus slid off the stool and checked the pot. The bisque was getting there. He took up a carton of cream and poured it in. Stirred. Watched the soup grow matte and thick. He tasted it for salt and found it a little too sweet, so added the salt. But not much. There were health concerns.

When he was satisfied, Eunice put him on fruit salad duty. Chopping mangoes, pineapple, peaches. Peeling grapes and slicing them. Drizzling on the lemon juice in a big glass bowl.

He thought about what he had said to Eunice about teaching poetry. He had meant to say something about how inadequate his education was. He had wanted to say that her lessons had a material substance to them, that they meant something to him. That she was a part of the real world that he longed to belong to. But now, squeezing lemons and drizzling their juice over the fruit, he could understand how stupid that must have sounded to her. Platitudes. Eunice didn't go around living her life awaiting a moment to dispense wisdom. She was in the business of living, getting by. Eunice was at the center of a whole universe that he couldn't begin to pierce and understand. It was a civic inattentiveness of the soul that had made him say something so stupid.

Eunice didn't need his benediction. His compliment was an insult.

It stung his pride.

Before service, they had a little break, and Seamus made espresso for them all. He poured them into the little cups and served Eunice and Lena with a cloth draped over his arm. Something he'd seen in a movie. And put on a bad French accent and said, "Mesdames."

They sipped at the kitchen island and moaned in pleasure. Eunice nodded in approval.

"You do have a way," she said.

Seamus nodded stiffly, then, because he couldn't help himself, he grinned.

"Don't I know it," he said.

Dinner service was in the dining room at the long table. They set out the plates, the cutlery, the glasses. Many of the residents were in wheelchairs and some bedridden. Others needed their attendants and nurses to help. Sometimes family. That night, there wasn't anything special planned. A small dinner of the bisque, the bread, the salad. An apple cider to celebrate the season. Just a little. The residents came in, dressed in soft clothes. Shawls, wraps, gowns, cashmere sweatpants, chinos, heads wrapped in turbans or bandannas.

This gray procession of the dying and their equally ashen family. The old, unmarried daughters and sisters, the stricken brothers and sons. Grandchildren. Nieces. They were only seven or eight for dinner tonight. Bert sat at the head of the table near his father, who was quite thin and severe. But he was dressed, fully dressed, in a sport coat and dress pants. Bert in jeans and his flannel looked so curiously mismatched. But they shared a heavy, dark intensity.

Dinner service under way. The clinking of spoons on porcelain. Seamus at the kitchen doorway, peering out over this assemblage. Their heads bowed over their bowls. Grateful, perhaps, for having something to do with their hands at long last. Eunice down in the mudroom, Lena washing the dishes.

Bert looked up then. Eye contact, curiously intense. Seamus thought about what he'd said out in the woods. Hating faggots like Seamus. Jokes about the dying. *Oh*, Seamus thought now. *Oh*. His dad didn't know. Bert was in the closet. That explained the misplaced rage.

Seamus felt powerful. That was the word for it. Powerful.

He smiled at Bert, gave a faggy little wave of his fingers just as the father looked up to see. And he raised his brows suggestively and turned back into the kitchen.

Lena was watching him.

"We got enough trouble," she said.

"Won't be any trouble."

"Yeah, not for you."

Seamus shrugged.

But he felt good.

Like he'd gotten something back for himself in the end.

Seamus rode up North First Avenue on the icy sidewalk. He hit a left and rolled down a slope, passing under trees. He was on the side roads, cutting through yards on his way into downtown. Occasionally, he set a dog off barking and pulling at their chain in a yard, or passed a family sitting down to dinner or watching the evening news. These illuminated windows of other lives, families, made him dizzy.

Then a set of high beams shot out overhead and dropped low. He pulled up on the sidewalk to let it pass, but instead the lights dipped out and he could hear the car on the road behind him, rolling along with a slow crackle. He glanced over his shoulder. A black truck was easing along behind him. The street was otherwise empty. Quiet. Houses and apartment buildings. He cut across the street and rode upward, pointing east. The car followed. The road grew narrower, darker. Inclined. Seamus pumped harder to gather some speed, and then looped back, cut down and turned north. There was a squeal and a rubber thud, like trash cans going over.

He gathered another burst of speed and pushed hard, his thighs burning. His back ached. The sweat stung the burn under the bandage. But he kept going. Was it Bert? Was he coming to collect his due? Seamus reached the top of the hill near College Green. He exhaled, easy. He knew where he was now. He glided down by the Co-Op, turned and hit Iowa Ave., which he took up into the heart of downtown. The undergrads hanging out under the lights near Joe's. Loud music coming from the bar on the corner. He saw Prairie Lights and Mickey's. Thought of dipping in there until he was clear. Then he rode up to Market and parked his bike outside of George's.

But then he remembered. It was a seminar night. His classmates would be in there. He peeked through one of the dim front windows, peering in with his hands over his eyes. He saw Oliver. He saw Ingrid and Linda. Helen. Some of the boys from the other group of poets. Laughing at the bar, in the booths. The music was loud. It shook the glass. He couldn't go in there now, showing up at the end of the night, knowing he hadn't been invited and why. He was tired. He had no patience for it. He needed to keep a lookout. He wasn't totally sure he'd ditched the black truck, whoever it was. If the driver was even after him, which they very well might not have been. He needed to stop being so paranoid. So sure of his own victimhood. It made him out to be like Beth and her Gorgon head.

He jogged up the street to the Fox Head. Fiction bar, but an off night for them, and so empty of writers, and at that particular moment also empty of locals. The bartender was about forty-five, balding, and skeletal in the face. He wore old band T-shirts and made a show of cleaning glasses. The bar was dim and loud, the pool table vacant for the moment. Seamus felt the emptiness of the bar acutely. There was no heat. He ordered a PBR, but the bartender kept looking down at the glass he was cleaning as though he didn't hear Seamus. After a few moments, he nodded and filled the glass and pushed it slowly across the bar. Seamus dropped the two dollars on the bar top. The bartender just looked at it, then, shrugging again, he picked up another glass and started wiping.

Seamus dumped himself into a booth near the side wall. The greasy window gave a view of the street and sidewalk, John's across the street. As he drank the PBR, he tried to keep his hands from shaking. Whenever a car was in the street, he slid low and peered through the window, trying to see the make and model. Never any trucks. Just small, compact cars belonging to undergrad parents or sensible people with real jobs. University ladies in stretch-waist pants. People going into John's. He checked his watch.

The beer did not help. But the second one did. Two men entered, ball caps low over their heads. Seamus sat at the bar after his third beer, saw no point in going back and stooping in the booth. He sat next to a tall guy in coveralls. The guy was drinking slow out of a bottle. He had a thick beard.

It was just the two of them at the bar, drinking slowly. The guy's friend came from the back of the bar where the bathrooms were situated. He tried to goad his friend into a conversation.

"I think you two can work it out," he said. "Don't give up on something good."

"It's not giving up if he's being an asshole."

Overhead, John Cougar, "Hurts So Good" playing slightly too

loud. Distortion in the speakers. He could feel the music in his teeth fillings. The guy next to him mumbling. His friend being persistent. Then Seamus felt something strike the back of his arm and he looked. It was the guy's friend.

"Hey, buddy. Tell him that he shouldn't dump his boyfriend."

"You shouldn't dump your boyfriend," Seamus said. The bartender slid change across the counter. The friend slid it back and added two dollar bills. The guy with the boyfriend about to be dumped looked mortified.

"I'm sorry. He's very drunk."

"So am I," Seamus said. Pointing the bottle end at the two of them. "Impossibly bombed, I'm afraid."

"Don't I know you?" the friend asked. He, like his buddy, was tall. Carhartt jacket, baseball cap pulled low. He was lanky and had a gap.

"No, but you could very easily. I'm Seamus."

"Hartjes," he said.

"Mouthful," Seamus said dryly.

"Fyodor," the other guy said.

"Bigger mouthful."

"Parents," Hartjes said.

"You guys Russian?"

"Black," Fyodor said. "Just black."

"Well," Hartjes started to say.

"Mostly black."

Seamus's neck flushed. "Oh. I didn't mean that about your names. I'm sorry."

"White man on the run," Hartjes said.

Fyodor shrugged.

"Don't listen to me, by the way. If you want to dump your boyfriend. You should. Don't let me stop you."

"He's a good guy. It's just hard. I guess that's always true. For everybody."

"Yeah," Seamus said. "Boy. That's the truth."

"That sounds suspiciously like the beginning of a story."

"I wouldn't know anything about it. I'm a poet."

"A poet! Man, no kidding. We had to bail on the last place because it was full of your people."

"Yeah. They're a bit like pack animals that way."

"You mean *we*."

"I mean *we*, yes," Seamus said, laughing. The song changed. Dylan. "Tambourine Man."

Fyodor put his bottle down and closed his eyes. He was blushing a little. Seamus knew it was time for him to get home and mind his own business for a change. But it was nice, sitting here with two people. After the night he'd had.

"Man, you ever just feel like. I don't know. Like you could just knock your brains out, you're so grateful the day is over?"

Hartjes eyed him and Fyodor laughed.

"White boys are crazy," Hartjes said.

"I think you're right."

Hartjes and Fyodor walked Seamus to his bike out by George's. Fyodor was driving home to the boyfriend, the one he was maybe planning to dump, who knew. Hartjes lingered while Seamus undid his bike. Hartjes said he'd walk Seamus as far as the parking garage down by the union. That's where he'd left his truck. Seamus said it was on the way.

They went up Market and passed the business school. It was dark but not late, just after eleven. The wind was getting sharp, though, coming off the river. Down by the parking garage, that tower of orange lights. Hartjes stepped in close to Seamus. Breathed on his lips. Sour beer. Seamus kissed him, then—remembering Bert, remembering the espresso—he pulled back. He felt bad about his breath. He'd rinsed his mouth, but he could still taste Bert. Hartjes smiled cryptically. Put his hand on the small of Seamus's back.

"You could come up to my place," he said. "Or . . ."

"I think I better just. Go home. Before I get into trouble."

"Fair enough," Hartjes said. "Give me your number, though."

Seamus typed his number into the phone and handed it back. Hartjes texted him and said he'd see him around if he wanted. Or not. Seamus said yeah, it'd be great. Then they split and Seamus was alone.

Taking his bike across the bridge. The wind was stronger then, slicing up his face. He looked up. The stars, he thought, had been watching him his whole life. They'd seen the whole thing go on and on. Him and the rest of all the people who had ever lived and ever would.

It was like living in a museum exhibit or a dollhouse. It was so easy to imagine the hands of some enormous and indifferent God prying the house open and squinting at them as they went about their lives on their circuits like little automatons in an exhibit called *The Late Americans*. A God with a Gorgon's head peering down in judgment.

What were you supposed to do in the face of that? Turn to stone?
Fuck.

He mattered so little.

Seamus lived in a studio apartment in the wooded hills that overlooked the rest of campus. The floor was creaky under his pacing,
and every so often it gave a sharp yelp, like a frightened cat. His
apartment was in an old house built back in the fifties or sixties.
There was something quite dense about the house, except in his
apartment, which had been cleaved from a larger room. You could
feel the difference in the strength of the wood, how it warped and
threatened to give way.

They were all living in such squares, carved from the greater
mass of history, from old lives.

In his apartment, he reheated some of the bisque he'd carried
home from the hospice and sat at his desk. A stack of discarded
poems gazed back at him with inert judgment—his compost heap,
he called it. Among the dashed, hurried fragments, quatrains and
couplets torn from the ends of other failed things, there was a crown
of sonnets about Alsatian nuns during the Thirty Years' War.

He had once read a historical account of a group of children who
had been stuffed into barrels and floated down a river in order to
avoid the Catholic authorities. Except that someone had made a
horrible mistake, the children's barrels had been battered by rocks,
and the children had all died horrible deaths. A group of nuns had
gathered by the riverside at night and waded deep into the water in
order to extract the children, or what there was of them that could
still be found. It was fable-like, the idea of a group of holy sisters

shedding their habits and wading in their white vestments into cold water to seek drowned children. For days after reading the story he had walked around feeling heavy with it, like he was the one who'd gone swimming with all his clothes on.

The poems had come out decently at first, or so he had thought. The lines glinted like cold stars, harsh and distant and perfect. But after he had completed them, each sonnet the story of a sister and a child, seeker and the lost, a call and a response or, rather, a silence, he found that he hated them. He had rushed through in the excitement of creation, in the blurry exhilaration of putting words down. Worse still, he had come up to the very edge of his technical ability, and had resorted in his more desperate moments to puns, to cheap tricks, to dodges of sentiment. There was a falseness to the poems, further illuminated by the stricture of the form itself. There was nowhere to hide in a sonnet, which was something that before had been the very point.

It used to seem to him that you could write about the past as a way of understanding the present. But now, his classmates wrote only about the present and its urgency. The very act of comprehension or contextualization was centered on the self, but the self as abstracted via badly understood Marxist ideology. The self in contemporary poetry was really some debased, abject manifestation of a system of wrongs and historical atrocities, shorn of their historical contexts or any real rigorous understanding. Their poems were complaints of hurts done and occluded. No one wanted to read his poems about Catholicism or Alsatian nuns or the apocalypse of the Thirty Years' War. They wanted to know how *he* fit in. Poetry was just a matching game, the poems simply cards.

He stared at a notebook that he had pinned open with paper

clips and weighed down with a ceramic bear. Then he took out a pen and set down the first lines of a poem that had come to him on the ride home:

How vast your works, O Gorgon Head—
the night, the century, the quiet, the cry.

2.

Beasts of the Field

Fyodor, drunk, out in his truck, listening to the engine click and cool. Golden light in the living room window. The porch light's bright halo in the damp cold. The glint of blue salt spread over the front steps in case of early snow. Out in the truck, listening to the engine click and cool.

Timo was staying over.

He thought about backing out and driving until he ran out of gas or ran off the road into the river. It was after midnight. Timo still up. Probably meant a fight—another one. It had been a long day at the plant. His teeth hurt from the screech of the hydraulic presses, the pneumatic hiss of the air guns they used to blast away the powdered snow of bone dust and flash-dried flesh. He was still in his coveralls, could still smell the ferrous odor of the blood, the peculiar salinity of the ice baths that had made his skin chalky and sensitive. What he wanted was a long shower and a long sleep. It had been a mistake to go with Hartjes to the bar. But go he had, and now he was drunk, head-heavy, trying to get up the guts to go into his own apartment.

Fyodor worked in beef, as a leaner. He cut away the pinkish fat and connective tissue from the dark red flesh, which was rather soft and delicate, like cloth or dough. You had to respect its natural geometry, the irregularities of how the muscle broke, the way it fell and lay. If you went too hard or too fast, you might ruin the cut, turn a luxury piece of beef into something better ground into chuck. What startled him at first was how little the meat resembled any animal at all by the time he got his hands on it. But then, he thought, if the meat reminded people of the docile animals it had come from, no one would ever eat it.

The difficulty of the work was in its capacity to lull you into a trance and then punish you for carelessness. What you needed was inattentive alertness. The noise of the machines made earplugs necessary, but you also had to be able to hear the shouts of the line leads, as sometimes conditions shifted on the fly. It was cold, too. And your hands got ate up from the sanitizer and disinfectant. The nitrates and the ice baths, the hiss and spray of liquid nitrogen. And there was the danger of the hydraulic presses and the constant, gleaming inner machinery that powered the belts. You sometimes got into such a rhythm, flying over the grain of the cuts, the fat coming away easy, like nothing, that you forgot yourself. Strayed too close to something and got your arm sliced open through your coveralls.

Most dangerous thing was thinking you had control when you didn't. It required a certain humility. But then, that was life.

Timo considered this work a variety of animal cruelty. He liked to say that Fyodor was a participant in a system that cost millions of animals their lives.

He and Timo had met on an app and had been together for about a year. The fighting about Fyodor's job had been constant, but at first, it had been a little hot. It had been a point of contention that

THE LATE AMERICANS | 55

let them work themselves up, and it improved their sex life because it gave the sex another dimension, some depth. The sex was a way of arguing without arguing, or the arguing was a way of fucking without fucking, which would hopefully *end* with fucking. Still, in some moments, Fyodor found it strange that their sex life was the result of an unresolved argument about what he did for a living. Timo was a vegetarian.

Out into the cold he went. The sky was clear and smooth. The street was empty, except for the rowdier undergrads down in the row of apartment buildings fronting the hospital parking garage. Loud music, shouting, windows up: they were having a great time. They didn't need an excuse for anything, Fyodor thought. They just went on living how they wanted. Time had no meaning to them. It moved over them like a stream. Time's passage. What could it mean when you had so much of it?

Up his own steps and into the front hall of the old Queen Anne, which had been busted up into apartments. Fyodor could hear something like classical music. He stood in the cool hall, pressing his head to the door, listening. It was piano. Timo never shared that part of himself anymore, not since those early weeks when they'd first gotten together. Now, he guarded that part of his life as if to share it would be some kind of betrayal of a promise he'd made to himself.

Fyodor found Timo lying on his back in the living room, listening to music coming from a small conical speaker on the table. He had one arm over his eyes and he was keeping time with his free hand. The music was melancholy.

"You're up," Fyodor said.

"I wasn't waiting for you. I was grading and needed a break."

"Fair enough." The clarification hurt Fyodor's feelings a little, but he wasn't totally sure why. "You eat already?"

"With Goran."

Fyodor poured a glass of water for himself and drank it at the sink, looking into the yard at the tall pine. Blue light from the neighbor's porch caught the ends of the needles. The sink was empty. He washed his glass and set it upside down in the rack.

"Must have been good to see him."

"I'm listening," Timo said. The music had grown louder but also more melancholy. Fyodor unsnapped the straps of his coveralls, pulled them down to his waist. Then he pulled at the black sweatshirt and thermal underneath. The apartment was warm. He should shower before the heat switched off. He watched Timo's hand in the air, seeming to shape the music as it poured from the speaker. There were bright spikes of something in the melody, a series of notes played rapidly and then revisited more slowly a few moments later.

Eating with Goran—that certainly explained the mood. Fyodor undressed in the small bathroom off the living room, then stepped into the shower and switched on the water as hot and as forceful as he could get it. The music was underneath the sound of the water pounding at the back of his head. He tried to unhear it, but it was so present in him now. Then it went away, and he realized that Timo must have turned the music off. This hurt his feelings, too.

He toweled himself off in the bedroom. Now Timo was heating something in the kitchen. Fyodor could smell tomato sauce, hear the brassy play of the potlids. His feet were so sore. Timo brought him a plate of pasta and sat at the foot of the bed while Fyodor ate it. He was grateful for the food—for the oily salt of it, the brine of the tomato sauce. They could hear, in the absence of the music, their neighbor moving above them. Signs of extraterrestrial life. Timo looked up. Fyodor watched the tendons of his neck, the swing of his eyes.

"That was nice, what you played earlier," Fyodor said.

"I better get back to grading."

Timo stood up. He stopped at the doorway, looked back.

"It's just music," he said. "It wasn't anything special." Then he left.

Timo's eradicating impulse, like everything was a battle to be won, was exhausting. Fyodor ate his pasta and thought about the argument in the bar with Hartjes, whether he should just cut bait with Timo and save them both a lot of trouble. These arguments—these petty, petty, passive aggressive fights about nothing that lasted for days. Why? And for what?

He dabbed up the red oil from the plate and licked his fingertips clean. There was a greasy sheen to his nails. He leaned against the headboard. His back was sore. His joints ached now that he had been sitting. The hot water had done its job pummeling him. He could sleep for years. But he got up, took his plate to the kitchen to wash it. He was running the plate under lukewarm water when Timo shouted from the bathroom, "It smells like a death camp in here. Why can't you just leave these work clothes in your truck?"

"It's my bathroom," Fyodor called back.

They did not live together. This was Timo's choice, and Fyodor had no complaints about it, really, except that Timo sometimes acted like they *did* live together. Timo said nothing. But then, coming around the corner, he leaned against the doorway and frowned like a spoiled child. Fyodor shook the water from his hands. "You don't listen to me," he said.

"You're just annoyed at me because you know your job is morally indefensible."

Fyodor leaned against the sink and gripped it tight. His head throbbed. One of the men at the plant, Tom Stein, had cut himself badly, and he'd screamed so loud that everyone could hear him over the roar of the belts and clank of the presses. The scream had made the enamel of Fyodor's teeth ache. Fyodor had picked up the man's slack, which made it a long, bloody day. His back hurt. His shoulders hurt. Fyodor thumped his fist against the edge of the sink and hummed three quick times.

"This is what my life is. You think that this is temporary, but it isn't. This is what my life is. What I will be."

"That's not true," Timo said with a bored drawl. "You have so much potential, and this is just murder, and it's awful that you do it. I'm not sorry for saying so."

Sometimes Fyodor thought Timo was the smartest person he had ever known. But there were other times when he thought Timo was a moron. Or, if not stupid, then just very naive in the way some black people could be when they'd grown up with money and parents who believed in them. They were both mixed, but apart from that they were nothing alike, and this at first had been thrilling to Fyodor. Someone so like him that he wouldn't have to explain the weirdness of not quite being one thing or another, while obviously being black even though he was also mixed. It was like a puzzle whose stated solution was obviously wrong but also irrefutable. If you were mixed, you were black. Fyodor had no issue with that. But Timo was irritatingly middle class, and sometimes that gave him illusions about how the world saw him.

Timo's naivety on the subject was cute. Sometimes sexy, like someone pretending to be dumber than they were. But sometimes, like now, Fyodor wanted to wring his neck. He looked so complacent and *sure*.

I'm not sorry for saying so was a thing you could say only if you'd grown up thinking you had options. Only if you did have options. But Timo wasn't totally without self-knowledge. He'd gone to college, Fyodor knew, and he was smart—so smart. Timo was a logician, which sounded a lot more fanciful than it was. Fyodor didn't really understand the term except that it involved math and strange symbols. He played piano and knew about music and art. In the summer the city put pianos out on the sidewalks for people to play, and sometimes, when they were walking home, the air fragrant and fizzy in the falling dusk, Timo would stop and play him something. Just a little fragment of something astounding and beautiful. The first time, Fyodor had been so startled by the effortlessness with which Timo pulled something wonderful out of the rickety old pianos that he'd stopped and choked on his beer. They were walking home from the bar. Fyodor with his brown paper bag, sipping discreetly. But then Timo had done that thing with the piano, and the whole world had shifted.

"Goddamn," he'd said.

Timo had just shrugged, moving toward him, and said, "That thing needs tuning."

But other times, like now, in the kitchen, Timo just gazed at him in bored hostility, totally unreachable.

Fyodor felt that if he opened his mouth again, what would come out would be not his own voice, but Tom's scream. Tom had taught Fyodor how to use the knife to separate the fat from the flesh, how to pull the fat away without stressing the muscle fibers, what to look for when you ran your hand along the cap. Tom, dark-skinned with a big gap. He was bulky and good, with hands so fast they were like elegant blades. Tom. How had he cut himself? He was so careful.

Fyodor closed his eyes. "I don't think we're gonna make it."

"Why do you want to be this way forever?"

"I don't want," Fyodor said. "It's not about wanting. Some of us don't get to want."

"Ah, the nobility of the working classes. Here we go. You don't have to work in this plant. There are other jobs. Other things you could do. We all have agency, Fyodor."

"You're right," he said. "We do."

Fyodor left the sink and crossed the room in three swift strides. Timo flinched. At the door, Fyodor took a deep breath. The air in the apartment was stale and too warm. Fyodor pulled the door open. Outside, on the front porch, everything was cold and dark.

"Please leave my apartment," he said. Timo squinted at him in disbelief, but Fyodor merely pulled the door open wider. "Please."

Timo did leave that night, and they didn't talk for the rest of the week. They didn't talk the following week. And then it was as if they had never been together at all.

Things went on.

Things always have a way of getting on.

Fyodor was in the café above the bookstore. It was where you could get the best espresso for the lowest price downtown, and on his days off he liked to spend time there watching the students, whose lives seemed unremarkable and therefore pleasant. It was mid-November, the end of the semester, and the students had an anxious, jittery quality. They were on Adderall and speed. Memorizing atlases of the body and columns of facts about various wars and catastrophes.

There had been a time when Fyodor wanted to be like them. When he still harbored certain ideas about what he might be capable of. But then he'd run into undergrads at bars and clubs, and he'd seen the way their eyes dimmed when they spoke to him and he tried to speak to them. The way they slowly became aware that they belonged to different worlds. He'd stopped admiring them then. They were just kids. This, he understood now, was why it hadn't worked with Timo.

He was reading a book of short stories by Garshin. Fyodor's own father was Russian. Or *had* been Russian, from a long line of Russians. He had named Fyodor after his great-grandfather. *Because you are Russian, don't let anyone tell you that you aren't,* his father had said. But fathers sometimes said things they didn't mean, or things they meant but that didn't really matter in the grander course of life. He hadn't spoken to his father in some years now. That life was behind him. Down in Alabama.

Still, Fyodor read the stories, experimentally, trying to see if something came back to him. Something ancestral and mysterious. There was nothing in the café that day. It was just clean, bright descriptions of ordinary life shifted subtly and irrevocably off course. Russian dramas of the mundane variety. The stories had nothing at all to do with him and the cold steel of the belts or the spinning blades of the saws. There was nothing in them at all that was the same as his life, yet he read on.

He wasn't the best reader. He and Timo got into fights about it—Timo would hold up his phone to show Fyodor something and then get tired of waiting for Fyodor to finish. Fyodor tried to explain that he had to go slow because sometimes his eyelids grew heavy and the words spun around on him. But he did like stories, and he remembered what he read. He could hold it in his head for a long time, turn it over. Poke at it. He liked to listen to Timo read in English and French. He didn't really understand the French, but he could feel the meaning deep down in the sounds of the words. But then Timo would tell him to get an audiobook subscription, or get tested for dyslexia, he was old enough now to do it himself. So, no, he wasn't a great reader. But he did enjoy the exertion of it. And the slow seep of the stories into his mind.

With the benefit of retrospection, now that they'd been broken up for a few weeks, he thought Timo was kind of an asshole anyway.

Then, as if he'd conjured him, Timo walked into the café with Hartjes, who waved at him. Fyodor waved back. Timo did not wave, which hurt Fyodor's feelings a little.

While Timo was ordering coffee, Hartjes came over to speak to him. "It's been a while," he said. "Hey, what's this about you two splitting?"

Fyodor didn't want to get into it, both because Timo was standing just a few feet away and also because he didn't know if he could explain it well. Any part of it felt insufficient: that Timo had not taken him seriously, that Timo was selfish, that they'd just wanted different things. All true, but Timo was also generous and funny, kind in his own prickly way. He was good to spend time with, and their arguments had a certain animal heat to them that made Fyodor hard and want to fuck him. The tension that had made Fyodor ask Timo to leave that night was also the very thing that made Fyodor want to be with him. But how to explain that without sounding nuts?

Nothing would sound sufficiently convincing or even truthful, and so Fyodor said bluntly, "It's complicated, but also stupid."

Hartjes smiled and sat down. He picked up the book Fyodor had been reading. "What's this?"

"Just some stories," he said.

"Garshin. Never heard of him," Hartjes said.

"He's Russian," Fyodor said.

"Figures. Though I never took you for the story type."

"What did you take me for?"

Before Hartjes could answer, Timo had come over with two paper cups of coffee. He pulled up a third chair, and there they were, the three of them.

Timo had a turn looking at the volume of stories. Fyodor's face grew hot. It was like being examined. He wished suddenly that he had just stayed in his apartment, where he'd spent the past three days feeling ill. He had bought the book just an hour or so ago, and he had read only the first couple of stories. He couldn't think of a good reason to explain to Timo and Hartjes why he'd bought the book at all, and they appeared slightly amused at him for it, like he was suddenly displaying altered behavior. Hartjes leaned back on the chair, and its spindly legs creaked a little. Fyodor took the book when Timo offered it back to him, and he shyly looked down into the surface of his coffee.

"I didn't know you liked Russian literature," Timo said. There was something mean and mocking in his voice. It was how certain of their mutual friends spoke to Fyodor when they felt he had done something out of character. When he offered to julienne the vegetables for stews, or when he delicately and with great tenderness lifted their quivering pets into his arms and spoke in soothing, quiet tones into their ears and they stopped shivering, or when his eyes grew teary at the conclusion of movies, as the music became soft and optimistic, like fine rain or mist on hopeful faces. In these moments he often saw himself through their eyes, and understood that they thought of him as something else entirely—as hard and stupid.

"I can read, you know," Fyodor said quietly.

"I didn't say you were illiterate," Timo said.

"How have you been?" Hartjes asked.

Fyodor drummed his fingers on the table. "I was a little sick the last few days, I guess. But I'm feeling better now."

"Good," Hartjes said.

"Sick how?" asked Timo. "You don't look sick."

"Because I'm better," Fyodor said. "Better people don't look sick, do they?"

"Whatever."

Hartjes sighed. "Well, this is lovely." He drank his coffee and then got up for a refill, leaving the two of them together. Timo did not look at him at first. Fyodor studied the grain of his beard. It was thicker than he remembered it. Dark red now, especially at the edges. His hair had a soft curl to it, especially where it sloped behind his ears. His neck was smooth, and Fyodor could remember the exact temperature and texture of that skin there, where he had kissed him, especially at night, when they were going to sleep.

He wanted—though perhaps want was not the correct word for it, because want implied something conscious, something of awareness, which was not present, and so it was maybe better to say that Fyodor felt, somewhere, deep and central to his body, a compulsion—to touch Timo. He slid his hand across the table, but stopped just before he touched his wrist, and the motion of his coming to a stop caused the surface of the coffee to ripple. For a moment, they watched the ripples in the coffee expand. The two of them were, for the first time in weeks, staring at the same thing, occupying the same space, watching it happen together.

"I miss you," Timo said. "I miss you, and I don't know what to do about it, except to say it. So I said it. There it is."

Fyodor touched Timo at the place where his sleeve pulled back from his wrist. The bones were firm, and the hair there was fine like cornsilk. Timo's eyelashes were thick with moisture. His nostrils flared subtly. Timo's thumb rested on the cup in front of him. Fyodor's fingers were laced together. Neither of them said anything because what was there to say? How could they bridge this impossible space? The rupture that had come about because of silence could only be fixed with silence, except that silence was no good for fixing anything. But silence and time were all they had. Timo's face grew red. He was embarrassed, Fyodor could see that. He had gambled and been rebuffed, but Fyodor wanted to reassure him somehow. He took Timo's hands apart and lay his palm against Timo's right hand, as if in benediction, and he closed his eyes.

"I miss you too," Fyodor said. That was only a part of it. But he could say it with his eyes closed, that was the trick of it. If he held his eyes closed, he could say some of how he felt without the burden of seeing Timo's face. That was pathetic.

"Okay," Timo said. Fyodor took his hand away. He cleared his throat. Hartjes returned.

They chatted a little in the halting, halfhearted manner of people who would rather be on their way, but who feel that they cannot without being rude. In the end, it was Fyodor who got up first, said he had to go. That there was something he had to do, and as he stood up, Timo flinched a little. Hartjes smiled and waved. They shared a hug. And then Fyodor wrapped his scarf around himself and went out into the cold and the damp gray of a winter afternoon.

Across the street, big white park service trucks had pulled in the Ped Mall. They were taking down the diseased ash trees. He had seen a little thing on the news about the trees, how before, back in the fifties or sixties, there had been elm trees all over Iowa City. But the trees had died of Dutch elm disease, and ash trees were planted to replace them. And now they, too, were dying.

Fyodor had never paid much attention to the trees in the Ped Mall. But now he could see that in the summer there would be no shade. It would be the sun beating down on all of them as they walked and shopped and listened to music on the square. The birds and the squirrels would have nowhere to go. It was sad. Too sad. The great dying off of things.

He walked over to the Bread Garden and bought two apples. He stood under the heat lamps of the patio and ate one, listening to the wind howl across the empty playground. He sat down and tried to read again but found it difficult. He kept thinking about Timo, how in the end they hadn't been able to say more than a few words to each other. It was unfair of him to be annoyed, he knew. It was his fault they'd broken up. But still.

When he realized he wasn't getting anywhere with the stories, he stood up. He put the other apple in his pocket for later, tossed the core in a garbage can, and walked away, leaving the book there on the table with his receipt for the apples. On his way home he thought about watching a movie, but he couldn't think of what to see. Nothing interested him. Nothing was good. Besides, movies reminded him of his dreams. Movies were uncanny and strange to him. Like something private playing on the outside. He always had too many questions about movies: How many people were involved in the shoot? Where had the camera been placed? How had they moved around while filming, recording? His thoughts all felt extremely literal when he watched movies, and he couldn't shake the habit of thinking that way. So he was caught between those two disconcerting feelings—that he was watching his own dreams unfold before him, but also that he was watching something fake but that almost approximated reality.

Lately, he had been dreaming about Alabama. It was always some version of the same dream. That he had gone home to visit his mother and could not leave. He'd lost his car keys, or his license, or he was his teenaged self again and couldn't drive. The dreams always twisted in some mundane, terrible way. An aunt said something cruel, his mother punished him for some childish thing, or else he just got frozen out by everyone and they refused to know him. No matter what he did, though, he could not leave. In the dream, they said things like, *We're family, why you wanna leave us?* Even as they were doing horrible things to him. Things that were not done to him in real life. Not really.

The worst things that had happened to him never made it into the dreams.

He'd been dreaming of Alabama ever since he got sick. And he wondered what it meant. It probably had no significance. Dreams—well, his mother used to believe in dreams. She had forbidden Fyodor to talk about his dreams with her. "I don't want that on me," she used to say. Meaning, what if it came true?

Fyodor did not watch the movie. He went home and sat on the porch, eating the other apple in the cold. When he was done, he lobbed it across the street where it split apart against a tree.

He wished he had said something to Timo. But he didn't know what.

Fyodor's mother called the day after Thanksgiving.

He had inherited to some degree her very pragmatic view of things—that you had to survive, and that survival was the most important part of life. *Hardship* was just what soft people called living. That sort of thing. But Fyodor knew that his mother saw in him a streak of something yielding and wasteful. When he was young, she used to catch him in the kitchen, drawing or arranging things on the shelves. Sometimes she caught him watching cooking programs on the special channel that was intermittently watchable on their TV. At those moments, he looked up to see her watching him with disappointment, and, later, with something like fear. She was afraid of what she saw in him, and her voice often trembled when she spoke to him about life. *You need to do something with yourself. Something good and honest.* When they spoke on the phone, she was always short with him. Wanting to be off.

And yet she called him and chastised him because they didn't speak more often. "If I didn't call you, we wouldn't talk at all." He didn't know what she really wanted from him. But he did know that she loved him. This was one of the fundamental truths of his life, although her love was at times inscrutable, indistinguishable from the routine rhythm and course of life itself. Love had been in the tension of his freshly made bedsheets, in the astringent cleaner she used on their bathroom and kitchen. Love was everywhere in their life. But then he had moved away.

"Boy, I'm tired of having to chase you around creation just to hear from my own kin."

"Ma," he said. He was lying in bed, sweating because the radiator was throwing out too much heat.

"What ailing you?" she asked, and Fyodor rolled onto his stomach. His shoulder was sore, and his knees ached. He had a body full of ailment, a list of complaints.

"Nothing."

"Don't sound like nothing to me."

"I said it's nothing, didn't I?"

"Not that you'd say. You act like someone want to rule your life."

"Nobody trying to rule my life," he said.

"I sure ain't."

"Didn't say you was."

"You ain't gotta say."

"Ma," he said, but his face was pressed into his pillow.

"One of them boys is dead."

"What?"

"I said one of them boys is dead."

"What boys?'

"Them boys," she said slowly, as if she were peeling away a curtain to show him a magic trick. Fyodor sat up on the mattress. He put his hand to his face and wiped at the stiff mask of oil and sweat.

"I don't want to try to figure this out, Ma. I don't feel well."

"Thought it was nothing ailing you," she said.

Fyodor let out a loose, hoarse laugh at that. Fair enough, he thought. But he felt elsewhere in his chest the corner of what she was trying to say to him. He suspected, slightly, that she was trying to say that one of his brothers was dead.

They weren't really his brothers anyway.

Fyodor's father had lived three towns over with his wife and their two children. Fyodor's mother had not hidden this from him. When he was growing up, he spent one or two weeks each summer with his father's family at their white house in the woods.

What he remembered most from those times was the smell of pine sap and freshly cut grass. The sap had smelled so powerful that it burned Fyodor's eyes and nose. His brothers were two chubby boys who looked almost like twins. They sweated all the time and smelled like okra, which strangely was their favorite food. The older of the boys was two weeks younger than Fyodor. The heat in those days was immense, powerful, almost like a living thing. The house was old and they cooled it with big fans shoved into the tallest windows. But the air wouldn't budge. The boys spent a lot of time running through strips of shade out in the woods, until one day the younger one fell down and broke his arm, and that was the end of Fyodor's time with his brothers in their house in the woods. That night his father packed up Fyodor's clothes, even the dirty ones, into a plastic bag and shoved them into the back seat. Then he told Fyodor to get in, and they drove for a long time in silence.

The car windows were down, and the air was cool. His father had his arm out the window, a flash of pale white. The shadows of the trees, like a corps of dark, conspiring monsters, sometimes broke suddenly, sharply into a wide-open field, flat and perfect, silvery under the moon. Fyodor thought about the smell of his father's aftershave, the scent of his soap. And the hard tightness of his jaw as he drove. When they reached Fyodor's house, his father turned to him and he said, "See you next time," like nothing at all had happened. Like nothing at all was the matter or wrong. And Fyodor felt a weight rise up from him. He felt it dissolve and fade, and he leaned over and hugged his father as tight as he could, and his father let him, and then Fyodor got out, and his father backed down the long gravel driveway, and was gone, and that was that, except for the place where the headlights had swung through the air—it seemed somehow like a lighter darkness there, channels of gray cut through the dark continent of night.

By the time Fyodor reached the front door with his bag over his shoulder, his mother was already there waiting for him. He was afraid she was going to hit him, but she didn't. She put her arms around him and she hugged him and kissed his cheeks and his forehead, and she said, in a voice he didn't recognize as belonging to her, that scared him because it was foreign and strange, "You didn't do nothing wrong. You didn't."

Fyodor never saw or spoke to his father again.

But now his mother was saying that one of those boys was dead, and Fyodor didn't know what to make of it, except that all his life he'd gone around with a soft piece of hurt just below his ribs, where he stored whatever disappointment or sadness he felt at his father and his brothers not trying to know him. It was not sharp. It was not hard. But it was a persistent, soft ache, like a sore gum through which a tooth threatened to rupture. And now one of those boys was dead.

"How do you know?" he asked.

"Saw your daddy. He said."

"What did he say?"

"That one of them boys was dead."

"No—I mean, what, exactly, how did he say it?"

His mother sighed. The baseboard clicked. She was somewhere windy, probably on her porch. He could hear paper crinkling, the soft hiss of television in the background. Her life had gone on without him. It was after dinnertime. She was probably watching *Wheel of Fortune*, or one of those crime shows, with the window cracked.

"He said the boy died. That's all he said. I'm not trying to fool you." She sounded annoyed that he had pressed her. He felt annoyed that she hadn't told him more. They were locked for an instant in a tense knot of silence, neither one seeming to know how to give way to the other.

"All right, then," he said.

"All right" was her answer. "I better go. I got these dishes."

Fyodor made an assenting sound, but she had already hung up. He rolled onto his back. His eyes stung from sweat. His stomach roiled. His brother was dead. A brother he'd never known except in the glancing, incidental way of their childhood. He didn't even know which brother it was. The older or the younger. He hadn't seen them in so long that he probably remembered them as being more alike than they actually were. Maybe one had a mole and one didn't. Maybe one was left-handed like Fyodor and one wasn't. He couldn't separate them. They were alike, unindividuated, a mass of white boy-dough. But one of them was twenty-nine and the other twenty-seven or twenty-eight.

They were men, not boys.

It was a shame that now they knew nothing at all of one another. But this was not their fault. Like everything else concerning their families, it was something done to them or for them, or whatever. His father hadn't blamed him for the younger one breaking his arm. It had been the boys' mother, a tall, tawny woman with a hard face

and mean hands. She used to pinch Fyodor when no one was looking. She'd reach under the table and squeeze his skin until he let out
a sharp cry, but by then she'd already have her hands back above the
table. When she bathed him when he was really little, she'd pinch
him between the legs. She wouldn't let him bathe with the other
boys. She'd make him bathe after them, and he'd sit in their gray
water, shivering because it had gone cold. Her cruelty to Fyodor was
of the bored, unremarkable sort. She reached for it when it was convenient, but otherwise left it alone. That is, she treated him fine until
she decided not to. Once, after Fyodor had given the younger one
his cup after drinking from it himself, the mother had come in and
slapped the cup out of Fyodor's hands and said it was disgusting, a
bad habit. Then she turned to the younger one and said, evenly,
Don't drink after him.

Still, it was a shame that one of them was dead. They were young,
too young to die, and their parents were too young to have lost a
child. It was unfortunate.

Fyodor left his mattress and pushed up a window. Outside, the
air was dense and cold. Everything glinted. The snow was lumines-
cent. The church bell tolled deep and resonant. There was a conifer
in the front yard, its branches heavy with snow. The sidewalks were
slushy and gray. No one was out in the streets. It wasn't late, but the
cold had kept everyone inside. Fyodor stretched until his bones
popped, then sat back down on the mattress and took up the book
he had been reading. But he found, every now and again, that his
vision went hazy or blurry every couple of pages. He couldn't see the
letters. He was crying.

The room cooled.

The baseboard clicked louder.

. . .

Laundromat day.

Fyodor knocked the snow off his boots as he stepped inside. When he looked up, he saw Timo near the back. They hadn't seen each other in about a month, not since the café. Timo still had the beard, and his body had changed. His chest looked broader, his shoulders wider somehow. He seemed more precisely himself. In a quantitative sense, as if there were more of him. He was wearing all black, jogging pants and a long-sleeved spandex shirt. His hair was shorter, but curlier. He didn't see Fyodor, so his face was calm and open, smiling slightly to himself as he folded his laundry.

Fyodor felt like he was seeing something he wasn't supposed to see. A hot pulse of desire raced through him. Something damp and wanting. He looked away, down to the gray slab floor, where he was still dripping snow melt. He stayed away from the back as he dropped his clothes near one of the machines and began to sort them into two separate washers.

Out came the coveralls. The bits of gristle and white fat that he picked from the fabric melted or turned stringy between his fingers. The coveralls smelled so strongly that he held his breath as he pushed them in. The lights were bright, too bright, drilling down into his skull. His head hurt. Fyodor counted out the quarters he needed from the plastic sandwich bag where he kept them. It was twice as much for the larger machine that held his coveralls. He slotted them in one after another. It was like a game. He scooped the dry powdered detergent. He waited for the machines to come to life, and when they did, he picked up his mesh sack and looked around for somewhere to wait.

Timo was looking at him.

Fyodor waved stiffly, all wrist. Timo waved back.

The laundromat was humid, though it was cooler up front where people kept coming through the door. A boxy television sat overhead, beaming news and weather at them. There was a remote control somewhere, Fyodor knew, but he'd never seen it. The channel was always locked on cable news, but never the same one twice in a row. This one was the conservative news. The volume was turned all the way down. The captions lagged, so that often a report of some gross disaster hovered over a cheery hamburger commercial, or news of a mass shooting in Florida framed a commercial about erectile dysfunction. Fyodor found it funny sometimes, but mostly, he wondered why it was that things couldn't work the way they were supposed to. But then maybe this was the way things were supposed to work, he thought. Maybe things were supposed to bleed together.

He couldn't sit near the television this time anyway because a group of undergraduates had taken that booth—four of them, all nearly identical in their fleeces and moccasins, eating chips and drinking Diet Pepsi, talking more than doing homework. Early December was finals season. Undergrads were everywhere. Taking every available surface for their performance of studying. A performance that they had been neglecting for most of the semester. You could always tell, like when someone showed up to hoop and holler in church on Easter and Christmas. There was something insincere in it. Desperate.

Fyodor walked past the line of machines, feeling dread as each step brought him closer to the back of the laundromat, where Timo was. When he got to Timo's table, he stopped and smiled as best he could. "Good to see you," he said.

"You can crash here with me if you want," Timo said.

"I don't want to get in your way," Fyodor said, but Timo just shook his head. He was folding his clothes and setting them up in neat stacks. Shirts and pants and underwear and socks, all of it laid out like the parts of an animal. "You look good," Fyodor said.

"Huh? Oh, thanks."

Timo's hands moved slowly and carefully. There was a kind of grace to his folding. He knew exactly what to do, where to place tension, where to pull, where to lay, how to truss up a garment so that it held together. Fyodor never folded his clothes right. Timo glanced at Fyodor's hands, and he pulled them away self-consciously. He had split two knuckles on his right hand into a bloody mess getting out of his truck that morning. His skin was dry and tight already, and in the bitter cold it had taken next to nothing to split it open. He'd hissed and howled, and the pain, while minor, had been first hot and then cold, as if it reached down to the bone. Now his knuckles were crusted over dark red. His nails were always in bad shape, split and chalky, but under the fluorescent lights they looked alien.

It hurt, but it wasn't as bad as it looked.

"How have you been?" Timo asked, studying his laundry very carefully. His tone was careless, casual.

"I've been all right," Fyodor said mirthlessly. "My brother died."

"Oh. Fyodor, I'm sorry."

"It's okay. I mean, it's not. Thank you," Fyodor said. He picked at the crust of his knuckles, which stung, and he winced.

"And your dad?"

"I don't know." Fyodor laughed a little at that. "That must sound strange to you."

"No," he said. "It's not strange."

"Come on, you don't have to be so nice to me."

"Fyodor."

"No, say it. We're not like you and your beautiful family. It's fine."

"That's not what I think at all," Timo said.

"Okay. Right. Okay."

Timo was holding a black T-shirt, larger than the others. Fyodor recognized the gray worn spots under the armpits. The specks of mint green paint.

"That's mine," he said.

Timo turned deep red. Fyodor laughed.

"You stole my shirt."

"You gave it to me," he said.

"Oh, did I?"

"Yes," Timo said. "Or maybe you left it at my place. I don't know. I didn't steal it."

"And you've been wearing it?"

"Yes. I have."

"It must be a dress on you."

"I'm taller."

"Still, I'm bigger."

Timo hummed, and he folded the shirt one more time and set it on the stack of other shirts. Fyodor smiled because he couldn't help himself.

"What are you smiling about?" Timo asked.

"I like the idea of you wearing my shirt."

"That's what you said when you gave it to me. Do you want it back?"

"I didn't say that."

"Yes, you did."

"I didn't say I wanted it back."

Timo took up a white shirt then and folded it, then set it on top of Fyodor's shirt.

"I'm sorry about your brother," Timo said. "I know you weren't close, but it's still hard."

"It is, surprisingly," Fyodor said. He leaned back in the chair, its cheap gray plastic warping slightly under the strain.

"What's so surprising about that?"

"Just that . . . I didn't expect it, I guess. For it to be so hard. I mean, I only saw him a few times. And the weird thing is, I don't even know which brother it is."

"Those are just details," Timo said, "you feel how you feel."

Fyodor wanted to laugh, if only because laughter might have precluded his crying. It was another of those moments in life when he felt he'd realized something about himself. Except he could not put into language what he understood or why. Sudden knowledge always made him want to cry. Because it brought with it a sense of relief—that it was okay, that he was okay, that the world would be okay. It was like when his mother had said on the porch that night that he hadn't done anything wrong.

Watching Timo as he shook out a towel and quartered it, Fyodor was overcome with great love and admiration. The long flexion of his arms, the precision of his fingers, the bored tension of his gaze. Timo noticed him staring, and he almost dropped the towel.

"Jesus, Fyodor. What is it?"

"I think," he began, but then he paused as if to draw a line through what he had just said.

"Well?"

"It won't sound right," Fyodor said.

"Try me," Timo laughed. "Come on. You're scaring me a little. What is it?"

Fyodor stood up. At the very back of the laundromat was a bright red door. Fyodor opened it and stepped into the cool, dark bathroom. He held the door open, and he looked directly at Timo, waiting. Timo remained at the folding table, surrounded by all the soft stacks of his clothes, and he squinted, seemed to think for a moment, and then there was the flash of recognition.

A channel had opened up and something clear and bright moved between them. Fyodor stepped backward into the bathroom and let the door go. Its pressurized hinges pushed it forward, but Timo caught the door before it closed. He came forward until he was standing in front of Fyodor in the bathroom. The door snapped shut. They stood in the dark room, with only the streetlights wicking through the skinny window overhead.

Timo reached for him, pulled at the drawstring of his pants. Fyodor reached for Timo, for the warm skin of his belly under the spandex shirt. Timo's body had been soft before, but now he was compact and firm. Not hard. But firm. They did not kiss. Timo licked at Fyodor's neck, and Fyodor bit the bony process of his clavicle. Timo dug his nails into Fyodor's lower back. Fyodor gripped Timo's throat. Timo pulled too hard on Fyodor's testicles. Fyodor raked his teeth across Timo's thighs. They took turns kneeling between each other's legs and sucking one another off. Timo tasted salty and clean. He watched Timo's head bob between his legs, and the soft crown of his head. The wet heat of Timo's mouth felt like kindness. Timo stood up and leaned against the cold white concrete of the wall under the window. Fyodor came up behind him and pressed his face into Timo's curls. There was a low groan. The damp press of their bodies. Timo arched against him and he reached back and guided Fyodor until Fyodor felt himself breach then sink through the resistance of Timo's body. He gripped the long metal safety rail in front of Timo's hips, using it to lock Timo in place, and they fucked there in the bathroom of the laundromat in the cold darkness, the world gleaming white beyond them. He came inside of Timo, who panted and whined and came hot and lush and sticky in Fyodor's hand. Fyodor extricated himself slowly. The bathroom smelled like piss and shit. They cleaned up in the sink, washing and rinsing. The tap was cold, and Fyodor flinched when he pressed the wet, coarse paper towels to himself. They left the bathroom first one and then the other. And they took up their places back at the table. Fyodor's body was still humming, still tight. His shoulders were tense. He had come, but he felt still that there was something unvented in him.

Timo looked pale. He said, "I didn't ask before. Are you . . . are you good?"

"Oh, yeah," Fyodor said. "I had a test a month ago."

"Okay," he said.

"Are you?" Fyodor asked.

"PrEP," he said.

"Oh, good."

"You should. Well, think about it."

"Insurance," Fyodor said. "Condoms. Usually."

"Yeah."

"I mean, I haven't, anyway."

"Haven't what?"

"Haven't. Since you. Since we. Yeah."

Timo nodded. But he did not say the same thing in return, which

Fyodor knew he shouldn't have blamed him for, but he couldn't help it. He felt a little angry about that.

There was a loud buzz then. Fyodor checked his laundry. It was time. He took out his clothes, their damp weight, their hardness. He tossed them into a red cart and wheeled them to the back, near the driers. He transferred them, trying all the time not to look at Timo. But he could smell him still, too, or at least smell the hand soap from the bathroom. It was on both of them.

They had never had sex in a public place before. It was strange that after their relationship had ended, they would still be doing new things together. Finding new ways to be together. It felt strange to have new history when it was all over. He snapped the machine shut, but then, in the reflection of the glass and the spinning clothes, he saw Timo looking at him.

"What?" he asked without turning. Embarrassed.

"Nothing," Timo said.

"It's funny. We never did laundry together," he said. "Before, I mean."

"And we had that fight about your clothes."

"Those fights," he clarified.

"Yeah. Those fights."

"I don't hate you. I'm not mad at you. Obviously."

"Why obviously?"

Fyodor turned then. He sat down in the chair. Timo sat, too. Between them were the towels and the shirts.

"Well, because of what we did. We wouldn't have done that if we were mad or hated each other."

"People fuck people they hate."

"I guess that's true. But I wouldn't."

At this, Timo laughed and flicked away a lump of dryer lint from the table.

"Did you like that? In the bathroom?"

"Yeah, I did."

Timo nodded, like he'd made up his mind about something.

"It's nice to do things together."

"I don't think that means fucking in public for most people, right?"

"You started it."

"Fair enough," Fyodor said.

One afternoon, in the new year, there was a shooting in Alabama.

A man had gone into a local bank and shot all of the workers and customers. It was such a strange idea. That a person could go into a bank and shoot every single person there. Had they all lined up and been shot down? Had they tried to run and had he just had excellent aim? It was a kind of miracle, bestowed by a bloody and ruthless god of carnage.

Fyodor read the news on his lunch break at the plant. He stood out in the parking lot. The sky was a tranquil blue. The trees at the edge of the parking lot swayed.

The bank was in the town where his mother lived. He had not been to Alabama in years.

He called her, but she did not answer. He called again, but she did not answer. He called again, and when she picked up, he almost fell to his knees in relief.

"What?" she asked. There were sirens behind her voice.

"Where are you?" he asked.

"At home," she said.

"Why are there sirens?"

"Oh, boy, I don't know."

"The bank," he said.

"Yes," she said.

"Are you okay?"

"It was some boy," she said. "Some stupid, stupid boy. Shot up everybody. They all dead."

"How many?" he asked.

"Seven, eight, I don't know."

"He shot all those people."

"Well," she said, like she meant to say something else, but she didn't. Fyodor felt stupid for feeling so worried. It seemed stupid to think that his life might intersect with the greater, terrifying course of life in the world. "You all right?"

"I called you, remember?" he said.

"That don't mean you all right."

"I'll make it," he said.

They got off the phone, but Fyodor couldn't get his hands to stop shaking. He got into his truck and turned on the radio, trying to find a station, any station that would ease the silence. He found a classic oldies station and slid down in his seat. The cab of his truck smelled like oil and dried blood. He could see his breath. The snow had turned soft, and the parking lot was bathed in filthy water. The plant looked like an elementary school. Set a short distance behind the main building were great silver towers and other steel structures. It looked, in this way, like a real factory rather than just a place where they took apart animals. Fyodor gripped the wheel. The music was familiar. He tried to think of that night in the car with his father, tried to remember what had been playing on the station, but he couldn't. How like memory to abandon him when he most needed it.

How like memory—so full of empty promises.

Fyodor really had thought his mother was dead. In those long moments before she picked up, he had really thought she'd been shot and killed. But she had been as indifferent to the fact of violence as she was to him. The violence hadn't pierced her life at all.

He tried to breathe.

His hands still shook. He wouldn't be able to handle the knife. He shut his eyes. The phone rang. He answered it.

"Hey—I just saw the news. Hey. Are you okay?" It was Timo.

"I'm fine. My mom's fine," Fyodor said. "I just called. She sounded pretty bored by it, actually."

Timo clicked his tongue. "Well, I'm glad she's all right. Still, fuck. I hope he fries."

"You do?" Fyodor asked.

"He killed like ten people. Normal, ordinary people. Running errands. Yeah, I hope he fries."

Fyodor clenched the wheel harder with his left hand. Something nagged at Fyodor. Something prickly, like coarse new wool.

"You hope he dies?"

"He's a murderer."

"Oh," Fyodor said.

"I mean, you don't think he deserves to live after what he did, do you?"

Fyodor watched a hawk skim low to the roof of the sandstone building before turning and shooting back up into the sky. It was an oppressively beautiful day.

"That just seems like a cruel thing to say, when it's already such a painful situation."

"Cruel is murdering people."

"And animals," Fyodor said.

"What?"

"That's what you think, right? That murdering animals for food is cruel."

"Jesus Christ. I am not having this fight with you."

"Isn't electrocuting him or injection or whatever, isn't that just as bad?"

"No, Fyodor, it's not, and if you can't see that, then we don't have anything to discuss."

Timo hung up on him, and Fyodor sat there with the phone still pressed to his ear. He could hear the air inside his own head. His ear was warm and sweaty. He tucked the phone into his pocket.

His hands smelled like the powerful cleaner they used when they left the line, so intense that it left your palms white and hard, and tingling. He could still feel the burn of it.

It was unfair of him to have said that to Timo, he knew. But Fyodor hadn't been trying to win a fight. He had been trying to articulate something about what he felt and thought. He had wanted to ask why it was that people found it so much easier to extend charity to the anonymous herd beasts of the field than to other people. Loving people was hard. It was difficult sometimes to believe that they were good. It was hard to know them. But that didn't mean you could just go on without trying. What he believed was that love was more than just kindness and more than just giving people the things they wanted. Love was more than the parts of it that were easy and pleasurable. Sometimes love was trying to understand. Love was trying to get beyond what was hard. Love, love, love.

Fyodor got out of his truck. His shift was starting back up.

When Fyodor and Timo had been sleeping together again for a while, they went to a show at one of the campus galleries.

There were supposed to be some talks by minor but charismatic artists who Timo had spent a week researching on the internet. For that week, Timo had been slipping into their conversation small references to the artists' paintings or to their philosophy, and Fyodor, drowsy from work and full of dinner, would nod as the conversation carried him along. This was a part of his effort to be a different sort of person, so that Timo would not feel quite so much like he was bad or stupid or whatever. Fyodor didn't find art pretentious. He didn't find it overrated. He wanted very much to like art, but he always felt more or less on the outside when he looked at it. Sculptures were easier for him because he could understand the manual nature of the work. But paintings, no matter how conventional, always felt cold and inert. Not that he couldn't appreciate their beauty. It's just that he was without a context. He found himself sometimes wanting to compare the postwar geometric work that Timo loved so much to certain cuts of meat he had handled that day—the marbling, the fat cap, the rich deposits of fat in their rhomboidal shapes, which were so beautifully and cleanly delineated that it was like they had been drawn by hand. But the one time he had tried, Timo had grown so angry at him that they hadn't talked for the rest of the night. They'd just laid there in Fyodor's overheated room, sweating

and stewing. Timo thought he was trying to reduce the work somehow. But that wasn't it at all. He just wanted a context.

But now here they were at the show in the gallery. Fyodor had
worn his best jeans and a chambray shirt with no burns or paint on
it. Everyone looked elegant and smart. He felt thick and slow. They
sipped champagne from small plastic cups. Fyodor took two at a
time and poured them into one cup. Timo lingered near his arm,
looking tense in the shoulders and in the jaw. Fyodor nudged him
gently and tried to catch his eye, to smile or laugh. At one point during the reception he brushed his knuckles against Timo's hand, but
Timo jerked away from him like a startled animal. They had driven
over in Timo's car, so Fyodor couldn't just leave, though he wanted
to. His shirt was too tight and his throat was dry the whole time
from the champagne and later from the gin and tonic he ordered.
He went out through one of the side doors and stood on the concrete
patio. There, he looked out over the frozen green pond to the hillside that sloped up behind the gallery. The lights inside cast a hazy
glow, and he breathed the cold air in deeply.

Fyodor still thought sometimes about the shooting in Alabama.
There had been four other shootings across the South in the last
month or so, each rising for a brief instant above the noise and
clamor of the news, the whole country looking in one direction at
one thing, burning a hole in the fabric of the culture. But then, the
next day or the next, their thoughts turned back to the common
demands of daily life. Everyone went back into the anonymous whir
of things, safe inside their irrelevance. He sometimes also thought
of his dead brother. He'd found out from his mother that it had been
the older one who had died, suddenly, from a heart defect. He'd

been out with friends at a bar, drinking after work, as common as anything. And then, just like that, he'd died.

Fyodor went across the patio onto the grass and the dirt. He crouched near the pond and leaned forward until he could see his own shadow on the surface. He put his palm flat to it and held it there, feeling how cold it was, how slippery. At the center of the pond, there was a place where the water was not frozen. It churned and foamed as a spigot there spat out new water. He thought he could feel the water moving under the sheet of ice, that he could feel the ice shifting. Maybe he could. He swayed in his crouch. His thighs burned. The hill was a sheer cliff face, fragile clay and mica, pale stone cut away in rectangular sheets. Fyodor glanced over his shoulder. In the golden light of the first-floor gallery, he saw the people of the party as if they were fish in an aquarium. He didn't see Timo anywhere. They were anonymous, elegant people who seemed a part of a different species. Nothing like the men at the plant, who were like trees that had been stunted by too much wind and not enough water. Hard chunks of men, their yellow teeth, their jagged hands, their flesh bronzed and burned, turned to leather almost. Nothing in his life had anything to do with this place.

Fyodor stood up. He wiped his hands on his jeans, and he thought, with a dull laugh, that he could have leaped into the pond and sunk through the ice and the water and no one at this party would have noticed or cared at all.

He joined the party again, this time hugging the wall, watching Timo from across the room, over the tops of the beautiful heads. Timo was handsome, smiling or laughing now and then with groups of people he knew from the university. But he never looked out toward Fyodor. Instead, there was a solid, dark, inward turning on

Timo's part, away from them all. Fyodor recognized this habit of Timo's. A way of getting along without requiring anything from anyone else. It was his particular way of being selfish. Fyodor drank more of the champagne. He drank white wine. He drank more gin. He grew more and more drunk, which he measured by the deepening of the gold light in the room and the haziness of the figures. By the time the artists were ushered behind a dais to deliver their talks, one dreary monologue after another, a procession of gray still shots or slow-motion video, Fyodor's eyes were barely open. He could feel the sluggishness of time. The wavering loose amalgamation of moments. Nothing was adhering to anything else. It all slipped by him. He was very cold by the end of it. And he realized that he was not leaning against a wall at all, but against a windowpane, and he was sweating, so his back was damp and then cold.

Timo looked up then, toward the end of the last talk, and saw Fyodor. His expression was sour and hard. Fyodor nodded to him blearily. He waved. Timo turned away. Fyodor was tired. His body was sore. Timo was being cold to him again, for reasons that were opaque. It was hardly fair. What had he done to deserve it? Nothing, he thought. He had done nothing at all to deserve any of this. He laughed quietly to himself. And then less quietly, and less quietly than that, until he was laughing out loud, and everyone turned to look at him. He doubled over laughing. The heat in his stomach expanded, reached up into his chest, and he just kept laughing, so hard his body shook and then hurt. Sharp pain down his back, along his spine, and then up his front to the base of his throat. He laughed, and then it was no longer funny and he stood up and wiped the tears from his eyes. People were staring at him, but trying to avoid his eyes. They kept looking away. Timo came up to him and said stiffly, "That's enough."

In the car, on the way home, Fyodor rested his head against the cool glass of the window. He kept his eyes closed, except that sometimes they hit a rut in the road and his eyelids parted and he saw a flash of streetlight or the glow of a passing building. Sometimes the darkness broke open and he saw into a person's life—folding laundry, walking, eating dinner, that sort of thing, all of it in rectangles of orange-gold light. People in their tanks like animals. The cold air helped his headache, helped the stinging in his eyes. It was a relief.

"Goddammit. We can't do anything without it turning into a fucking circus," Timo was saying. The music on the radio was distant and hazy, an old standard. Fyodor sat up. The car made him sway. He tried to hum the song, but he was out of rhythm.

"Fucking nonsense," Timo said.

"I'm drunk," Fyodor said, as if by way of explanation, but Timo just shook his head.

"Obviously."

"I'm sorry," Fyodor said, but it just made him laugh.

"It's not funny."

"I know," he said, but the laughter persisted. He coughed. Put his head back against the window. "Did you have a good time?"

"No, as a matter of fact, I didn't."

"Well, I'm sorry about that." Fyodor's hands were sweaty. He held them clasped in his lap, ran his thumb over the ridge of his other thumb. His hands felt filmy and greasy. The car smelled like pine air freshener.

Timo leaned forward at a stoplight and turned on the heat. It rattled faintly and then settled into life. The air was warm on Fyodor's knees and thighs. He thought he'd fall asleep right there. Timo looked at him. Fyodor could see him in the window, a nearly translucent reflection. He recognized the course they were on. They were going to Fyodor's house. There were trees overhead, clustered close to the street. Snow dripping, like rain almost. It was late March.

"What was that back there?" Timo asked.

"Do you remember that day we talked about the shooting?"

"What?"

"You said you hoped that man fried. That he died because of what he'd done."

"I don't want to talk about this."

"I didn't say anything at the time," Fyodor said. "But I don't agree with you. I think killing people is wrong. It is always wrong. Even if you do something really awful or heinous. Nobody should get to kill you."

"You butcher animals for a living. Don't lecture me about capital punishment."

"But, see, that's the thing. You act like . . . ," and here Fyodor closed his eyes. His mouth felt acidic. He smacked his lips several times, like that would help surface the words. He could feel his mind reaching for them, searching out the contours of what he meant to say. Yet it all felt useless somehow. Like nothing he said would matter much. They had passed the old church on the corner, which meant they were close to his house. He sighed. "I mean, what, you want to kill me, too? Because of my job? Because of how I feed myself? You think I am a murderer."

"You're right," Timo said. "I do think you're a murderer. And I hate your job. And I think that if you walk into a bank and shoot a bunch of people, yeah, you deserve to die. Like an animal."

Fyodor nodded slowly. There it was. He reached out like he could grab the point out of the air and hold it. He folded his fist around it. The point was solid in his hand and he turned to hold it in front of Timo's face. He opened his palm.

"That's it," he said. "That's cruelty."

"What?"

"You said *die like an animal*. But you don't think animals should be killed. So that's cruelty. Isn't it?"

"Get out of my car, Fyodor. You can walk home."

Fyodor nodded. He closed his palm. He got out of the car. His balance was okay. He could make it. The snowdrifts had turned filthy and porous. He kicked some of the brittle snow and it went down dry and hard, like flakes of dandruff. He grunted with satisfaction.

Animals lived and animals died. They were friend and they were food. They began and they ended. All that separated humans from animals was bitter hypocrisy. They were all just upright beasts, walking on their hind legs, baying at electric moons. They were nothing. But they had in them the dignity of life, a right to be. He had not always understood this. But he understood it now.

When he got home, twin headlights fell across him as he slid his key into the door. He turned back and put his hand over his eyes so he could see. There was Timo's car in the street, pulled up into his usual spot. Timo got out and stood there with his hands in his pockets. Fyodor understood then. Timo had followed him down the three houses until he had made it home. It was kindness. It had the indifference of love.

Fyodor raised a hand. He pushed the door open. The front hall was stale. The stars above them were cold and white.

Work in the morning.

3.

Ivan the Terrible and His Son Ivan

van and Goran did not talk about how long it had been since they had fucked. They did not talk about how long it had been since they had held each other and fallen asleep. They slept together, woke together, ate together, and otherwise went about their lives as though nothing at all had changed, though of course everything had.

It was not denial. It was something else—fear, perhaps, or a lack of caring.

They fought about dumb things, like who used more electricity or who used more water. But it was really a fight about them not fucking. Whenever Ivan tried to initiate sex, Goran was tired. Whenever Goran tried to initiate sex, Ivan felt cold and far away from himself. They couldn't get themselves to align. They kept misfiring. Ivan slept on the couch, which aggravated his joints. Goran hid his pain medication. Ivan left glasses of water perched on Goran's keyboard.

The not fucking had a cause, though they were not willing to face it. They were both graduate students, Goran in music and Ivan in finance, but Goran had family money. That was the beginning and the end of their trouble. Money made things easier, in one sense, when you had been raised without it. Like the first good gulp of air after a long run. But then came the burn.

Ivan felt like he could never get the upper hand. Goran paid most of their rent and most of their bills, paid for their groceries and their toiletries. What Ivan had to spare, he sent home to his parents or otherwise saved in dribs and drabs for some time in the near future. Goran never made a fuss about paying for things, until he was drunk or mad or irritated about something Ivan hadn't done to his exact specification. Then it was, *The least you could do* this and *The least you could do* that, all in this tone of passive-aggressive reproach. He could barely remember why they'd gotten together in the first place. But then if he left, where would he go? He couldn't afford a place on his own. He couldn't afford anything. He was at the end of a bleak period in his life, finishing out an MBA in hopes of getting a decent job somewhere, anywhere, a job that would let him pay his parents back for all they had done for him. Goran didn't understand that. He had money. So much money that it fell on him like dust or snow, floating down in great tufts from his parents and grandparents.

Goran said he spent the money so freely because it wasn't really his. He was adopted, a black kid in a white family, studying music in the Midwest. Trying to be a musician, trying to figure out what it meant to be a musician in the world today. The money, he said, had been earmarked for some white kid who'd never been born. And so he'd slotted into that kid's place. Whenever Goran talked about race, about being black, Ivan felt guilty for forgetting that he was black. Goran only ever brought it up when he got sad or drunk and talked about the money he'd spent earlier that day on dinner or lunch or buying a friend a new jacket for the winter. The gifts had the outward appearance of generosity, and Ivan thought of them as such, but there was something so pitiful underneath the giving, and Goran made him think it had to do with being black and having money from his rich white family.

He'd said that to Goran once, early on, as they were walking around the Ped Mall eating frozen yogurt. A jazz trio was playing at one end of the pavilion, and a black guy with a relaxer was singing acoustic covers of Michael Jackson songs at the other end. Goran had been talking about how he wished his parents could understand how difficult it was seeing the news of the black kid who'd been shot by police in Ohio. How hard it was for him to see that. *We don't understand*, they kept saying. *We tried to do right by you. We love you.* Goran did a cruel imitation of their voices. And Ivan said, *I wish I had your parents. Rich white people sound really nice right about now.* And Goran had stopped and thrown his yogurt at Ivan's head. *Fuck you*, Goran said. *My people are dying and you're full of self-pity.*

Ivan had almost replied that those were not Goran's people—not the black boy who had died playing with a toy gun, not the black boy who had died in Florida for walking home in the rain, not the black man strangled to death in New York, or the black man shot in the car while his children watched him bleed. They belonged to a dark fraternity of modern martyrs, and Goran belonged to a rich family from the Chicago suburbs, grown obscenely wealthy for their early invention of key manufacturing technologies and the reconstitution of American slavery as they exploited the labor of the working industrial class. But he did not say that. What did he know. It wasn't his place. Instead he'd said, *I'm sorry. You're right. I don't get it. And I'm sorry I don't.*

He tried to keep a low profile in both their relationship and their apartment. He tried to wash the dishes and fold the clothes and look after the trash cans and recycling. He tried to keep things good and running smoothly, and when he had a thought, he kept it to himself. Goran had enough going on. Goran liked to say that he was struggling to figure out where he fit. Where he was in the world. Mostly he just seemed so sad and so lost, and Ivan wanted to comfort him. But they couldn't get it to work, so they drifted along.

Their apartment was a one-bedroom on the second floor of an old house at the corner of Iowa Avenue and Van Buren. Their downstairs neighbors were two roommates, painters in the MFA program. The man was pale and had a perpetual look of sleep deprivation. The woman was sullen and muscular, with buzzed platinum-blond hair. They were not a couple, though Ivan saw them often at the corner co-op buying discount organic produce, wearing matching overalls or jumpsuits. Ivan sometimes saw the man sitting on the shared front porch, smoking. The man would hike one leg up against his chest while the other one dangled low over the shrubs. The woman walked a large, barrel-chested gray dog that did not belong to her. Ivan knew it wasn't hers because he never heard it. What he did hear from downstairs was their music. They played jazz standards and bluesy renditions of songs from the Great American Songbook, but what they played most of all were show tunes. They loved Cole Porter. They played *Anything Goes* with Patti LuPone over and over. He could feel it under his feet.

Some nights, Goran went to the poet bar and Ivan stayed home. Goran was sleeping with a married poet who had two small, blond children. Ivan had seen them in the café talking. Goran reached out and touched the man's forearm, and the man glanced around furtively and then withdrew. Ivan assumed the poets, like dancers, all slept together. As if they were a restless pack rubbing against one another for heat in the winter. Iowa was a kind of cultural winter—they had all come to this speck of a city in the middle of a middle state in order to study art, to hone themselves and their ideas like perfect, terrifying weapons, and in the monastic kind of deprivation they found here, they turned to one another. Every dying species sought its own kind of comfort.

When he was alone, Ivan sat at Goran's keyboard. He could play fragments of songs from the radio, but he couldn't play anything complete. Once, while Goran was doing the dishes, he'd sat down behind the keyboard and played part of something from a band he liked, but before he'd even reached the end of what little he could manage, Goran threw a glass from the kitchen into the wall opposite Ivan's head. It burst into a powder that dropped in fragments onto the keyboard, spraying into Ivan's hair.

"Goran!" Ivan stood up slowly, carefully.

Goran was standing in the kitchen archway with soap dripping from his hands onto the carpet. His expression was hard and cruel. He said, "Don't be stupid."

Ivan had spent days picking the glass from the carpet. He ran the vacuum over the spot every day for weeks, but he could always feel the glass beneath his feet, pressing at him from among the fibers.

Ivan lived on student loans, amassing a pile of debt in order to study the meteorology of money. His parents couldn't help him because they had wrung every penny from their lives to send him to ballet school, first in Boston and then later New York, where it had appeared likely that he would make a life for himself—until it turned out that his tendons were bad and wouldn't heal, and at the age of seventeen he found himself needing to make other plans.

His mother was an elementary school teacher, and his father was a city mechanic for Boston who worked on the buses and the trucks and machines that broke down in the water sanitation plant. The strain of paying for his tuition those ten years had been hidden from him, except on Christmas breaks and summer vacation, when he came home and found his parents diminished and tired. They scraped and saved. They accepted money from their church and from their parents. They poured all their resources into him, until nothing was left for them. The summer he turned seventeen, Ivan remembered, he had lain awake in his bed, thinking how stupid it all seemed. To have given so much and to have tried so hard, only to come up against the hard fact of biology. He had lain in bed for hours and hours that summer, burning up with anger, until he vibrated with it. What a cruel fact of the world, that you could live your whole life in sight of what you want most and still find yourself unable to attain it, because of some vicious quirk.

He decided to study finance because he knew he could make a living that way, enough to support himself and his parents. While at school, he worked in restaurants and construction, in the cold and heat and the disgusting slush of Boston's outer suburbs. He got accustomed to driving all day to a job site, working, and then driving the winding roads and blind curves to Somerville, only to wake up and do it again the next morning.

But he worked and studied and saved, and he graduated, and now at twenty-five he found himself at the tail end of his MBA, needing to bridge the summer in New York or San Francisco because he couldn't do finance right in Iowa, unless he wanted to stay here permanently, which he did not. He didn't have enough money to make it possible, and yet needed it very much to be possible. In this way, Ivan's life hadn't changed very much.

That January, he was helping his friend Noah build a shed out in the country. The land belonged to Bert, who owned several properties around Iowa City and the outlying areas. He bought up old houses and converted them into apartments to be rented by gangs of undergraduates and grad students. Ivan lived in one such apartment with Goran, though Bert was not their landlord. Noah rented from him. Bert was white, flabby, and wore thick glasses. He looked like one of those men from *America's Most Wanted*. Sometimes Ivan looked up from where he was squatting on the ground, tying something to a stake, and found Bert staring at him. Noah would laugh and say, *Don't mind him.*

The wind chapped his knuckles, but the work was good, and it left him feeling tired and hot. On bright days, he lay on his back in the bed of the truck and listened to the gray wind comb the grass flat. The fields were muddy. The spindly trees on the edge of the forest swayed.

Noah was in the dance program at Iowa. He'd grown up in West Des Moines, half Japanese, half white, and for most of his childhood he'd been an elite gymnast, until he got bored with it. He'd found the other boys tiresome in their intensity, and he used to get weird looks from their parents, like they were always scoping him out to see if he was outgrowing their own kids. In ballet, every boy was a little princeling. Ivan knew it well, the way teachers fawned over the boys, even the ones with bad feet and lazy tendencies. In ballet, if you were a boy you were a precious commodity, rare and exceptional, even if you were mediocre, and he said the music was better anyway. He liked dance. It suited him.

Ivan had first seen Noah when he attended a fall dance recital. It was some modernist nonsense, and the choreography wasn't very good, but Noah was good in it. He had a fluid easiness to his dance, natural in ways that some people were forced. It was hard for Ivan to watch other people dance. He missed it so much that it hurt his stomach. It tired him out, too, because he found himself memorizing the choreography, twitching with the little shadow motions it took to get it down cold in the spine. But that night he'd just watched Noah dance, and later he bought him some drinks at the bar.

Noah said he had auditions coming up, now that he was graduating. Auditions that would determine the course of his life. Ivan said he could understand that. He had some interviews coming up, too. If he was lucky—*fuck*, if he was lucky. Noah said he was getting a very late start, but that was life, what could you do. Sometimes it just snuck up on you. Ivan laughed. Yeah, it was like that.

A large blond dog roamed the allotment. Noah called him Dota, after the video game, and gave him food from a bag he kept in the back of his truck. He said Bert told him not to do it, which was why he took special pleasure in feeding him and driving him around. Bert had said that the dog was wild and was full of fleas and ticks, and Noah's eyes gleamed when he told Ivan this, as though they were coconspirators. Sometimes, Dota climbed up onto the truck bed next to Ivan and lay over him. It was warm under his weight, and Ivan would fall asleep that way despite the cold.

One afternoon, after they had knocked off for lunch, Noah went on one of his walks in the woods. Ivan and Dota climbed into the truck bed to nap. Then, seemingly the moment he closed his eyes, Ivan was startled by a sound like distant thunder. Dota jumped to the ground and let out a long howl. There was another sharp crack in the distance. It wasn't thunder at all but rifle fire. Recollection, as firm as the sound itself, swept toward him as if across a great plain. Dota went in circles, yipping and dancing anxiously.

Ivan dialed Noah, but the sound of the ringer came from back over his shoulder in the truck cab. He leaped to the ground next to Dota. Another shot, the cracking wave of the sound. Was he supposed to go into the woods after Noah? Or stay where he was? He had no way of knowing if he was in danger. He waited. The wind changed direction. A bitter sulfur smell carried to him. So close. His fear sharpened.

But then another sound came over the tops of the trees—laughter. Noah's voice. Ivan ran, jumping over the low ditch, to reach him at the edge of the woods. Noah was taller than Ivan, with thick, dark hair. His smile was crooked. He had a little tear of a scar near the middle of his lips.

"Fuck," Ivan said, gripping him by the shoulders.

"Oh, hey," Noah said.

"Didn't you hear those guns?"

Noah laughed louder. His breath was hot on Ivan's cheeks. Ivan shook him, and Noah just laughed louder.

"Those weren't guns."

"What?"

"Bert left some air canisters in his burning barrel. Fool."

Ivan dug his fingers harder into Noah's shoulders. The wind had turned and went back through the trees. Dota danced at their feet, leaping up and putting his front paws on Noah's stomach. The dog barked twice, then looked back at Ivan and barked at him, too. His tongue was purple, spotted pink like a reptile.

"God," Ivan said. "I thought. I thought."

Noah laughed as he gripped Dota by his fur.

"Your face," he said.

"God," Ivan said.

After they pulled off from Bert's place, Noah and Ivan found a deserted stretch of road to park. They unbuttoned each other's flannels, and there in the creaking cold of Noah's truck cab, they jerked each other off while Dota panted hot into their faces. Their hands were still stiff, still hard from building the shed, and they had splinters in their palms, dried mud caked under their nails, but under their clothes they were clean and smelled like the sea. Ivan bent over the center console and took Noah's whole cock into his mouth. His pubic hair was dark and bristly. It tickled Ivan's nose and lips. Noah shivered and asked if it was all right if he came in Ivan's mouth, and Ivan only nodded and grumbled, and there it all was, hot and slimy on his tongue and the roof of his mouth. Noah did the same to him, but Ivan couldn't stay hard, and after a while, he just pulled up his pants on the seat and said it was all right.

Dota lay his head on Ivan's lap. He was too big to be in the cab with them, but it was too cold for him to ride in the back. Noah's truck was old and lacked a CD player, but some guy Noah knew through his weed man had rigged it to play music from a cell phone. Noah drove with his chin on his left hand, his right lazily guiding them along. They listened to Rachmaninoff, which was not Ivan's favorite, but which Noah preferred to the exclusion of almost everything else except Tupac.

The road was easy, a stretch of slick darkness running through yellow and brown fields. They sometimes passed houses crouching in oncoming crepuscular light, and it was like a painting of the dark interior of this country. Houses stripped by the wind and lesser fortune: white clapboard or crumbling brick; low, dark roofs; large front windows or slits of gold light in falling evening. Hills rose fitfully at the turns in the road, wild grass tufted out of their backs like fur. There were scraggly trees and frayed rope hanging from their branches and large tires sitting in yards or propped against sheds. The whole commonness of the world was before them.

"It's depressing out here," Ivan said.

"Is it?"

"Look," he said, motioning toward the windshield, to the houses they passed on either side of the road, but Noah shrugged.

"I don't know. It just looks like people."

"This is America. Why do they live this way?"

"You're American. How do you live?" Noah asked sharply.

"Not like this," Ivan said.

"Are you sure?"

"Whatever," he said, though he knew this was not an answer.

"I told you before. If you need more money, there are things you can do."

"I'm not going to sleep around for cash," Ivan said.

"That's not what I mean, and you know I don't do that. Not with Bert."

"Oh, so it's a love match?" Ivan put his head against the glass.

Noah drew to a stop on the gravel shoulder of the country road. They were tilted a little into the ditch. The engine rumbled underneath like a drowsing animal. Dota picked up his head a little. Ivan stroked him.

"Don't be so naive," Noah said, leaning forward to brace himself against the steering wheel. "All I mean is, there's this site. You can sign up. Make videos. Get cash. It's easy. I do it. Some of the other guys in the program do it. Super simple."

"Porn? Your plan is porn?"

"I'm sorry, but some of us don't have trust funds. Including you."

Ivan exhaled. This wasn't the first time Noah had suggested making videos of himself, but Ivan hated even the most mundane forms of social media. Getting online felt like subjecting himself to the whims and feelings of other people, and he had a hard enough time doing that in person, with real people. He couldn't imagine a legion of invisible watchers, their eyes upon him at any moment, scanning a perfect re-creation of his past actions.

"Your body is fucking amazing. Why not use it?" Noah asked.

"My body is shit. My knees are on fire, just from building a shed. I'm not some dancer anymore."

Noah blew hot air from his nostrils. He drummed his fingers on the dash.

"You make me sick," he said after a moment. "You make me fucking sick. Why complain if you're not doing anything about it?"

"I wasn't complaining."

"Why do people live like this?" Noah said in an unkind version of Ivan's voice.

"Why are you being so mean to me?"

"Because you're wasting it all."

"Wasting what?"

"Everything," Noah said. But he put the truck back into drive and pulled back onto the road.

Ivan did not know what to say to that. He had thought he understood something about his life, but now he thought he understood nothing at all.

Noah put him out in the cold and was gone.

Ivan stood on the porch until he had gone numb from the cold.

Goran and Ivan went to a party at Noah's apartment up the street. The sky was clear and dark, and a few hard stars glinted over them. Goran had just come from a late practice, and his brow was still damp. Occasionally he shivered or said something under his breath, directed not at Ivan but at someone else. Whenever Goran came home from rehearsal, the day's conversations leaked out of him like a vapor. Rebuttals and redirects, subtle realignments of facts spontaneously burst forth.

Ivan had spent the day applying for summer internships. His head swam with the details of his résumé, neat columns of type shifting in holograph before his eyes. Their shoes scraped and slipped. Goran reached out to grip him. His hand went to Goran's back, held him steady. It was a good, solid kind of contact.

They didn't speak.

Noah lived on the second floor of a house on Jefferson Street. People spilled down the stairs of the front hall, out onto the porch and into the yard. The lights in the first-floor apartment were on, but the shades were drawn. As Ivan and Goran walked up the driveway, Goran pointed to the silhouette of a man moving.

"That's where Timo's boyfriend lives."

"Is Timo going to be at the party?" Ivan asked.

"Maybe. They might be broken up. It's never going well with them."

Timo was Goran's friend, maybe more-than-friend. They'd had a thing before Ivan got in the picture. Timo worked in math, in some way, and he was dating some townie. They were always breaking up and getting back together, which Ivan understood. Sometimes it was like that. Some days Goran took his married poet on dates to the café where Ivan worked, and on those days he saw Timo coming in after the poet left. They would nod to each other, he and Timo, and that was the extent of their communication. Goran saw Timo often. They ate dinner and went to concerts at the auditorium. Once, Timo had come to their apartment to return a record, but Goran wasn't yet home, was still on his way. Ivan offered Timo water, but Timo didn't accept. They stood there awkwardly for the fifteen minutes it took Goran to get home. Then Goran and Timo left together. The record was on the table. It was a Rubinstein recording, with an old, yellowed album cover. Ivan put on the record and listened to the long opening passages of the first piece. It was somber and yet contained a real brightness.

Ivan missed music. He missed moving to music. He missed dancing. He played the record all the way through and then started it again. When Goran returned, a little drunk, a little happy, he climbed onto Ivan's lap and kissed him. They fucked while the record played itself out, then fell asleep, oblivious to its hiccupping, scratching silence.

The next morning, Goran was furious when he woke and found

the record still spinning. It was unreasonable. The record had been playing when Goran returned, after all, and he could have stopped it himself. Ivan felt that they were both complicit in leaving the record out and in whatever damage might have occurred to the record or the stylus. But Goran didn't feel that way, obviously. Instead, he said from the other room, "The least you could do." But then went silent. He left the apartment and didn't come back the whole day. It was the last time Timo had come to their place. The last time they'd fucked.

Goran kept his friends to himself. He and Ivan didn't do a lot of social mixing. Their lives were like those dumb little toys you made in school with oil and food coloring and vinegar and sometimes water. Just lying there on each other, but never mixing.

The silhouette stopped in the middle of the window, turned, and receded from the shade, going deeper into the apartment. They climbed the steps. Goran reached over and rapped at the window to see if someone would come to check, but no one did. They went into the front hall and climbed the stairs to Noah's apartment, squeezing by people on the stairs, their faces shiny with good times and good drugs. It reminded him of ballet school, where the parties had been spontaneous in a low-key, illicit way. Some of the older dancers had still older boyfriends and girlfriends or people they fucked. It resulted in a caravan of cigarettes, cheap vodka, cheap beer, cheap tabs of ecstasy, and not very cheap ketamine.

The drugs were, at first, a part of it. A way of asserting their dominance over their bodies, over their parents, over the paternal order of their instructors and the needs of dance. Their way of being independent, being alive in their flesh, until they had to wake up at the first gray slice of dawn and pour themselves into tights and limber up before morning class. The drugs were, at first, just another way of putting on the pelt of how they wanted to be seen. Beautiful, young, but older than their years, wise in that they could get their bodies to do what they wanted. Ivan remembered very clearly being fourteen and looking to one side of the studio, seeing boys just a little younger than him having fun and playing games of flexibility, seeing who could get their spine to bend back and down and grip their ankles, toppling over and laughing like kids. They *were* kids. And then looking to the other side of the studio and the boys no more than a year older than him, looking down through the studio windows at the streets below, something adult in their bored nonchalance, the way they were whispering to one another—making plans, Ivan knew, to smoke during lunch. That's how young they still were, that they made plans to do something *bad*.

Climbing the stairs at Noah's party, his hand at Goran's back, Ivan could see in the eyes of these young people, too, how desperately they wanted to *be*—and how desperately this hinged on being *seen*. That if no one witnessed you in the state of freedom, then you were not free. This seemed, to Ivan, really sad. He wanted to grip their shoulders and tell them to leave and to go and just be, just get the fuck out and do something with themselves. They still had time, they were so young. But what right did he have? He was not older than them. Not old enough to justify giving them orphic warnings from the shores of his second life. But he did know something about wanting to be finished with a part of your life before you were really ready, how you could trick yourself into thinking you knew so much when in fact you knew nothing at all. These dancers.

High, glossed out of their minds, riding a wave of pleasure. They were so fucking alive. And they were dead already. And it broke his heart.

Oh well, he thought.

The music wasn't loud, but it was excessively percussive. Ivan could feel it on his chest and his cheeks. Every bit of loose water in his body fizzed and shook. Goran took their coats through the apartment to the bedroom. Ivan went in search of beer in the kitchen.

There were about twenty people at the party, but because Noah's apartment was small, it felt like more. Everybody touched everybody else. When Ivan bent over the sink to grab the beers from the slushy ice water, he felt someone's warm breath on the nape of his neck, as intimate as if someone had slid their hand under his shirt. He stood there, his hand submerged in the basin of water, clutching the bottles, the breath coming on and coming off his skin. There was pressure in his lower back and between his shoulders, the square front of another person, the implication of human solidity. The dark, fine hairs on the sides of his neck grew heavy and damp from the breath, and when he looked up into the window that offered the reflection of the room back to him, he saw that it was Noah's friend Bert pressed up against him. Their eyes met in the window, and Bert inhaled deeply, so close that Ivan could feel the wetness of his lips and the slick, firm cartilage of the tip of his nose. It grazed Ivan, landing at the very back of his skull, as purposeful as a finger, and then Bert stepped away.

Ivan took the beer through the crowd knit together in the kitchen and found Goran sitting on the couch arm. He handed him the beer—light, cheap, still dripping. Goran took it from him and held its head toward Ivan. Ivan tucked his own wet beer under his arm, where he had grown sweaty and hot, and he reached forward to twist the cap off Goran's beer. It came away easy, and Ivan put the cap in his pocket. They toasted, and Ivan stood awkwardly next to Goran, but he kept having to shuffle to get away from the door that opened and shut to let people in or out.

The thing about a party was that no one could decide where to be. Noah was nowhere to be found. But there were dancers and poets, painters and would-be novelists—a shaggy bunch. Noah's weed man was here, and the air was also filled with the scraggly vapor of marijuana, like a localized cloud system. The lights were low and throbbed their amber light, rendering all the faces familiar and strange at the same time. Ivan felt like he had met everyone before, but also like he'd been dropped onto an alien planet.

Noah appeared with Fatima, one of the dancers from his program, on one side and the downstairs painter on the other. They were laughing and falling over one another. Noah reached out and put his hand on Ivan's shoulder.

"You made it," he said.

"I did."

"Goran!" Noah shouted.

The painter—was his name Howard? Richard? Pritchard? Leonard? Lennart? Something like that. Ivan could almost recall it. Fatima was the only black person in the dance program, which marked her out. She had started out in ballet the way they all did, but had switched to modern in undergraduate. The modern dancers were a dense core of five or six, and they held themselves back from the other dancers as though they were superior, and perhaps they were. Modern was technical and demanding—part acting, part contact sport, part nervous breakdown. The person who ran the modern section was one of those philosopher artists who shouted Wittgenstein at the dancers as they worked their way through the tangled knot of his choreography. It was less a dance than an institutionalized destruction of the self.

Ivan often saw Fatima at the café, where she worked extra shifts as a barista. The other dancers gave her a hard time about it, because it somehow made her seem at once less serious about her art and also more dedicated. They resented the implication that they wanted it less than Fatima because they didn't work for it as hard as she did. The idea of judging the worth of art based on the artist's rigor and dedication—there was a dreamlike logic to it.

Fatima put her arm around Noah's waist, and he kissed the top of her head as though bestowing a benediction. Ivan laughed.

"Is everyone here already high?" Goran asked.

"That's what happens when you're late," Noah said with a kind of song in his voice.

"It's a party. You can't be late to a party."

"So say the stragglers," Fatima said.

Goran pretended to be put out by this. He folded his arms across his chest and pouted. Ivan ran his fingers through Goran's hair, but as he did so, he saw Fatima's eyes on them. A look of consternation and fleeting irritation. She hummed in the back of her throat. Goran nudged Ivan away from him.

"How quick come the reasons for approving what we like," said the painter neighbor. Noah laughed loudly, squeezing the painter neighbor's side.

"Jane Austen. Who knew painters could read?"

"And not just Kant, right? Shocking," the painter said.

"Well, this is above my pay grade," said Fatima as she unwound herself from Noah and stuck out her hand to Goran. "Let's go get you faded."

Goran took her hand and rose from the couch. Noah took his place and patted his lap. Ivan lay on the couch so that his head was on Noah's knees. The painter took Ivan's place on the edge of the couch and watched them with an amused, warm look. He wore black overalls and a pink wool sweater. His hair was shaggy and dyed a bad copper color. Dark circles under his eyes and a chewed, raw lip.

"You two look like a fucking painting."

Noah thrilled to this compliment and Ivan could feel the muscles in his thighs tightening. He looked up and watched Noah preen and pose, swinging his shoulders forward and back, tilting himself away and then toward Ivan. The painter nodded vigorously at each of these silly poses, as though he were considering them.

"Yep, just like Repin. *Ivan the Terrible and His Son Ivan.*"

"My name is Noah, not Ivan."

"It's an allusion. An homage," the painter said, laughing. "Dancers. So literal."

"What's this painting?" Ivan asked. The painter looked momentarily surprised, and then he blushed.

"I don't, really. Well, it's like. Hmm," he said.

"Don't posture!" Noah said.

"I'm not," the painter said, but he was.

"Busted," Ivan said.

"No, no. There really is a painting called *Ivan the Terrible and His Son Ivan.* It's like, kind of a pietà? I guess?"

"Pietà? Isn't that about Jesus and the Virgin Mary?"

"I'm no virgin," Noah said.

"We know," the painter said. "It's hard to explain if you don't know anything about Russian history."

"I am Russian," Ivan said.

"You grew up in Boston."

"I mean, yes, but my parents are Russian. I am Russian. Sort of."

"An allusion," Noah said.

"No. Yes. I mean," the painter said, rubbing his neck. Ivan sat up and put his arm around the back of the couch. Noah leaned back so that his head brushed Ivan's arm. He looked so warm and happy to be there that Ivan, without thinking, leaned over and kissed him on the lips. When he withdrew, he saw that Noah's eyes were closed, and he was smiling. The painter grew quiet and still. Ivan was resting on his haunches on the couch, his arm trapped under Noah's head, the warmth of his body, the distant noise of the party bathing them.

"I think it's more a painting about man's inhumanity to man."

"That's Sartre," Noah said, without opening his eyes.

"It's Burns, actually," someone interrupted. It was a guy with reddish hair and sad brown eyes. He didn't look like he belonged to anyone.

"Oh, a poet. Someone let a poet in here," the painter said. Then he stood and gave the poet a loose hug. "This is Seamus."

Noah nodded distractedly. Seamus gave a tight wave. Ivan nodded, too, following Noah's lead. A poet. He had not known many poets in his life. Or any. Or maybe just some. A few. He'd seen poets in New York, at parties and at openings he'd attended, pretending to be older, more interested in things, than he was. Just letting that whole life of gleaming white rooms and champagne and coke in the bathroom wash over him, leaving no trace. But those poets had been adults. This poet was in a denim jacket and loose white sweater, looking not quite finished. Stafford. That was the painter's name.

"Well, Seamus, welcome to the demimonde," Stafford said.

"*You* brought the poet," Noah said. Seamus flushed.

"I didn't *bring* him. I mean. I invited him. Among others. A loose cohort."

"Jesus, not the day care."

Ivan felt a little sorry for Seamus. But then he seemed fine, if a little embarrassed.

"Seamus has a poem coming out in a *very* prestigious journal." Stafford raised his eyebrows suggestively. "It's a great poem."

"What's it about?" Noah asked, yawning.

"That's not really . . ."

"It's not a memoir," Stafford said. "A poem isn't *about* something, right? It just is." He smiled at Seamus, who looked like he wanted to throw up.

"I was just being polite," Noah drawled. "I don't really give a fuck. Congratulations, though. That's cool."

"I'd like to hear about your poem," Ivan said. Noah laughed. Seamus nodded.

"Cool, yeah. Maybe I'll tell you all about it." He made a dweeby little maneuver with his eyes, ducking his head in fake enthusiasm.

Noah laughed again. Ivan hated the falseness of it. The meanness. Noah's eyelashes were damp with sweat. His skin glossy and clear. Ivan kissed him again, this time on the corner of the mouth, and Noah parted his lips just slightly, so that Ivan could taste the warm, metallic interior of his body. There was something charged and hot in the kiss, though it was not a good kiss, when he pulled away. Noah's eyes opened just a little, and Ivan could see the slick blackness of his iris sliding around.

They hadn't talked about that last time in the truck, a couple of weeks ago, when Noah had asked him if he was sure his life was so different from the people's in the houses they passed. There was a question in Noah's eyes and in the posture of his mouth. A question Ivan could not answer. Or, rather, he could answer it, but he wouldn't, because his feelings were still a little hurt. Instead, he let Noah's head rest on him, because it was all he could do in the way of apology without receiving one first. Noah closed his eyes again: let it ride.

"Garshin, the writer, was the model for the younger Ivan in that painting. He threw himself down a flight of stone stairs. And, like, he died. Later. But he died."

"Jesus," Noah said. "Are we back on that?"

"What a way to go," Seamus said.

"I mean."

"It's a lot," Ivan said. "It's a fucking lot."

Noah was studying Seamus. Ivan put his hands across Noah's eyes.

"You're being weird."

"He's all right," Seamus said. "I don't mind."

"What happened to you?" Noah asked.

"I got burned," Seamus said. He leaned closer to them on the couch and gestured with the back of his fingers to a circular scar that had mostly healed. Noah squinted, touched the mark with his fingertips.

Seamus jumped and yelped, and Noah jerked back. "Oh, fuck, I'm sorry!" But then Seamus just laughed. Snapped his teeth at Noah.

"Got you."

Noah gave him the finger, slapped his chest.

Ivan's heart was beating fast, and he tasted acid in the back of his throat. Seamus had gotten him, too.

"Okay, I like you slightly more now," Noah said. "Why am I not higher? Why?" He pushed up from the couch, looped his arm around Stafford's neck, who'd been watching them with amused detachment. Then he took up Seamus's hand in his own as well. "We're getting fucked up."

Ivan watched them leave, feeling suddenly so heavy and tired. He sank lower on the couch and closed his eyes, tried to catch his breath for a moment.

Goran returned without Fatima but seemingly riding an azure cloud. Ivan was holding his warming beer between his thighs. The moisture soaked into his pants and into the cushion. A little damp spot in the world.

"Here you are. Frozen in place," Goran said.

"Yep," Ivan said. He'd taken off his boots, was sitting there in his gray socks. The party had entered a quiet phase, or maybe Ivan had simply acclimated to its noise, but either way it wasn't so hard on him anymore. Goran sat next to him and put an arm around his neck. Sure enough, he had the skunky odor of marijuana. Ivan's knees had begun to burn.

"How are you liking this party?"

"It's all right, I guess. Same as any party."

Goran hummed.

"How are you liking it?"

"Fine enough," Goran said. He put his feet on the glass coffee table. Across the room, two women stood close, talking and holding hands. The night was ending. The porch had emptied about a half hour before, but the kitchen was still dense with bodies, an over-crowded nucleus. They would fission eventually. Give themselves to the night on their way home, trailing behind them their scents and their sweat and their voices, a comet trail of the time they'd had.

"You don't seem happy," Ivan said.

"I'm not."

"I'm sorry."

"Don't be if you're not."

"I am."

Goran sighed. "This is tiresome."

Ivan came closer to Goran, but Goran turned away. Ivan traced the curve of Goran's neck. There came a laugh, small, stifled.

"Hey," Ivan said.

"Don't mock me."

"I'm not," Ivan said. "Why do you always think I'm mocking you? I'm not. Hey. I mean it. I'm not."

Goran turned to face him directly. It was alarming. It felt as if it had been years since they had looked at each other this way. Goran's thick eyelashes. His eyes. The playful, annoyed curve of his mouth. The tension in his brows. Unremarkable human face, but familiar to Ivan. Goran's nostrils flared just slightly.

"Then act like it."

. . .

There was a small, stiff envelope taped to their door. Ivan turned it over and found the painter's name: Stafford. Inside the envelope was a postcard on which the painter had written a small note:

The humanity!
~S

The postcard was a small print of a painting. An old man clutching a younger. A look of dazed horror in the old man's eyes, almost cartoonish in size and emotion. The younger, dying man had some sort of bloody wound. There was terrific tension in the arms, the way the younger man braced himself against the floor. The faces were ghoulish and terrified. A large staff lay on the floor, thrust away from them. The men seemed possessed by fear of what they had done, of what lay ahead. The old man wanted to take it all back, Ivan could see. He wished he could undo what he'd done. The card had a smooth, tacky surface. Ivan tucked the card inside his jacket pocket.

Goran was out with his married poet again.

Ivan hung up his coat. It would be a while before he heard back about his applications, before he'd know if he got a spot or an interview. In the meantime, he trudged through his classes, nodding off as his professor droned on about accounting practices, about means of incorporation. The part of class he liked best was the case studies, thick packets of data on companies that had risen and fallen and been destroyed in the grand concourse of the market. He found it quite pleasurable, really, to read over the data preceding a decline, trying to pick out in the sea of numbers where the tide had started to turn, however imperceptibly, against the company. The infirmity in the organism of commerce.

He had applied to several firms and banks in New York, offices dotting the island of Manhattan. He had not been back to the city in a long while. Not since he left ballet school. That long, solemn train ride to Boston with his father's old army duffel, full of clothes and tights, tucked under the seat. He'd felt like a soldier returning from war. It was snowing then.

He missed, in a silly way, summer in the city. The heat shimmering in the glass of the skyscrapers, and the cool shadows of Chinatown and the Lower East Side. He did not miss the stink of the river in summer. But there was something in the way people had of lying out in the sun, exposed and vulnerable to the eye. The whole city seeming to perform a radical opening of itself to expel heat. That was something he missed very much. Summer in Iowa, because he could not afford trips home to Boston, was more depressing. It was more a radical closing and folding in. Whole streets deserted during the heat of the day, the Ped Mall a white sore of concrete and dying trees. Summer in Iowa was a closed fist. Nowhere to run except to the movies, if you had cash for it. And even then. Even then.

But then he'd been young in New York. Well, younger. When you were that young, nothing mattered except your body and what you could do with it. He'd lived wholly by that body. Until it turned on him. But for a while, fuck.

Still, the matter of getting back there. Even if he got a job in one of those banks, he'd have to find a place. And pay: Rent. Security. The ticket up. The ticket back. The price of a U-Haul, unless he decided to sell off all his shit. Storage. Not for the first time, he thought of asking Goran. But he already asked Goran for so much.

Needed him for so much. Sometimes he couldn't tell the difference between how he felt for Goran and what Goran did for him. He needed a little juice of his own. A little magic.

Then there was Noah. His advice.

In the back of his sock drawer, Ivan kept a camera he'd used to record himself in his ballet days. He'd bought it with money he won in a dance competition. It had been a stupid purchase then. It was even more stupid now. But he'd at least gotten a couple of years out of it. These days, he seldom used it. But now, remembering Noah's words, he took the camera from its place in his drawer. He set it on the top of the dresser and crouched in front of it. His knees burned. His thighs ached.

The camera had a red, flashing light. It was angry like a pulse.

Ivan took a deep breath, waited. Below him, the painters were playing the score from *Evita*. Ivan didn't know what his face was doing in the camera's gaze, if he looked sad or angry, calm or anxious. He only knew how he felt: a tight quivering in his stomach like a plucked string, the tension in his knees threatening to give way, the quick-slow hitch of his heartbeat. He felt uneasy in himself. At odds with his body, like it disagreed with what he was making it do. It was true that his body had become a rebellious thing, surly and uncooperative. But so, too, had his demands. When he was a dancer, he'd known what to ask of himself, but now he felt unformed and unyoked. What was he to do with himself now and forever? It had been eight years. Surely, he should have had some idea by now. But no. That life of his was gone, and in its place was only a series of vague demands issuing up out of the dark of himself: food, sleep, sex. It's all he had.

He might begin again, he thought. Might find something in all of this. Some small, human thing. Ivan undressed himself in front of the camera, and he crouched again in front of it. He would try, he would try. He would let himself do this.

It was, after all, possible.

The videos surprised Ivan in that they were not difficult to make once he began to record himself. He emptied his mind of expectation or thought. Let the movement come from where it came from, let it do what it would do. He touched himself and felt nothing. He slid out of his clothes and felt nothing. The camera caught everything. Every flicker of motion, every shadow. He did not move toward anything. He did not decide upon anything. It began in the body and ended in the body. When he gripped his cock and stroked himself, it was the body. Ivan watched himself remotely, feeling cool satisfaction at the smoothness of his movements, the easiness of his figure. He filled himself and emptied himself with his fingers, slicked from his mouth. He slid himself upon rubber implements, pushed them into and out of the place where he was clenched tight and hot.

Sometimes he came, and sometimes he did not, but there was no pleasure in it. There was nothing in it at all, except the satisfaction afterward of having moved. He recorded himself for only short periods of time. It was the time constraint that imbued the clips with meaning. When he played them back and watched them, it was like seeing someone else's body. He chopped the clips in strange places so that they cut off unexpectedly or dropped into darkness, while the audio played still. Sometimes he was just off frame, and there was only the faint impression of his shadow upon the wall, the suggestion of motion. He posted the first clip to the microblogging site and sat alone in the dark of the apartment, waiting for something, for anything, to happen.

A few minutes later he deleted the clip, but then he reuploaded it. He held his breath. He deleted the clip. He reuploaded it.

The next day he received a notification that the clip had had fifty views, and he had a subscriber. When he realized that there was a steady initial trickle of people coming in, he uploaded another clip and another. Three clips freely floating through the servers of a microblogging site, all showing bits of Ivan. His face and his cock and his stomach and his back, all fragments of himself digitized and transmitted. It felt silly and easy. For him to post these clips, and for other people to respond by paying him monthly for access to them. Even the ones he'd given away for free. But pay him they did.

How stupid. How very stupid.

In early March, Ivan mailed his parents two checks for three hundred dollars each. It was not enough. But it was something. It was nice to be able to shave off a little bit and give it to them. His mother called to thank him. Ivan was on the rowing machine at the gym and had to get off to take the call. He stood out in the cold under the rec center awning. Snow falling in mounds and drifts. He could see the hospital back and above him, somber brick and stone against a heavy gray sky.

"You didn't have to send," she said. "You didn't. How can you live if you send."

"It was okay," he said. "I had extra."

"What extra?" She was suspicious. Doubtful. "You not eat? How can you eat if you send?"

"No, no," Ivan said. "Eating is fine. I'm good. I just had extra. Please."

"Your father is happy. I am happy. We are happy. But how you eat if you send?"

Ivan laughed, but his mother got upset at his laughing. That was how it had been in ballet school—her pleading with him, worrying over him. Once, when he failed to return her call—he'd dropped his phone down a grate—she'd gotten on a train and come all the way to New York from Boston. He found her waiting for him after class, worried. When she saw him, she nodded and touched his face and said she was happy he was okay. Happy he was alive. She cooked him soup on the hot plate in his subsidized housing, and then she got on another train and was gone by the time he had to leave for evening class.

"I'm okay," he said. "I'm okay. I promise. I just had a little extra."

She paused. Then she said she'd use it for Easter dinner at the church. To make a big meal.

"You should use it for yourself," he said, a little annoyed. "It's not for that. It's for you."

"Is for me, yes."

"No, not for church. For you."

"Yes, is for me."

Ivan shook his left arm hard to wake it back up. He was cooling down too fast in the snow.

"How can it be for you if you give it to church."

"Is not for church, is for me. For God. For you."

"Okay," he said. "You can do what you want, I know. And Papa is happy? Okay?"

"Papa is good. Very happy."

"Okay. Then I am, too."

His mother said goodbye, and Ivan hung up the phone. He stood a little longer in the falling snow, looking upward, telling himself it wasn't so bad, this thing he was doing.

Back in the gym, he set his phone at the base of the machine and got back into rowing position. He got the camera app open and set it to record. He did a few reps to warm his muscles again, to get back into the rhythm of things. When his thighs felt loose and his muscle had some give to it, he took a deep breath and gave himself over. He didn't look into the camera's tiny dark eye. Instead, he fixed his gaze on the wall, where a Hawkeyes banner hung. He gazed at it, his vision so tight on the banner that people going into and out of his line of sight were just blurry figures. The hardness of the handle, the smell of the cord heating as it wound and unwound around the flywheel. But he kept going, gliding along the machine's course and back, pumping himself bigger, faster, harder. His posture erect, perfect as he had been taught. His knee burned like a motherfucker, but he felt loose and good and kept going.

At home, he stripped and showered. Then got his laptop and opened the footage. He adjusted and cropped and put on a black-and-white filter. He blunted the sound and overlaid an audio clip he had pinched from an ASMR channel of gym noises. The sound of his own breathing went away, replaced by this stolen audio, shorn of context. But it made the clip feel authentic. More itself.

This grainy clip, five minutes long, shot up the axis of his thighs, centered on the dark expanse of his crotch. And the bulk of his chest and arms. He didn't know what other people saw in this video except the implication of sex. The same way you sometimes felt when you passed someone on the street and could see the suggestion of their body, their strength, through their clothes, or when they turned and you caught their gaze, and you could imagine how they would look lost in pleasure.

Life was full of such moments, the self momentarily exposed. What he and all the other people on this site were doing was harvesting such moments, not through happenstance or spontaneity but using some apparatus of mass production. Like the fields upon fields upon fields of corn and soy out by Bert's place.

The relationship between sex and what he did in these videos, he thought, was the same as the relationship between the way people used to farm and what had become known as agribusiness. He could understand the elegance of it, the sophistication that came with scale and concatenation. It was the same thing in banking. He wasn't interested in *business*, in any of that entrepreneurship bullshit that was really just prosperity gospel for atheists. No, he wanted something more than that: He wanted to be a part of that rarefied class that got to skim the money from the money. They who got to set the invisible laws by which the whole of the world functioned. Ivan had grown up thinking that dancers and choreographers and the great geniuses—Balanchine, Robbins, Joffrey, Ailey, Diaghilev— were the inheritors of the priestly class, the keepers of culture and legacy. But now he understood that the new priests were the bankers. The financiers. What was culture compared to the brute, terrible force of money and its ability to make and remake worlds?

Ivan uploaded the video from the rowing machine, stretching out his sore knee as he watched the progress bar tick upward. When the clip was fully uploaded, he closed the site and put his laptop away. Then he lay there on his bed, thinking of the conversation he'd had with his mother.

Your father is happy. I am happy. We are happy.

Ivan curled up into a ball and thought that it was good they were happy. He had done this with his body. He had done something good and right.

Ivan was with Noah when he heard back about the internship.

They were loading scrap tin onto Noah's truck with Bert. He was puffing with the exertion, his blotchy face gone blotchier, and his glasses all fogged. The wind was particularly scathing that day, whipping down on and through them in gray waves. Sometimes it blew in bits of gravel from the road. They landed on the tin like hail.

Noah and Bert were carrying the tin across the ditch and dropping it down by the truck, and Ivan had to bend and lift it up. The tin kept pulling on stray threads in his gloves, and he wished he'd brought the leather ones. Bert stood up and whistled.

"Boy, it's a bitch out here today."

Noah slapped him across the belly and said, "You're the one who said it had to be today."

Bert shoved at him, then laughed, and they went back down into the ditch and started throwing the tin up the other side. It clattered as it fell. Ivan checked his phone and saw the email notification. It was from one of the smaller banks in Manhattan—not his first choice, but still beyond what he'd expected to get. The title was ambiguous, just, "re: SIDOROV, IVAN D." He felt his stomach drop. Surely, if it was good news, they would have called. Surely.

Noah poked his head above the lip of the ditch and called his name. But Ivan was just looking down at his phone until the screen went dark.

"I think I just got rejected from my internship."

"Bummer," Noah said.

"I got your internship right here," Bert called.

Ivan looked at the two of them in the ditch. Noah in a hoodie and overalls, oversized leather gloves. Bert in a white sweatshirt streaked in dirt. Red fisherman cap low on his head. Looking old next to Noah. He thought for a moment that this could be his life: Loading scrap in ditches. Hauling tin. Working shifts just to keep his head over the lip of a ditch.

Noah went from laughing to frowning.

"Hey, hey, Ivan. Come on."

He saw his whole future closing down in front of him. But then, but then, but then—he swallowed.

"Sorry about that."

"Did you open it?"

"No," he said. "It just. They'd call, right? If it was a yes, they'd call."

Noah nodded. Then climbed out of the ditch and took his hands out of the gloves. His palms were dry and ashy. Ivan handed him the phone.

"What's your code?"

"Nine seven three zero five," he said.

Noah typed the code into the phone. Ivan couldn't bear to look at him. His mouth was dry, his heart going hard. He turned. Looked at the tin in the truck bed. Bert had climbed out of the ditch.

"What's going on?"

Noah didn't answer. Ivan watched the flat horizon. The dark

mud and the flattened grass running all the way back to the old house. Dota jumped down from the truck, and Bert clapped his hands hard and loud.

"Get, get on, now!" He stomped, and Dota yipped happily. Bert lunged and Dota took off in a blond flash around the truck and out to the fields. Ivan turned.

"Well?" he asked. "What, do you have to decipher it or what."

Noah looked at him, then down at the phone and then back up.

"You got it," he said.

"No, you're lying."

Noah grinned. "Yeah, I'm lying."

"No, you're not," Ivan said. He reached for the phone. It was a long email, one that began not with congratulations but with a long description of the applicant pool. How many applications there had been, from how many different parts of the country and the world. A description of the bank and its services, its history and clientele, a set of descriptive remarks about the fit and the kind of associates they were looking for, hoping to find. Down and down the column of text ran, words and phrases bolded and underlined, dates in the future that made his stomach hurt with possibility. And then, at the very end of the email, *Please confirm receipt of this message to schedule your interview for later this spring. We hope that you will be able to join us and look forward to hearing from you.*

Was this? Was this? Was this? Was this—it? Was this the moment it all became possible?

"Oh my God," he said, turning to Bert and Noah, who was still smiling.

"Told you!"

"You must be happy. New York, though. So expensive."

"He's got his ways," Noah said.

"Yeah, but it's not going to be cheap. That's my point."

"Shut up, let him have his thing."

Ivan's hands shook. "Oh my God."

"You said that already," Bert said.

Goran was at his keyboard. He'd been practicing Chopin for the spring concert in the Music Department when Ivan had told him about the internship. Goran had stopped playing and stared into the wall above the keyboard. There was a shadowy indentation where he'd thrown the glass earlier that winter. Ivan sat on the couch arm, watching him, waiting for some sign.

"I don't understand," he said at last. "You're moving to New York?"

"It wouldn't be until summer, but, yeah, it's looking that way."

"Interesting."

"That's a funny way of saying congratulations."

"I just mean. You didn't ask *me* if I wanted to come with you. Or if I even *could*."

"You graduate this year, Goran. I mean, come on. I'm not blindsiding you with this. I'm bringing it up because I hope it can be a thing we do. Together."

"That's not what you did at all," Goran said. "You brought this in and you put it down in front of me, and you're like *Surprise! I have something awesome! It's great!* It has *nothing* to do with me. You did this and it has nothing to do with me. That's so fucked up."

This was not true. Well, it wasn't entirely true. Well, it was entirely factual, but it was also the least generous possible reading of what had happened. Goran turned on the stool and gazed up at him, his slender eyebrows arched. He had a quietly, passively furious expression.

"I think that's an unfair read of it, but okay."

"How would you read it?"

"That something good happened for my partner, and I'm happy for him. For once, it would be nice if you could be happy for me."

"Wow, the maudlin quotient just got very high in here right now."

"Fuck you."

"What a change of pace that would be," Goran said with an exuberant opening of his arms.

Ivan pressed his palms to his cheeks and tried to calm himself. The back of his mouth was ringing again, a sharp, persistent vibration.

"How are you going to afford being in New York, anyway? I doubt that pimp of Noah's pays that much for the shitty construction you guys have been doing."

Goran was smiling. Ivan went into the kitchen to get an aspirin from the cupboard above the sink. He chewed the aspirin into powder and gulped it down with hot water.

"I have money," Ivan said.

"Oh, do you? And how's that? You get a paper route?"

"Why are you being so negative?" Ivan asked.

Goran was in the kitchen doorway. He shrugged. "I'm not. I'm being practical."

"No, you're being an asshole. And I don't understand why. All I ever do is walk around here like a kicked puppy. I stay out of your way. I take up no space. We hardly even see each other. I don't even think you like me anymore, Goran. But this. This is just. Beyond."

"Maybe I don't like you."

"Yeah, I'm getting that feeling."

"But so what if I don't like you? We're together. Sometimes I don't like you, okay. Sometimes I hate the way you look or smell. Okay. Fine. I'm an asshole. But I still want to be with you. That counts for something, right? That's something."

Ivan closed his eyes. He tried to remember what it was like when they were good and together and all right. He tried to imagine what it was like the first time they met on the app and made plans to see each other outside the auditorium at night. They'd stood on the bridge and looked at the lights of the auditorium, gold and tiered like a delicate rock formation. Then they'd walked around the river path and talked all night about music, about ballet, about where they spent their afternoons, best place for coffee, how to dodge the undergrads.

That night had been so good, like something out of a dream. And they were so far from it now.

"I can't make you happy," Ivan said.

"You do make me happy. This is me happy. I am happy."

"This can't be happiness. If this is you happy, then I don't think I understand what happiness is for."

"Sometimes happiness is just letting people feel how they fucking feel," Goran said.

He looked the furthest thing from happy. He looked pissed off. He looked annoyed. He looked like he was going to cry. His eyes welled. He bit at the inside of his jaw, then sat down sharply at the kitchen table, trying to catch his breath. Ivan sat down next to him, reached for his hand, and for the first time in a very long time, Goran let him.

"I think you need to be needed," Ivan said. "And that's not something I can do anymore."

"Oh, great," Goran said. "You've decided you don't need me anymore either, and you're just bailing. Cool."

"What do you mean? Stop being so cryptic."

Goran didn't say anything. He just looked down at the table. Ivan understood then.

"Your poet. This is about your fucking poet," he said. Ivan stood up. Goran followed him into their small bedroom.

"I'm not proud of it."

"Well, I do things I'm not proud of, too. I don't make it your problem."

"Yeah, like what? Hauling scrap metal?"

"Making videos of myself beating off so I can send my parents money, for one. How about that."

Goran stared, his mouth a little open, and then, drawing it closed, he said, "You're what?"

"Like I said, I have the money. I don't need your charity or your benediction."

"I can't believe—you're making porn?" Goran said.

"Why? You watch porn. We watch porn. Porn isn't bad."

"No, but—that's different. You're making it? You won't fuck me, but you're making porn."

"You're literally fucking a married poet. Oh, I'm sorry. *Were*."

"Now *you're* being sanctimonious."

"Please don't be selfish, Goran. Please."

"You're selfish!"

"I'm selfish?" Ivan asked. "Me? I am selfish? Me."

"Yes, you. This is selfish. Stop it, right now."

"You are being unreasonable," Ivan said.

"Why are you doing this? Do you want attention? Is that it?"

"No," Ivan said.

"A pornographer. Imagine. I'm sure the investment bankers will love that."

Ivan knew it was hopeless to get Goran to understand anything about the money part of it. Goran had a trust fund. He'd come from wealth, moved with wealth as though it were a different, better kind of element. Goran wouldn't understand why someone like him, like Ivan, would need to make money, make enough of it to get by, to ensure a future for himself and his family. Goran didn't need to think about the future because the future held no mystery to him, except in aesthetic terms. But Ivan couldn't live on aesthetics. There was anger flashing in Goran's eyes. Disgust and hatred.

"Why is this so difficult for you? What did I do wrong? I don't belong to you," Ivan said. "I'm a person. I don't belong to you."

"That's right, you sure don't," Goran said, and that was the end of the argument.

Ivan sat on the edge of the couch, and Goran went back to playing the Chopin. It was clear to him now why Noah had said what he'd said in the truck. He understood now how cruel and simple the question had been: why do people live this way? The answer was, because they must.

It was late March—a cold spring.

Things got worse between them after Ivan told Goran about the videos. Ivan moved out, and for a couple of weeks they didn't really talk at all. Then Goran asked if they could talk, if they could try to figure out how to be together again. Ivan wasn't sure what he wanted, but after he'd let Goran pay their bills for so long, he felt like he ought to at least try.

They met at the café where Goran had gone on those first anxious dates with his married poet. Fatima let them have espresso for free.

"How are you?" Goran asked. It had been a few weeks since Ivan had moved out.

"The same. You?"

"Ditto."

"Good," Ivan said.

"I don't know about that."

"I'm sorry."

"Aren't we all," Goran said. He put his chin on his hand. Spooned the crema from his espresso. "Oh, you left something."

"What?"

Goran took from his jacket pocket a small postcard. Ivan recognized it right away as the card given to him by the painter from downstairs. He couldn't help but laugh at it.

"I found this in my coat."

"I thought I left it in my coat," Ivan said.

Goran laughed. It felt like forgiveness.

"Thank you," Ivan said, taking up the card and creasing it.

"Ouch," Goran said.

"What? Oh, it's fine." He creased the card again, and again until it was too tight to make smaller. He dropped it into his shirt pocket.

"It was an interesting painting," Goran said.

"The model for the younger Ivan was a writer, Garshin. He killed himself on some stone stairs," Ivan said.

"You don't say."

"In real life, Ivan the Terrible killed his son."

"How Shakespearean."

"Some say it's cursed—people keep trying to destroy it. The painting, I mean."

"Cursed image," Goran said, laughing.

"I don't believe in curses," Ivan said. "I think it's all just bad timing." It was a lie. Ivan did believe in curses and destiny. He believed it all.

"You just might be right," Goran said.

It was the first time Goran had ever said Ivan was right about something. It was nothing. A fleck of mercy. But it was, Ivan knew, his way of trying. Of being better. The weeks apart had softened Goran in some almost indiscernible way. The bristly outline of his nature was a defense mechanism for some inner anxiety.

"You can put your sword down," Ivan said. "I think, if it's going to work, if we're going to be in it, we have to decide we want to be in it. Not because you need me or I need you. But because. We want to be in it. It can't be the way it was."

"I know," Goran said, nodding.

"No, like, don't just say you know because you want to get through this part fast. It can't just be over because you want it to be how it was."

Goran nodded, then, catching himself, stopped. He took a deep breath and held his hand out on the table.

"Okay," he said. "Okay, we go slow. We go easy. I want to be a better version of myself."

"I like you how you are," Ivan said. "I just want you to be nice to me."

"Steep price," Goran said.

"Please."

"Okay. Okay."

Ivan put his hand in Goran's. In the closing of Goran's palm, Ivan thought that things would be all right between them. That it would work out, and they would go to New York and be happy. They had to get to the end of the semester. To the end of classes. To the end of work. To the end of this particular phase of their history.

"I'm going to try. About the videos. I'm going to try," Goran said.

"I know," Ivan said. "I get it."

4

The Kings of Norway

Goran didn't hate pornography on principle.

"If it were *you* making the porn, I wouldn't mind at all. If it was literally anyone else, it would be great. Fine. Wonderful. I love it. Power to you. Means of production. Yes. But it's Ivan," he was saying.

"That's logically coherent, but kind of fucked up," Timo said with a laugh. He liked Ivan, who had a melancholic, downbeat humor like Charlie Chaplin or Eeyore.

"Be on my side—come on."

"I did say it was logically coherent, which considering the circumstances is kind of a minor miracle."

"A regular friend would say *dump him*."

"Would they, though?" Timo asked.

Goran shrugged, but Timo did wonder if that was true, if someone else would say that they should break up over Ivan making porn. "I mean, what's the specific issue here? Is it that he hid it?"

"I *wish* he'd hidden it!"

The clips, maybe ten or fifteen in all, ranged from thirty seconds to ten minutes. The video and sound quality were pristine. It was possible to pause the video and count the freckles on Ivan's chest.

The acts portrayed were almost shockingly mundane: flexing, running his hands across his stomach and shoulders, a variety of suggestive poses in incredibly thin underwear, and later, masturbation with deep, chuffing breaths, or the slow insertion and extraction of fingers and other implements into and out of himself.

Sex never seemed the object of the clips, from what Timo saw. They never really included the viewer. There was something fiercely forbidding in watching Ivan, as though he were unwilling to let the viewer escape what they had done by trying to include themselves in his pleasure. Even his orgasms were hateful, partial.

Timo had seen the first clip because Goran had forwarded it to him. A short, almost perfunctory video in close-up on the lower half of a male face mostly in shadow. Impossible to tell if it was Ivan or someone else. The mouth in a casual, bored expression. Then, around the halfway mark, the man stood and there was the slow procession of the chest and stomach, the arms coming into view. And then, the tip of the penis coming to rest like a sleeve on the dresser. It lay there for another few seconds, and then the clip ended. Timo played the clip over another dozen or so times. He noticed the gradation of shadow falling across Ivan's pubic hair. The subtle shifting of his stomach as he breathed. A piece of paper fluttering on the edge of the surface on which his penis rested. How, as Ivan was pushing up to stand, there was just the slightest jostling of the camera, a micro-blur of motion.

In the background, you could see the comforter hanging slightly off the bed to the floor. There was substantial room tone in the video, but because of Ivan's proximity to the camera, it was possible to hear his breathing, and as he stood up, his elbows popped. Over the successive viewings of the clip, the texture of the video changed, deepened, the way a word begins to come apart when you repeat it too often, sounding not more like itself but stranger somehow. The more Timo watched the clip, the sadder it made him, and when he began to watch the other clips that sadness became something else, more complicated, as if the watching were a sieve through which his emotion was being passed over and over again, and in the refining, more of its distinct character emerged.

In the end, Timo had not been aroused exactly—except what was arousal if not the generation of feeling? So perhaps he had been aroused after all. He did not say this to Goran, because it would have made Goran feel worse. But what he suspected was that Ivan had not been making pornography at all. It seemed like he'd been after something else. Yet the place where Ivan had posted the clips was a social media site for amateur porn. People could subscribe to his channel for twenty dollars a month, which allowed them access to all his clips. The first link Goran had forwarded Timo was the only clip available for free. Timo had subscribed using his PayPal and a fake username to see the other videos. According to the site, Ivan had something like eight hundred subscribers. When Timo did the math, his vision grew slightly blurry at the scope of it.

It was enough to live on.

"Oh, Goran," Timo said. They were in the café sitting alongside the front window. It was one of those gray Saturdays in early spring—dense with cold under an opaque sky lit like a blank movie screen. Goran had put his head down on the table, sulking, which was a bad habit, and Timo felt sorry for him, which was also a bad habit. "Do you want to go?"

"Yes. No. Yes," Goran said. "I should practice anyway."

"Mind if I tag along?"

"Nothing better to do?"

Timo shook his head.

Last Friday, Timo had asked Fyodor if he wanted to see a movie that was playing at FilmScene as part of their queer cinema series. It was a movie about gay German cops, one of whom was closeted and one of whom was not, and the trouble this caused. You know I don't like movies, Fyodor had said. They gave him a headache. And he had a shift on Saturday, so they couldn't be out late. Or he couldn't, but Timo could. He'd go, if Timo wanted.

Timo said it was stupid, that they never did anything except eat and sleep and fuck, and when they did something, it was always like begging the parole board for special pardon. It wasn't a relationship, it was like fucking work release.

"You don't know anything about work release," Fyodor said with his jaw clenched. "You love talking about shit you don't know anything about."

"Spare me, our lady of working-class piety," Timo said.

"Why is it," Fyodor asked, "that everything we do is on your terms? And when it isn't, you have to be so awful to me. I'm not your scapegoat."

"You're being defensive."

"I went to the stupid art show, didn't I? I'm trying here. I'm trying so hard to stay in this thing. I want to. I'm not saying I don't want it. But you gotta meet me, Timo. You gotta."

Timo held his breath, tried to be another kind of person. But it killed him to let the record go uncorrected this way.

"It wasn't stupid, and it wasn't even a show. It was a talk."

"Jesus," Fyodor had said.

Timo wondered if they were about to break up again. He saw

Fyodor hang his head low and try to calm himself down. Timo tried, too. He sat on the end of the bed and put his hand on Fyodor's arm. But that was all he could do. He hadn't had it in him to make Fyodor feel *secure*. It was so tiresome having to make a grown man feel like he had something to offer.

"You are not an easy person to be with," Fyodor said. "Maybe we're just too different."

They went to bed. And they got up, Fyodor very early in the black cold, Timo much later in the morning. They texted at first, little bit here and there, on the first couple of days. Hey, hey, how are you, okay, you, okay, sleep, bye. Fyodor was fine—working too much, eating too little, sleeping not nearly enough. They'd only recently gotten back together after some time apart. Some difficult and strange months away from each other in which Timo wondered why they'd been together in the first place. At the time, he had missed Fyodor terribly. But the minute they were back together, it was the way it always was. Fyodor was reticent. Difficult to talk to. He gave nothing away. Gave nothing up. And sometimes the only way to get anything out of him at all was to pick a fight. Arguing was the most fluent part of their relationship. Arguing and fucking. But there it was.

So, no, Timo didn't have anything to do, not really. There were the papers to grade from the introductory logic class he taught undergraduates. And then there was his own coursework. Each of the grad students in the departmental seminar was responsible for reading the assigned paper of a guest lecturer and coming up with a question, which was due to the department secretary two days before the lecture. These questions were then distributed to the visitor and also to the other students, so that each might have time to consider one another's contributions. This tended to result in after-hours gossip and low-level humiliation. Timo couldn't figure out whether you were supposed to be ironic and not take the question very seriously, come up with something stupid and simple, or apply real rigor to the exercise, do some research, read all the lecturer's papers, support your question with reference citations. No matter what you did, people made fun of you for it. Wanting either too much or too little.

Timo could go to the art library if Goran didn't want him to come along. He could do some reading. Or grade. Or pretend to grade. But he would rather have listened to Goran practice. Goran downed the rest of his coffee and shrugged.

"Do what you want."

Timo dumped his coffee into the plastic bin by their table and they went out into the gray cold. Goran had on a wool cardigan, and he wound his thick black scarf around his neck. Timo zipped himself into his bomber jacket, which was inadequate to the wind. The corner across the street had recently been turned into a construction area: what used to be a bank had been knocked down and its lot dug out into a muddy cavern rimmed with gravel. A rickety cage and some concrete barriers were all that kept people from dropping in. They went along the sidewalk, their shoes scraping.

"Is it the Chopin today?" Timo asked.

"No," Goran said. "I'm doing some stupid thing for the ballet class. Debussy."

"Oh. Well. That's nice."

Goran sighed and shook his head. He had thick hair, uncombed, and he wore round glasses. Goran had a funny walk, as if his center of gravity kept changing with every step. He walked in a series of forward almost-falls, like a drunk person trying to be sober or a sober person pretending to be drunk. Goran hated Debussy, Timo knew. But he played for dance classes for the money and for the practice, and also for a certain sense of superiority. *They're just a bunch of gay jocks, that's all*, Goran said of the dancers. *Empty in the head, clomping around.* Sometimes, when they were drinking, Goran would get up from the floor and do a pirouette or a fouetté, for a moment so graceful and beautiful that it hurt to look at him. But then he'd stagger slightly and drop back to the floor too fast, too hard, making the table rattle, and Timo had to close his eyes at the shock of it.

Timo could understand why Goran hated playing the classes. In what was now another part of his life, he had studied the piano very seriously. He still had a pianist's hands, wrists, and posture. Goran liked to say it was the first thing he'd noticed about Timo when they first met, at a mixer for gay graduate students: *You had a rod up your ass, like all the pianists I know.* But that was long ago, and Timo hadn't played the piano in almost two years. The piano wasn't the reason his parents had split up, but he couldn't separate the two things in his mind. The better he got at piano, the more his parents fought and the faster their money ran out, until it was time for him to go to college, and there was nothing left in either the marriage or their savings account. They were surgeons, it was true enough, and Timo had come up in the so-called Black Upper Middle Class in D.C., but what differentiated this from the regular Upper Middle Class, meaning *white*, was that there was less money and the money was less durable on the whole. Where did it go, all that cash? Everywhere and nowhere—and then 2008 sucked it all down and down, out and out, and obliterated their affluence. Timo went to a sturdy

college in Ohio, paid for with a trust fund from his grandfather,
who had invented a very small part of a machine important for the
scything of corn. In the end. This was all that had been left. He paid
for his other expenses by playing classes, and he came to appreciate
the repetitive nature of such work. Sometimes, he liked to see how
much he could deviate before the ballet master gave him a sharp
look and said, pointedly, *Again*. The dancers had an aloof, feral quality to them, like coyotes in a zoo. Their shoes squeaked on the floor
as they leveraged themselves forward and through the air. Loose
screws rattled, and the mirrors shook as the dancers landed. They
didn't notice him, or look toward him. They were always apart from
him, apart from one another too, even though they were squeezed
together in rows, formations coming together and then undone.
Goran hated the repetition. He called it *pretentious scales, that's all it
is. They want me to go in and play them a fucking waltz and then walk
out. That's it.* Timo himself hadn't minded that so much at the time,
when he played. It had been a way to absent himself. But that was
over now.

Goran's practice room was on the third floor of Sayers Hall, three
buildings down from where Timo taught introductory logic and
precalculus every Monday, Tuesday, and Thursday. They often ate
lunch together on the benches that lined the quad, complaining
about their students and their classes, their schedules and their departments. Today, the quad was empty and windswept. The grass
was damp with snowmelt, and thin dark branches of the trees
shifted listlessly. Sayers was on the hill that overlooked the northern

half of campus and the river, an ornate gray building with a forbidding oak door that was heavy to open, and Goran had to lay his shoulder into it to open it. They went up the stairs, and all around them was cool silence.

It was an artificial silence—the rooms in Sayers were soundproof, locked chambers of warm, recycled air. Goran nudged the door open with his hip, and the room was drenched in harsh light. Pink foam egg carton hung on the wall. At the center of the room sat a grand piano, glossy and stern.

"She's a beaut," Timo said, whistling.

"Yeah, yeah," Goran said.

"They certainly don't have a grand at the ballet studio, though."

"No, it's a shitty upright," Goran said, frowning. They dropped their coats on a chair in the corner. Timo sat next to Goran on the bench, and Goran stretched his arms over his head and back. Their voices were plush, insulated. It was only when Timo listened very carefully that he could hear the mosquito-thin drone of the lights overhead. It was the sort of room that made you want to whisper. The air just ate your voice.

Timo's palms ached. He hadn't been on a bench in years. He felt the familiar, involuntary tension in his fingers, the tightening in his lower back. He looked away.

"Do you want to give it a try?" Goran asked.

"No—you go ahead."

"All righty," Goran said. He had his arm wrapped around himself and was stretching.

"You know I don't play anymore."

"I'm not twisting your arm," Goran said.

Timo laughed a little at that, and marveled at the clarity of the sound coming from him.

"Jesus," he said.

"I know. It's kind of maddening," Goran said. He sat with his hands in his lap, looking down at the keys. Timo sat on his own hands. His shoulders had opened.

After Goran had gone through his scales—he always started with scales, as if in fealty to an old teacher—he moved on to the Debussy. Timo admired the easy vigor of Goran's playing, the way he lunged through the difficult passages. Sometimes his arm brushed Timo's, and he'd look up just a little bit as if startled to remember that Timo was present. But he didn't ask Timo to move, which felt generous. Timo could feel the vibrations of the music under the seat and in the air in front of him, which grew heavy with sound. The fine, dark hairs on his lip and chin hummed. The physicality of the music was in him. He could taste it, almost. It felt like a real, concrete thing in the world with them. His knuckles ached. Goran nudged him. Timo pressed his chin to his own shoulder and looked down at the slender space between Goran and himself. Goran had put a hand on Timo's leg. The bench was worn, and blond patches poked through the black paint like the whorls of a fingerprint.

"It's all right," Goran said.

"I know that."

Goran looked at him full on. Timo's face grew hot. He hid behind his shoulder. Goran's hand on his leg squeezed once and then withdrew. Goran went back to the Debussy, but the sound of it was distant from Timo. He watched the solid weight of Goran's fingers as he depressed the keys. Playing was a little like dancing that way—the physicality of it, the precise dimensions of the room and the keys, everything as unforgiving as the sides of a polygon drawn on paper. It was the reason that Timo had given it up for math, like trading one brutal occupation with space for another. He could understand the arrangement of finite physical quantities. Goran played the piece to an end, and Timo got up from the bench.

"That was good," Timo said.

"It was shit. Slop for the pigs."

"Maybe so." Timo laughed. He settled on the edge of a chair across the room. Goran squinted at him, reached out, flexed his fingers.

"You're so far away," he said.

Timo crossed his legs. Goran leaned against the piano and rested his chin on his arms.

"Are you still thinking about Ivan?" Timo asked. Goran hummed in assent. "Have you talked to him about it?"

"No," Goran said with a sigh. "What would I say?"

"You might try something like *Please stop making porn*."

"But it's his body, isn't it? His right?"

"Sure. He doesn't have to listen," Timo said.

Goran tapped the heel of his palm against his forehead.

"Money for sex."

Timo regretted now, more than just a moment before, having said anything. How stupid he'd been to say anything when it wasn't his place. Goran had fixed him with a stare like a faithful blood-hound having caught the scent of something alive and fearful. Timo searched himself for purchase, for something to hold on to, but there was nothing there. He slid down the slick, inner surface of himself like a lizard in a glass. What could he say in the end except, "Sorry."

Goran snorted at him, then lay into a braying chord, and then another, until he was layering them on top of each other. It was harsh and grating, a pot-banging sound that Timo recognized. It was from the sublime middle section of Chopin's Ballade in G Minor, offered to Timo not in apology or rebuke but in the random yet purposeful way one begins a conversation with a friend after a long absence as if no absence had taken place. Goran was playing it too forcibly, too wildly—even Timo could tell that much—but he wasn't playing it for practice or for beauty or for enjoyment. He was playing the Chopin to let something out of himself, the way some people tuck hair behind their ear or chew on their fingernails. It was Goran's habit, as casual as anything else.

Timo braced himself against the back of the chair and held his breath, because even though the music was loud and forceful, it was also beautiful. Goran's playing was beautiful. Here too was a sieve through which feeling filtered. Goran was passing his feeling through the contained network of the music, its strictures, its measures, its chord placement, the ridiculous fingering of it, pouring himself into it and emerging undiluted. Goran's shoulders opened like a pair of wings as he played. His hands were quick and large as they swept and descended. His face a mask of annoyed thrill. Timo wanted to tell Goran that this was like Ivan's pornography, that it was not so bad and he needn't worry. Timo laughed a little even as the hairs on his arms stood up—Goran couldn't help himself.

At the end of the ballade, the frenzy is supposed to turn tender, wistful. But Goran skipped that part now. He played even the soft parts with such vicious intensity that it was as if the madness just kept going, endlessly, until it vaulted into the waiting silence of the room, which vibrated, thunderstruck.

. . .

They ate dinner downtown, despite the fact that neither of them had much money. They ordered a charcuterie board and two glasses of wine each. It was early evening, and despite the season, Goran had convinced the staff to let them sit outside: *Here, look, the chairs are already here, and a table, no it's fine, we'll take it, no, don't worry.* Timo always felt embarrassed when Goran did this, massaging their circumstances until they exactly matched his own desires. Timo was accustomed to taking what he was given and not questioning it.

The sky overhead was woolen and low. The wind had a grainy, chastising quality to it. They drank red wine and snacked on cheese and bread, olives and pickles. Goran had prosciutto. Timo was a vegetarian. There was a small sideboard of mustards, ranging from very sweet to earthy and spicy. They licked the grease from their fingers. They ordered a second round of food. Jellied nuts and boiled peanuts spiced with pepper. Roasted tomatoes and feta. It didn't amount to a full meal, but there was pleasure in the act of eating.

The wine was decent, which was just the sort of thing that people in graduate school said about wine. *Decent*, as though they had a long and mysterious history with the act of drinking wine and could discern its various nuances and flavors. But Timo's classmates and his peers all drank the same cheap wines, sometimes ironically and sometimes earnestly, and he wondered how they so easily and readily constructed an air of aloof superiority. Not quite damning the wine they drank, but withholding approval. Timo thought that if they actually hated the wine or thought it poor in quality, they might have said that or said nothing at all. When someone truly disapproved of something, they seldom said it. Why would you? The quality judgment had nothing to do with the object being assessed, he thought, but it had everything to do with proving that one possessed the faculty of discernment. They all were going around all the time trying to prove themselves, litigating the case for their own worth.

Look at me, look at me, look at me—I matter, don't I?

Timo was guilty, too. He drank his wine down to the sooty bottom. Goran was rolling the miniature cucumbers around his plate.

Money and sex. A fear of solitude. Silence and noise. Goran was inspecting his phone intensely. Timo hummed idly, his eyes glancing restlessly around. Cars sliding on the damp streets. The crane across the street in the construction area. Something eerie about its solemn head, bent as if in prayer. The construction zone with its gravel and packed earth like an abandoned civilization.

"You didn't do your grading," Goran said.

"No," Timo said. "I didn't."

"Don't you think you should?"

"I'll get to it," he said. The wine's bitter aftertaste somehow more pungent in the descending night.

"And how is Fyodor?"

Timo smiled and then shook his head. Fyodor was not a subject he and Goran talked about. They didn't talk much about Timo's life in general. Their friendship was not predicated on the equal exchange of information—they had only become friends after the fact of their fucking. On that day when they'd first met, Goran had been the one who talked about himself. And just like that, maybe especially after the sex, they had fallen into a pattern as resolute as the line of succession of the kings of Norway.

Still. Goran didn't really care about how Fyodor was. He didn't care about much of anything, except himself and what was on his mind. It was, Timo knew, a version of the behavior Fyodor perceived in him: self-involvement. Still, Goran was talented and funny. Some people got to be selfish, didn't they? They were special and their selfishness was a part of that.

"He's well," Timo said.

"That's nice," Goran said, but he was already changing the subject. "Hey, do you mind if Ivan joins us?"

"Oh?"

"Yeah, he just got out of class. He wants to come over. I told him it was fine." Goran dropped the phone on the table. Did Goran want Timo to say no? Did Goran want him to say yes? Did Goran want him to forbid Ivan from coming to them? There were no clues to what Goran wanted. He'd asked *after* inviting Ivan, so maybe it meant nothing. But then, a few moments later, they heard a shout from across the street, and there was Ivan, tall in black anorak and black tights, jogging toward them. He pulled up a chair next to Goran and took off his coat. His sweater was bright orange. His beard was thick. His voice was hoarse, like he had a cold.

It was strange, after watching his videos so many times, to see Ivan in the flesh. Here in his warm animal body, the flaring of his nostrils, the way the orange light from inside lit up the red undertones in his hair, the sensuous slope of his mouth. He put his arm around the back of Goran's chair and leaned back in his own. There was a raw, hot quality to the air around him. He said he'd run there straight from class. Realizing that he was staring, Timo looked down into his own plate, where the discarded shells of boiled peanuts lay like the husks of mollusks.

Ivan still had a dancer's grace and muscularity. His movements were precise but smooth, like a practiced habit. He smeared three different kinds of mustard onto a slice of bread, folded it, and ate it like a kid in a cafeteria. He chewed with anguished pleasure. Timo thought involuntarily of his latest clip, the way he'd come as if against his own will, a thready, gritty cry in his throat. Timo thought involuntarily of the way *he* himself had come watching the clip, clutching himself through the mesh of his running shorts, how he'd reached the point of orgasm by surprise and caught his body off guard. In that moment the two of them had been connected by an invisible channel, by some strange, dark luck in the world, and their pleasure had been joined like a permutation in a probability question. Timo grew hard and then flushed with the remembrance of it.

Goran propped his chin up on his hand and watched Ivan split the cornichons with his teeth.

"You eat like a dog," Goran said.

"I'm hungry." Ivan ate more of the bread and more of the meat. He rolled the prosciutto around four pickles and swallowed without chewing it.

"So we see," Goran said.

Ivan drank the rest of Goran's wine, then leaned over and kissed his shoulder. Timo shivered. The cold was deepening.

"What have you done today? Loaf?"

"I practiced."

"And you—?" Ivan pointed his voice at Timo. His eyes were warm.

"I watched," Timo said.

"I bet you like to watch."

"I do."

"He should play," Goran said. "He used to play."

"I remember," Ivan said. "I'd like to hear you play sometime. Goran practices but never lets me hear him actually play, not really."

"Sometimes the practice is better," Goran said. Ivan looked at him briefly but then turned his gaze back on Timo.

"Well, I don't think that's likely. I don't really play anymore."

"You're in math, right?"

"Yeah," Timo said.

"What kind?"

Timo shrugged out of habit at the question, which he was often asked when people had no idea what else to say to him. A pointless grasp at specificity, leading nowhere in particular. In America there was, increasingly, an idea that math was supposed to be a simple, concrete thing. Pragmatic. And it wasn't just sulky teenagers complaining about learning theorems and proofs. The question also found its way into grant writing and grant evaluation. The public had a distrust of, an animosity toward, so-called public funds channeled into what they considered frivolities. The American economy ran on *What good is this to me?* But there was no easy translation for Timo's research, no convenient gloss he could spritz over it.

"Logic," Timo said. "I thought Goran would have told you that by now."

"Ah—set theory, that junk?"

"I'm bored," Goran droned.

"Yeah, exactly, that junk."

"You know, you could make some real money if you came to finance," Ivan said.

"Like you?"

"Yeah, I mean. I'm not like *you* or anything, but it's a lot of math. You'd love it probably."

"Isn't that what tanked the economy in 2008?" Goran asked.

Timo laughed. Ivan nodded soberly.

"Yes, but, I mean, it's all regulated now. It'll never happen again like that. And anyway, they were profitable again by 2010. Read a book."

"Right, because this is America and we love regulation of the markets," Timo said.

"But have you seriously never thought about it? I mean, it could be amazing."

"Timo wants to be an academic," Goran said. "Last gasp of the great bourgeoisie."

"More like the fading bourgeoisie," Timo said.

"I'm not talking about that. I'm talking about *money*. Making a living. I think I'm good on the sell side. I think I got that. I can do that. The numbers, I mean. That stuff is abstract, for me. But selling. Quick calls. Decisions. I think I got that."

"And is that what you want to do with your life? Quick calls and lots of money? Being decisive?"

"No," Ivan said with another ambiguous smile.

Timo nodded, though he didn't fully understand the nature of Ivan's smile or the conversation, which had gotten away from him. In truth, yes, he had given the matter of his future some thought. He'd given it a great deal of thought. But he felt he lacked sufficient information to make a decision. What he wanted, more than anything, was a clear answer presented to him out of the blue. He felt that if he just kept staring at the initial conditions of his life, something might occur to him. Or he might ultimately be left with no choice at all, and so his fate would be sealed. His future was so muddled.

"But it's sad you quit piano," Ivan said. "That seems like a real loss. Goran said you were talented."

"I didn't *quit*. I just. I don't know. Started doing something else," Timo said. He sat on his hands, crossed his legs under the table. Ivan leaned toward him. Timo could smell his sweat. His hair was thick with moisture. Goran sat back.

"What's the difference?" Ivan asked.

"Leave him alone."

"I didn't love it enough," Timo said blandly. He shrugged in indifference. But his heart caught as he said it, and the indifferent cool he wanted to project collapsed in on itself, so that he felt exposed and quivering. Like a child trying to act out profundity.

The water carafe sweated. The waiter returned, a bleary blond man. Did they want more food, more wine? Ivan ordered a glass, and another board of meats. Timo was full. Goran ate the rest of the pickles.

"As for myself, I'm starting to think I should just go to law school," Ivan said.

"Don't you have an interview for a bank in New York?" Timo asked. Goran just looked bored, like he'd heard this all before. People in graduate school were always talking about going to law school, except for the people in law school, who talked about going into real estate. Painters, dancers, poets, and even scientists dreamed at their desks of the law, of a codified system that ran through all their lives and kept them from bilious harm. What they wanted was something that made sense and made money and could convert their temporary suffering into something more stable and right.

Goran had been raised in a family of lawyers and dentists. This was not news to him. Timo's parents were surgeons. Timo didn't know what Ivan's parents did. From practical people they each had come, and now they lived out the wet amphibian prologue to their adult lives, dreaming of law school. But it was still jarring to hear Ivan say it.

"Yeah, but, who knows, right? I have the interview, and they could decide they hate me. I'm not cut out for the quant stuff. It's so computational these days. If I go in and they don't want me, then what?"

"You're mostly done with your MBA."

"Sure," Ivan said carelessly. "Yeah. I am. But, you know, next steps. If you don't get the right internship at the right firm, you're stuck cooking the books for cow farmers. Law school, you know, could be great. A lawyer's just a lawyer."

Timo said nothing for a moment, only thought of the clips, of the amassing of all that money. It made a kind of brutal, craven sense to him now.

"It's expensive," Goran said.

"I know," Ivan said shyly. He looked sideways at Goran. Like a kid seeking permission. Timo's palms were sweaty against the seat, numb from the pressure of his sitting on them. He drew his hands from beneath him and folded them on his lap. "Maybe a bad idea."

"No, that's not what I mean. I think, if you want, you know, do it."

"No, no, bad idea."

"No, no."

"No. No."

"No, no."

"No."

It was like in the practice room. The sound of their voices was a solid thing moving among them and through them. Goran and Ivan's voices bled together until it was one unbroken stream of speech. It was unbearable to think that this was all humanity had to contain their feelings. These mean kernels of sound. It was cruel. Timo's mouth filled with an acidic heat. He tried to breathe through his nose. He tried to be present. He tried to be there.

No, no, no, no, no, no, no, no, no, no—what stupid little words.

Goran and Ivan were laughing. They leaned against each other and kept saying *no*. They rubbed each other's arms, kissed each other's necks. They held each other tight. Ivan tickled Goran, who writhed and jerked, and they jostled the table.

Timo swept the water carafe to the ground with the back of his hand, and it broke open with a loud, wet crash. Glass gleamed in the shadow under the table, caught by the white streetlights. Goran looked at him as if from at a great distance. Ivan's eyes grew wide.

But at least they had stopped.

It was a lie that Timo had not loved piano enough. He had loved it very much, but in a way that was difficult to describe. It was apophatic—he could only describe it through its negation. He only understood how much he loved the piano after he had given it up. Even that decision in hindsight seemed arbitrary, a whim. An act of petulance. But he had loved it, and he still did. Every day, he felt like a struck tuning fork, vibrating all the time. Except that it wasn't pitch he was tuned to but something else, some horrible frequency cutting through the universe. Loss, he thought. It was loss.

After he said goodbye to Ivan and Goran, Timo did not go home. Instead he headed off to the small office he shared with the other teaching assistants. He climbed the dark stairs in silence, and when he got to his office, he locked the door but did not turn on the lights. He sat in his chair and took out his phone.

There were messages from his mother and his father. There were three text messages from Fyodor—first saying *Happy Birthday*, and then *I love you*, and then *Call me when you're free*.

He called up the first of Ivan's videos again, and when it was over, he watched the second and the third. He watched all fifteen clips without breaking, so that they formed a kind of film. Back to back, end on end, the clips were jerkily of a piece. The same filter. They grew longer, as though the clips themselves were growing more confident in their ability to exist. The acts contained within the clips grew less abstractly sexual and then more concretely sexual. Until he reached the final clip, uploaded just a few hours before, in which Ivan, dressed in the same clothes he had been wearing at dinner, filmed himself stripping out of his Lycra and sweater. He filmed himself growing more and more naked. He turned from the camera to pull down his tights. His back was long and smooth, furry at the lower spine like a tender mammal. His arms were taut and strong. The flexion of his ligaments, the veins running down his forearms, and the plump heft of his ass. His body was beautiful and alive. His shoulders were two swinging blades. The room was his room as it was always his room. The same blank walls, the same comforter on the floor. The soft hiss of his clothes, the snap of the elastic being pulled and let go. Ivan rose back to his full height. You could see the slow, unfurling motion of his hand working at his cock, but not the cock itself. Only his arms, the steady pistonlike motion of it. Then, the angle of the hip changing, shifting, as he turned back toward the camera, but as his eyes lifted to meet the camera's gaze and as the shadow of his cock fluttered into view, the clip lapsed into a complete darkness, five seconds of crackling darkness, and then the clip ended. That crackling darkness, which was of a different quality than the darkness in the room. The blackness of his screen radiated outward into the darkness of the office. The slick darkness of the screen licked the air. Timo's forearms were cool and damp. He shivered.

Timo grew hard again. He put his hand over the mound between his legs. Squeezed himself. There was the funny tickle of wetness, the prelude to desire. He squeezed his legs together, which only made it worse. He opened his pants. He held himself, the warm animal of himself, his pulse beating like something desperate to claw its way out.

He held his cock that way, in his office where he taught, where he drank his coffee, where he talked to the other students in sporadic conversations, hard and beating. He didn't jerk off. He didn't come. He felt cold. The wind pressed on the window. He tucked himself back into his pants.

The grading went on for twenty or so minutes. Their mistakes were all the same. He had taught them wrong, he saw, could see just where he'd gone wrong in explaining the proofs—they hadn't even known where to begin.

He knew that he was not a gifted teacher. Among his students were many provisional admits who had to make up for deficits in their high school education. They were not stupid, but they certainly were not smart either, and he resented this, their need for him to educate them. What he wanted was for no one to need him, to require of him nothing. Because that way he wouldn't have to feel this way, this awful terror at comprehending his own failure.

He put his head against the desk, hating the feel of himself.

. . . .

It was a little before eight when Timo left his office. He went down-stairs, crossed over Pentacrest, and took Jefferson down by St. Mary's. The lights were on in the high window beneath the steeple, which rose and rose into the deep, smooth vault of the sky. Across the street, the parson's house sat stubby and sincere. Never was there a more midwestern house. He peeked through the screened porch as he passed and saw two shadowy figures playing cards and sipping from mugs. A space heater glowed in the dark.

At the end of Jefferson, he jogged across the street to Fyodor's house. The broad front windows were eerily gray. He climbed up the porch steps and pushed into the front hall, which smelled like salt and mold. Old shoes. He could hear the dancers above them. A party of some kind.

Fyodor's apartment seemed empty at first. But then, he turned the corner into the kitchen and on the little table, there was a cake with three candles burning. Fyodor was sitting there with his head down, asleep.

Timo stood in the kitchen doorway, looking at him. This sleep-ing man. This dumb cake he'd probably paid too much money for at the co-op. He looked so peaceful. Timo sat at the other end of the table and watched the candles melt. They were those trick candles. But they had burned down and down through themselves. The wax was perilously close to the cake. He wet his fingers and pinched out the fire. The little sizzle and burn against his fingertips.

Fyodor snored loudly and woke himself. He looked up blearily and then jumped, startled by Timo's presence. Once the candles were out they were more fully enclosed in the dark, but the blue light from the neighbor's porch still reached them. Fyodor wiped at his mouth with the back of his hand. "Happy birthday," he said.

"Thank you," Timo said.

"I didn't know when you'd be back. I thought earlier, but then. I don't know. I think I fell asleep."

"You did."

"Sorry."

"It was nice."

"That feels like a loaded comment," Fyodor said warily. But then he got up and turned on the light so that they could see each other.

It felt really tawdry and cheap to apologize. Like something people would do in a movie in the face of a kind gesture. But they weren't movie people. They weren't little trains set on their track running their preset courses. Free will had to enter into it somehow. Agency. A tendency toward messy, mundane complication. He was sitting across from Fyodor, whom he loved. Whom he knew. Fyodor, another living person, breathing and thinking, feeling. How to make his own feelings understood? How to say, *I see you, I love you, I'm sorry*? But sorry was just a cheap, dirty little word. It presupposed an orderly world. It presupposed that it was ever possible to make up for what had come before.

Instead, Timo stood and took a knife from the rack. He cut a wedge of cake. Carrot. Vegan. It was the co-op cake, thick and stodgy, but he cut it and set it on a plate, which he pushed in front of Fyodor. He cut his own slice and sat, not back at his end of the table, but next to Fyodor.

They ate in silence, ate without looking at each other, and when they were done Timo washed their plates. Then they moved over to Fyodor's couch, and Timo read him a story by the writer Garshin, who Fyodor had been reading lately, or trying to read as part of his *trying*. The story was called "Officer and Soldier-Servant." Fyodor lay with his head on Timo's lap, listening. He was asleep before the end of the story.

Timo did not move. He did not get them into bed. He sat with Fyodor's sleeping weight on his lap, looking through the window at the empty side yard. Over them, the dancers and their party went on. He felt a little like crying then. Not because he was unhappy. But because he felt, for the first time in a long time, like he had done the right thing. That he had chosen to do something good. He had done right by another person, not thinking of himself.

He looked down at Fyodor and marveled that it was possible that someone could trust him enough to rest with their head on his lap, not thinking he might harm them or do something monstrous to them. That a person could trust him, even after all the dumb fighting and arguing. It moved him. Most people would not have cared. Or noticed. But Timo noticed. Timo cared. Fyodor, sleeping.

The apartment grew cold. But still Timo sat there with Fyodor's head on his lap. His own legs going to sleep, tingling and then dropping off entirely. He rested his head against the back of the couch and slept, too.

Upstairs, the party went on.

I just want to be serious about something," Goran was saying. They were in the café. It was Monday. The rain was cold, but the sky was bright, silver almost. There was ice on the ground.

"You are serious," Timo said.

"I mean about my life."

"You're right," Timo said. "You're right."

The café was filled with the noise of undergraduates. Timo looked out from his spot in the corner at them. They all looked the same. Like small, desperate creatures, fearful and alone in the world. A barista banged on the counter to dislodge a hard pat of espresso.

"Ivan and I are over," Goran said.

"I'm sorry to hear that. I'm really sorry."

"It's not the porn thing," Goran said. "It's the law school thing. Or New York, I guess. He's leaving." Timo laughed at that, but Goran just shook his head. "He doesn't know what he wants. And it made me realize that I really need to get fucking serious and stop floating around. No more classes."

"You mean, you're going to lean fully into your trust fund," Timo said.

"Fuck you." Goran was anxious about the money his grandparents had left him. He felt guilty for having it, and sometimes he suggested that his guilt had something to do with his having been adopted. Timo did not regret saying what he said. But he did regret the hurt in Goran's eyes. He was serious.

"I'm sorry."

"Anyway, I can't be wasting my time. I have to get down to work. I'm no spring chicken."

"You're absolutely geriatric."

"I was a prodigy, once."

"I remember," Timo said. It was true, Goran had been a prodigy, of minor but robust gift. You could tell he'd gone to conservatory from a young age. It was in the way he played. Like obeying a set of rules even as he broke them. He had a terrifying sense of pitch. But Timo had been a prodigy, too. Or maybe everyone was a prodigy if they worked hard enough and long enough and became, at a young age, competent at a thing. Perhaps what people misjudged for prodigious talent was really just unexpected competence.

"Fuck you. You don't believe me," Goran said.

"I do. I do."

"You don't."

"I do."

"You don't."

"I do."

"Anyway. I think you should get serious too. Get back into it."

"That ship has sailed, I'm afraid," Timo said. "You know that."

"But come on. Like. It's not the way it was when we were kids, man. Like, there's a whole fucking world out there. Beyond Chopin competitions and grad school. Like, music is so much more than what we used to think. You could be—"

"A popularizer?" Timo laughed bitterly. "I'm going to start a YouTube channel and explain what tonics are? Maybe I should be the fucking pornographer, huh?"

"Don't be like that—it's not what I meant. You know it."

"You just mean, you can go on to a concert career, like you were trained for, and I get to do the slop for the hogs."

"If music matters to you, you'll do anything for it. You know that."

Timo could hear in Goran's voice something like how he must have sounded to Fyodor when they fought. The strident righteousness of a certain path. The certainty you could only get if you were just slightly delusional.

"No, thanks," Timo said. "But I am happy you are taking your music more seriously."

"I was thinking it was something we could do together."

"Like a band? A duo?" Timo laughed again. "There's an idea."

"I don't think it's absurd. People do it all the time."

"People who have access to instruments. To connections. To practice space. To money. Yes."

"You aren't poor," Goran said. "Why is everyone always acting so terribly pious about money. You grew up in a suburban monstrosity just like me."

Timo drummed his fingers on the table. Not just like Goran. There had been money, yes. More than some people. More than most people, in fact—but running out all the time. Running down and down, through a sieve, into some black hole. It was one thing to have money and to know there would be money tomorrow and tomorrow and tomorrow. It was another to have money and watch it shrink and vanish day over day, knowing that it would end sometime soon. And it was yet another thing not ever having enough. The whole world was just a series of nested shell games involving dwindling sums of money, everyone a little worse off than the person next to them, until you got to the very bottom, where some people had nothing at all.

He had not understood that at first. Even having come through it, he hadn't really understood it. He had understood only his own private deprivation. And that what felt secure to him was what felt secure to everyone. That his values were the *real* values. But now he saw how dumb that was.

The white men on the television were always talking about it, weren't they? The great vanished American middle class. That's what his parents belonged to. They'd had money, and then the bedrock on which that money had rested was eroded by tariffs and taxes and the outsourcing of capital and labor abroad. The giving way of agriculture and industry, the crumbling infrastructure of midcentury American fortunes destroyed in the hypercharged realities of the neoliberal/neocon nineties. Reagan, Bush, Clinton, now Obama: It was all gone now. All used up. Or at least reconfigured and locked behind ever more severe sets of restrictions. You needed money to access the money, and what they were left with, the hundreds and thousands of families that had once had enough money to ensure the next generation's comfort—what they were left with was nothing, just the bitter memory of the houses they used to own. Tracts of land that used to belong to so-and-so up the family tree. And to say nothing of the whole black thing. Generations of beige upper-crust blacks marrying beige upper-crust blacks, all those women in their pearls and the men in their Harry Winston watches. All that time spent signifying that they came down from a long line of free folks, ten, twelve generations out of slavery, free of that ancestral taint of bondage. Forget the whole respectability politics of it all. That nascent but very present idea that if they'd really been worth something, them slaves wouldn't have been caught in the first place. All that wrong-headed nonsense handed down along with the money, which shrunk over time. But Goran didn't know about any of that. His family was white. Goran's family still had money. Timo's family did not. So, no, not just like Goran at all.

"Music is all wrapped up in that other stuff for me," Timo said. "You know that. It's best to let it lie."

"Excuses!" Goran said, smiling. He was amused by this. "That's just an excuse not to try! But I won't twist your arm. Think about it."

Timo smiled back. "Okay. Yeah. I'll think about it."

They went on smiling at each other, each knowing that it was a lie and that they had come to the end of something. Timo had fallen out of love with Goran in that moment. And Goran could see it. But they couldn't bring themselves to say it. To acknowledge it. So they went on smiling, and then they were laughing at their table in the corner, while it rained and grew cold and the café grew loud and then warm and then empty, and the whole world, the whole procession of its events marched on without a single notice or care that there in their tiny, obscure particle of the galaxy, two people's hearts were breaking over and over again.

5

Gorgon Head

After Seamus wrote those opening lines, a curious yet ordinary thing happened: the poem seized up on him and shut itself away.

Those lines had come with a shape and a sound, and he felt that if he could just wedge the poem open, he might manage to scoop the rest out. He sat at his desk for many hours at a time, waiting for the poem to open and reveal itself to him again, but nothing came. The opening lines had seemed to be the end of a long period of silence in his writing. But instead, they had been only an illusion, or some other form of silence.

Still, he could not bring himself to consign it to the compost heap. Something in it still felt alive, and whatever it was would not let him go. So he went to class and he went to work. The snow fell and melted and fell. Ice coated the roads. In the mountain west, ancient trees burned, and in the South, cold killed the grid and people went without food or power or water.

Thinking that it would provoke the new poem out of him, Seamus gathered his Alsatian nun poems. Reading the poems back over, he thought there might be something in them—or, at least, in his original urge to write them. In his first year, his classmates hadn't liked his poems at all. They had mocked him and called him a colonizer and a Catholic sympathizer and apologist for the horrors of empire. Where were the drone strikes? Where were the anticapitalist critiques? Was it enough to write after old forms if they had nothing to offer the atomized world of today? Where did *race* enter into it? Where was the indictment of whiteness? But maybe just letting his classmates have all the say was a way of being afraid.

All of that had made Seamus feel trapped, stuck deep in the dark thicket of the poetry program. But there was a world out there. Bert had burned it into his face. And maybe, maybe, all this grad school shit was just pretend. If he couldn't believe in his poems. If he couldn't believe enough to get through this doubt. This fear. Then he was not a poet. There had to be something out there outside all of this, and he had to believe it.

What he needed was some sign that he might emerge from graduate school into that larger, outer world.

Submission. That was what they called it when you sent your work out. When you put your neck on the block and awaited the cold clarity of the blade. You had to believe in the eternal. What came next, after they lopped your head off and hoisted it high in celebration. You had to believe that, in that moment, you became something greater, grander, larger. Submission required belief.

He gathered up the Alsatian nun poems and emailed them to a reader he knew at *The Paris Review*. When he clicked send, he wanted to throw up and retract the email. But he could not figure out how to call it back. It was totally delusional. He had sent poems to *The Paris Review* throughout undergrad, but he'd never even received so much as a form rejection. Still, he thought, maybe by sending the poems, he could at least stir something loose. Get some juice going. Instead, it just made him miserable. Now, not only was he unable to write, but he was checking his email every ten minutes.

Week after week, he sat in the seminar room, looking out over the treetops down by the river or watching eagles cut down and snap up distracted ravens. Inside, his classmates talked over poems about their grandmothers picking cotton or the silver mines of Utah. Linda workshopped a poem about an abortion. Ingrid and Garza sat on either side of her, gripping her hands as she told the story behind the poem.

"I was alone. That's what I remember most, lying on the bed, my feet up, and I never felt so fucking lonely. And for a minute, like, I really thought, am I about to get rid of the only person in the world who will love me?"

Seamus looked around the room. Their eyes were all red-rimmed, even Oliver's. Linda's writing wasn't bad. It was fine. Good sometimes, even, in flashes. But it wasn't poetry, and he couldn't bring himself to say that Linda was an essayist more than she was a poet. That her poems were, in the words of a fictional Robert Lowell in an Elizabeth Bishop biopic, "observations broken into lines." There was no shame in that. It took a certain skill to write good sentences, to make good observations. She had that, at least. It was not a minor gift. The faculty of observation. But she lacked a poetic intelligence.

Yet she had learned—somewhere, here, probably—that a poetic intelligence could be elided with certain tactics. *There* was a word: Tactics. Emotion. Feeling. Her piece had a lot of feeling and it corresponded to something painful and true in her life. But that did not make it poetry. Autobiography was not sufficient.

Seamus sat with his arms folded, looking at the white sky and the black branches shifting against it.

"You have something to say?" Linda snorted. "You wanna tell me my abortion is fake?"

"I've never met your abortion," Seamus said, but then, growing more serious, "I guess I just don't feel there's much in it."

"Wow."

"No, I'm being serious, for once," Seamus said. "It's not a diss, or whatever. I'm not coming for you."

"Coming is probably a big problem for you," Ingrid said.

The professor cleared his throat. "Please."

"Forget it," Seamus said.

"I want to hear it."

"Don't put yourself through it for him," Ingrid murmured.

"Yeah, white men have no business talking about our bodies," Noli added.

"Well, I'll just cover my eyes so I can't perceive you." Seamus did cover his eyes then, but no one laughed. He dropped his hands. "I'm just saying that this is very moving. It's very, very moving. But what is it other than that? Is this a poem? It's functionally equivalent to, what, like, a slasher movie? A children's story?"

"Oh wow, fuck you," Linda said.

"I can't believe this," Helen said.

"I'm not trying to be inflammatory," Seamus said.

"Perhaps . . ." The professor trailed off.

"Great, yep," Seamus said. He was already getting up and taking his bag with him.

Another day on the bridge with Oliver then, another early class.

"We can't keep getting tossed out," Oliver said. "It's really fucking with me, Seamus."

"I wasn't even trying that time. They're so tingly."

"It's not like you gave them a compelling reason to read you in a generous light."

Seamus sighed. He didn't have it in him to spar with Oliver, too. He leaned on the rails. The river was totally frozen, dusted with snow. His eyes teared from the wind.

"Whoa, you must be depressed if you're not taking the bait. What's the deal?"

"Man, I am so blocked. I am so totally fucking blocked. I had. Like, a few weeks ago, I had this. Poem. Just. Sitting right there. You know? Like, I had it. And I lost it. And. It's gone on me."

"The worst."

"Yeah. The worst."

"But it's not like you've been trying, though, right?"

"What?"

"You haven't submitted for like a year, Seamus. I mean. Is this really different from that?"

Seamus did not know how to answer immediately. In one sense, yes, it was different. In another, more broadly speaking, no, it was not. He had not written. He had tried to write, yes, but hadn't really written anything alive in so long. But he'd touched something. He stuck his hand over the river. He'd been so close.

"It's different," he said. "This time it is."

"Then," Oliver said, rocking forward over the edge of the bridge, "no choice but to go after it."

Oliver righted himself and jogged to the end of the bridge.

Seamus followed, slowly, feeling the bridge sway beneath them. At the riverbank, Oliver climbed down onto the river and stood with his arms stretched high above his head. He inhaled and yelled as loud as he could.

The river was empty except for them. Cold. The air was close. In the silence, Oliver's yell doubled upon itself and became a battalion of yelling voices. He motioned for Seamus to join him, and Seamus climbed carefully down over the rocks and the frozen mud. He stood on the ice. It felt dense under him. Heavy. Yet he could also feel Oliver's weight through the ice. It groaned under them. Overhead, eagles wheeling, skirting the tops of North Hall and beyond. The dorms with their gleaming glass fronts. And back across the river on the other side, the houses and frats. What peace.

Oliver panted from his yelling. His lips were chapped and red. He slid over to Seamus and gripped his shoulders.

"Get after it."

"It's a poem, not a deer."

"Poems and deer, man. Same shit."

"Now you sound like me."

"Then you've taught me well," Oliver said. He hugged Seamus. The warmth of it, the strength in his arms, made Seamus want to cry. It was so much the opposite of how it had been with Bert in the woods that night.

No. Do not think of it.

Seamus turned as he did whenever Bert came back to him. He turned from the thought and redacted it from his memory. No. Not that.

"Now let it out. And get back to work."

"No. I'm not doing that."

"I won't let you go until you do," Oliver said. He went to put Seamus in a headlock, and Seamus yelled loudly directly into his face. Seamus's throat was raw at the end of it. But he did feel good after it. There were footsteps on the bridge. Two people peeked their heads over.

"What the fuck was that?" one of them said.

"Mind your business," Seamus called up.

A few months after the thing with Bert in the woods, Seamus had gone to a party with Stafford, the painter, whom he knew only because Stafford stole paper from the poet office in the liberal arts building. Stafford taught a gen ed art appreciation class, and sometimes they talked about art. Sometimes they talked about music. Sometimes they just fucked. But Stafford had asked him to go to a dancer party, superior because poets were not usually involved.

On the way over, Seamus mentioned that *The Paris Review* had taken a poem of his—one of his poems about the Alsatian nuns during the Thirty Years' War. At the party, Stafford kept telling people about it, which embarrassed him but also made him feel good. Proud, like he'd achieved something in his art—though there was nothing more mortifying than feeling proud of publishing a poem. It said something about how needy you were. How hungry. But that publication was the first real, true thing he had done with his poetry. It made the silence of the new poem stranger, more curious and brutal.

There, in the haze of booze and weed smoke, talking to dancers, giving them a hard time, he'd glimpsed a familiar figure out of the corner of his eye: Bert. A jolt of recognition in the flaking scar on his face, pus-green at the middle, dark angry red at the edges. From the burn. Bert.

Seamus swayed, his vision going swimmy. Stafford took his arm and brought him outside to catch his breath, and when he asked what was up, Seamus thought he might have just imagined it. That Bert wasn't there after all and he was just making it all up in his mind.

He had not been able to write since then. The poem had gone silent on him. Somehow, the poem and Bert had gotten all mixed up together. Sometimes, still, when he rode home from the hospice on his bike, he thought he could hear the truck following along behind him, invisible, but there, coasting right up to him. He dreamed of Bert. He woke with the taste of Bert in his mouth. He could still smell him.

That night outside of the dancer party, he had told Stafford it was nothing.

That was the winter of Bert. Lingering. Squinting in at Seamus out of every darkened windowpane and from every corner. Sometimes at the hospice, during dinner service, he could hear Bert's loud laugh carry back into the kitchen. And each time, he excused himself to go down into the mudroom, where he locked himself in the bathroom and waited until the residents were back in their rooms and visiting hours were over.

Spring semester was thesis semester, and because no other professor would have him, Seamus was once again in seminar with the professor. Along with his classmates, as they shared an adviser. He considered this both bad luck and also bad decision making on the part of the administration. But he could get by. He knew how to get by. At the end of their first meeting, the professor asked to see Seamus outside.

"This is your last semester," he said.

"Yeah, don't threaten me with a good time. No, I know."

"Thesis semester."

"Yes. I know."

"You haven't participated in over a year, Seamus. I can't . . . You can't. It's not. You have to submit."

"This some kind of kink thing?" Seamus laughed. They were in the hall. His classmates were passing them, eyeing them up.

"No. It's not."

I don't know why you just don't write," Stafford said. They were lying on the floor, catching their breath.

"Right, like it's so simple," Seamus said. Stafford had just come on his stomach. It cooled in a pearly puddle, seeped into his navel. Stafford lit a cigarette and Seamus motioned to the window over his desk. Stafford stood up to open the window, his knees and ankle bones popping. He had a languorous stride. Seamus wiped the semen from his stomach with the corner of his bedsheet.

"I just don't think anything is achieved by making things harder for yourself, that's all."

"Yeah, well, you don't have a pack of witches breathing down your neck." Seamus rolled over and put his face in the pillow. Stafford sat on his desk, puffing smoke out the window. The cool air felt good. Stirred up the sour smell of his dishes and his soiled blankets. He had to find a better way to live. Meaning his apartment, but also, perhaps, poetry. He couldn't go around with his guts hanging out, feeling sick and miserable, trying to push at something that wouldn't give.

"Maybe you're just not a poet," Stafford said. He flicked ashes through the window. Seamus turned to look at him.

"That's kind of a fucked-up thing to say, no?"

"I just mean. We get so hung up on these labels, like *poet, painter, dancer, grad student*—it's all because we're godless faggots and our world has no central organizing theme anymore."

"That almost scans," Seamus said.

"Almost? Fuck you." Stafford grinned. "No, I'm serious. It's very Marxist. Total collapse of values. All that remains is labor and capital."

Stafford with his compact body and platinum-blond hair. His strong neck and shoulders, turning nonchalantly to flick ashes out the window. There was a trapezoid of light on his shoulder, some bright fragment torn from a greater plane.

"Maybe so. But poetry," Seamus said. He lay on his back and put his hands behind his head. "Poetry. That's worth staking your life on. My life, anyway."

Stafford drew on the cigarette and watched him. The angle of light changed. The trapezoid faded. They were in a different attitude then.

"Well," Stafford said, joining Seamus on the floor again. "If it's worth it to you. Just blow up whatever's in your way."

Seamus took the cigarette from him and drew on it himself. He could taste Stafford in the filter. Stafford watched him, waiting for him to exhale. He held his breath.

Seamus tried not to think of Bert.

He tried to think of his mother and his father. He tried to think of his grandparents. He tried to think of Mr. Fulton. Eunice and Lena. He tried to think of the women in that first kitchen in Rhode Island. Michigan in the summer. Watching his father do Shakespeare at the summer festivals. He ran through the litany of things he wanted to say in the poem, and what he wanted it to do. He thought of Beth's bad poem. So many months in the rearview now. It seemed irrelevant, now that he had decided upon this course of action. But he needed to write. That was all there was to it. He needed to write. To be writing.

The problem was that he had all these ideas about what writing meant. And what if he wrote and it turned out that he was nothing.

Would that surprise him terribly, to be nothing?

Was that quite so shocking?

No.

He had learned that lesson.

He thought of Oliver on the river before break. The volume of his yelling. That's what he needed. Just to let it go. Let it out. He opened his notebook to the opening lines again. He had repeated and scratched through and repeated the lines dozens of times across dozens of pages, going through many notebooks.

He set them down again, just once more, as if to remind himself:

How vast your works, O Gorgon Head—
the night, the century, the quiet, the cry.

Seamus worked on the poem for three days leading up to the deadline to submit for the next seminar. He blasted away at the poem, writing first long lines and then short lines, huge stanzas, then one great column. He tried prose poetry. He tried a sonnet, but it wouldn't give. He tried wrapping it up in a sestina, thinking that it would force the poem open like scrambling a Rubik's Cube, but it remained illegible to him. He wrote on the computer and on a pad. He tried ink and graphite. He drew it. He wrote it. He dreamed it. He ate bits of his drafts, thinking this would help, somehow. But his stomach hurt, and he couldn't shit. He drank coffee cold and stale. He drank whiskey. He smoked in the snow outside that had come at last, after threatening for days. His back grew sore. His legs grew numb. His fingertips were singed from striking his lighter. He had cigarette butts in his pockets. He masturbated furiously until his underwear were stiff with semen. His cock grew raw and chafed. He stared at it for long periods of time, thinking that he might have caught something from Bert. He wrote long emails to his teachers at Brown and to Mr. Fulton, whom he later found out had died two years before. He found this out because he also looked up various people from his life on the internet and searched out their obituaries. He looked at time-lapse videos of plants blooming. He sketched a layout for a small garden in his front yard. He looked up the prices of tropical plants. He reread *Othello*. He read the first five pages of Proust. He masturbated more. When he came, his body seized up, and for a moment he thought he'd snap in half. He wiped his semen on his mattress. He wiped his semen on his chest hair, where it grew hard and opalescent like the interior of a clam. He called Oliver, but Oliver did not answer. He sent text messages to Oliver, but Oliver did not answer. He sent a picture of himself naked to Oliver, but Oliver did not answer. And then he sent another text after the nude pictures: *just kidding man pick up*.

He texted Stafford. He texted Hartjes. They talked in the fragments of gay men: hey, hey, sup, u, nothing, hard, tired, good day, morning, hey, sup, nothing, writing, cool, u, nothing, lunch, good, working, writing, sup, you. There were moments when being gay made Seamus feel less than literate, but also, he liked the anticipatory heat of it. What it might lead to. In this case, nothing. They just texted each other a few pictures of their dicks, their bodies, said, *so hard, want you so bad*. And, once, panting, he and Hartjes jerked off on FaceTime, telling each other scenarios in which they were touching, stroking each other. What made Seamus hardest was when Hartjes said, *I can feel you. You're so warm when you're clenched up around me. I can feel you*—it felt so personal. So pure and good. When Seamus came, he was embarrassed. After the FaceTime, they didn't text anymore.

But all of this was writing, too. All of this, those three days, was writing. Even the not writing. Even the jerking off to avoid thinking about writing. About the impossibility of the writing. Trying to hammer out a shape for the poem. For the feeling. For the thing he'd come through that night. Bert. The truck in the street following him home. Hartjes outside the parking garage. The curious loneliness of his life. His parents. His father. He tried to write a poem that was all of it, and yet bore no sign of any of it. Because that was a true poem. Something that had no sign of what had made it.

That was what mattered to him. The invisibility of the thing that had gone into it. It was not cowardice. It was not fear. It was intention. It was purpose. It was the thing he wanted most. To hide. To see but be unseen.

It was three days, but finally the poem came. He emailed it to his classmates in the middle of the night, and the next morning he deposited a copy in the front office. After he had turned in the poem he walked home and stood on the bridge. A loose snow had fallen in the night, and the world, that morning, had a damp, woolen quality to it.

The sky was heavy and low to the ground, and the air was thick and cold on his cheeks. The green water of the river was sluggish and smooth as it flowed under the bridge. His face was stiff from the cold, and also from not having bathed. He could smell himself, powerfully, the scent of musk and the odor of having stayed in his flesh too long.

When he got home, Oliver was on his stoop waiting for him, his hands tucked deep inside his dark coat. He looked up to see Seamus.

"Yo," Oliver said.

"Hey," Seamus said, feeling shy, feeling nervous because of the text messages, because of the naked pictures, because of the desperation, which now felt like the worst kind of confession.

"So, that was unexpected, huh?" Oliver said.

"I'm sorry about those pics, man."

Oliver blinked, and a look of confusion fell across his face. Seamus exhaled through his nose, and his breath was a white cloud. He could feel the film across his teeth.

"What?" Oliver asked. "Oh, no. I meant the poem. It's fucking great."

"Oh, fuck," Seamus said. "Oh, fuck." He crouched to the ground and put his hands through his greasy hair. "Oh, fuck."

Oliver came to him and crouched down beside him. He put a hand on Seamus's shoulder. "Are you all right?"

"No," Seamus said. "Fuck."

It was strange in a way. He had forgotten, in the span of time it took to walk back to his apartment, that submitting the poem to seminar meant that other people would read it. They would know. This had been a part of the plan, but in his writing, he had lost sight of it. He wanted to make himself small. He wanted to make himself tiny and invisible. He shivered. The poem was too much about him. It was too much about Bert and the woods and his parents and his grandparents and too much about how it hurt not to be wanted in the way you wanted to be wanted. Too much about the things he had balled up and discarded. It was base and crass and there was too much of his flesh and bone in it. He hated the poem, but hated more that he had liked the poem. How it had outmaneuvered him. You were supposed to be in control of your poetry. Its workings. But he couldn't control anything. And he hated that.

"Seamus, man. That poem was fantastic. You don't have anything to worry about, what's wrong with you?"

He couldn't say it, he knew. Not to Oliver. He wavered on his feet in his crouch. He shivered. The world grew indistinct. The cold was in his mouth. He wet his lips.

What could he say? He laughed hoarsely.

"Yeah, it was whatever. Thanks." He stood up, his knees popping. "I did it at the last minute."

"Really?" Oliver asked. "It felt *worked* to me. It was great." Oliver's hand was on his wrist. Seamus felt warm.

"You want to come up?" Seamus asked.

"Yeah," Oliver said. "I do."

When Seamus emerged from the shower, Oliver was sitting next to the window in the knockoff Eames chair he'd pulled over from the desk. He was spinning a pencil on his fingers. He'd taken off his coat, and he wore a green flannel shirt and gray sweatpants. He had crossed his legs and resembled a professor.

Seamus was warm from the water. His hair was wet. He sat on his mattress. Oliver moved to sit next to him. They kissed with uncertainty at first. His hand found Oliver's furry stomach and then slid down into the front of his pants where he was half hard. Their kiss grew more certain, like a slowly darkening bit of fabric. Oliver lay down on the mattress and pulled Seamus on top of him. He pulled away Seamus's towel, and then Seamus pushed down Oliver's pants, and then they were naked. The room was damp and cold. The light through the window was pale and shallow. It was like something strange and unknowable. They jerked each other off at an erratic pace. Oliver couldn't stay hard. He kept saying sorry, kept looking away from Seamus's cock. Seamus was hard, but his cock was sore. When he came on Oliver's thigh, he felt something hot and stinging race through him. Oliver gripped Seamus. He bucked his hips. His eyes were wild and desperate. He kept saying, under his breath, *Please, please, please,* and Seamus gripped him tighter and pumped Oliver in his fist. At the last moment, Seamus bent down and took Oliver into his mouth. He tasted fresh and clean like new snow. Then the slick salt of his semen. Oliver let out a lowing, grateful sound.

Bert was in the room with them. Just months ago, in this exact posture—this exact configuration of submission—he had let Bert use his mouth. He had let Bert use him. He had wanted to be used.

To be run over the edge of someone else's want to sharpen it. But Oliver didn't grip the back of his head and fuck his mouth. Instead, he stroked the shell of Seamus's ear and whispered *Please* and begged for mercy. It was the opposite of being with Bert. Of that moment in the dark in the woods in the cold. Seamus looked up and saw Oliver's face contort in pleasure. Like he'd been touched by some distant, divine force. It was the premonition from the bridge those months ago. Hurt and want and need and pleasure, all at once. He sank deeper on Oliver's dick until he felt it at the back of his throat and opened and tried to swallow Oliver whole. Not just this part of him, not just this moment. But all of him and all he had ever been and all that he would ever be. As payment. He wanted to totally nullify Oliver. To pay him back for coming here and being genuine in response to a poem. A fucking poem.

But Bert was in the room, and Seamus was on his knees, and Oliver was in his mouth—it was all wrong and all right and all fucked up. Oliver moaned, and he came in Seamus's mouth, and Seamus swallowed and thought to himself, *Amen.*

After, they lay next to each other on the mattress. The room was very still. It was late afternoon. Seamus made Oliver some bisque, which he ate quickly. The light turned blue, and they touched each other again, and Oliver this time wrapped his legs around Seamus's waist and asked him to recite his poem when he entered him.

Seamus was too embarrassed at that. Looking down at Oliver, splayed out on this soiled and sullen mattress, he couldn't bring himself to recite his own poem. Instead, he laughed nervously and said, *Shut up.*

Sex with Oliver was not something that Seamus had known he wanted exactly. Sex with Oliver had not seemed like a possibility. In their first year, Oliver had gone around with several girls in the program and in the art history program, where he often took classes. Oliver appeared steadfastly heterosexual. And yet now they'd had their mouths and hands all over each other. He'd been inside of Oliver, the dank, dark corridor of his body. They had smeared and slathered each other in spit and semen and sweat, and other, darker fluids. His back ached from where Oliver had dug his heels hard. Oliver hid his face behind his arm. The snow was falling again.

"I didn't know you could write a poem like that," Oliver was saying sleepily. "I had no idea."

"Stop talking about it," Seamus said. "It was cheap, anyway."

"It wasn't," Oliver said, and then again more quietly than Seamus thought was possible, "It wasn't."

"What's this about anyway?" Seamus asked. "Did you come over here to seduce me?"

"No—I don't think so anyway. It wasn't like that. I just wanted to say how much I'd liked the poem. I guess."

"You fuck everyone with a poem you like?"

"No," Oliver said. "It wasn't that. I don't know. You looked so sad before, I guess. Outside. I couldn't help it."

"God," Seamus said. "Pity sex."

"I'm sorry," Oliver said. "No, it wasn't pity."

"It sounds literally like pity." Seamus sat up. He was angry. He knocked Oliver's bowl over, and the spoon clattered around in it loudly. The floor creaked.

"I wasn't pitying you. I just said you seemed so sad before."

"This is pity. Great, thank you," Seamus said. He pulled on a long shirt and stepped into dirty underwear.

Oliver was sitting up on the mattress now, too, with the thin sheet pulled across his legs. His body was soft and pale. He almost glowed. Seamus cleared his throat.

"You maybe should shower or like, I don't know, leave."

"Seamus," he said.

"*Oliver*," Seamus mocked. A loose, grainy heat was building up inside of him. Pity, he thought, pity, what was worse than pity.

Oliver sighed. He stood up, towering briefly over Seamus. He dressed himself and then, at the end, turned back to glance at Seamus one last time.

"I loved your poem," he said. "I thought it was brave."

Seamus shut the door in his face.

Bravery had nothing to do with poetry, Seamus thought. He dropped Oliver's bowl in the sink, where it split apart with a dull clank. He washed each part with slow, angry caution, thinking, *Fuck him, fuck him, fuck him, he doesn't know anything.*

At the seminar, he took his usual seat next to Oliver, who would not look at him. He kept trying to get Oliver's attention, but every time their eyes met, Oliver just looked away. Linda sat next to him and gave him a vague, appraising smile that he resented slightly. Helen sat next to Linda and didn't look at him either. Someone had put on a pot of coffee, and the small room filled with the smell of cheap, bitter beans.

They were all in their coats and scarves, sweaters and sweatpants, everyone slightly flush-faced and damp—from snow, from exertion, from sweat—and he could smell their soap and beneath their soap, the heat of their animal bodies. Ingrid came in with the professor. Her hair was luminous in the winter light. They were laughing quietly, and his hand was on her back like he was leading a horse. The professor's voice was low and raspy. He took his seat in the circle ahead of Seamus, and for a moment there was eye contact between the two of them. Seamus felt like all the slack had been pulled from the space between them and their eye contact was a taut cord connecting them. The professor hummed cheerily.

"This week's packet was quite the strong one," he said, looking around at them with sheepish pride. "It's an honor to read your work."

This was his Liturgy of the Word, the way he began each week, to settle the nerves. Seamus felt ashamed at how relieved he felt to hear it. He dug his thumb into the side of his thigh and pressed hard, though he could not feel it except in the joint of his thumb, which bent back and threatened to snap.

"And some new faces in the packet, as well," he said, which made Seamus's neck hot. Oliver coughed quietly.

"Well, how shall we begin? A reading, maybe—"

"Excuse me," Helen said. The professor blinked dully, then gave a slow nod. "Some of us were talking before, and . . . we don't feel like it's fair?"

"What's not fair?" the professor asked, and the room began to shift uncomfortably, a murmur rose.

"Um, like, it's not fair that we have to read poems that are clearly mean-spirited and, like, that degrade our work?"

Seamus watched the play of expressions across people's faces: some with eyes wide with surprise, some with keen grins, some with the thrill of spectating. Others were looking at him with what looked like more than the usual disgust. He was accustomed to people not liking him, thinking him mean or petty or superior. He was accustomed to having people roll their eyes at him, but he hadn't even spoken yet. Seamus was more and more certain as the silence went on that people were looking at him. Oliver was drawing a series of concentric circles in his notebook.

"Would you please elaborate, Helen?" the professor said, but she shook her head stiffly.

"I don't want to give the piece any more of my time, frankly. It's unfair. I just wanted to speak up."

"Well, who is it?" Seamus asked sharply. "Say it."

"Don't speak to me," she said. "You don't get to speak to me."

"I think we should calm down a little," Oliver said.

"Don't call her hysterical," Linda said.

"I didn't. I just think we should calm down is all," Oliver said.

"We *are* calm," Linda said.

Oliver looked from side to side, and seeing that he was also being watched sharply, he grew quiet.

"What is this mean-spirited poem?" Seamus said. "And, actually, I guess, a better question is, are we just here to read things that make us feel good? That seems silly."

"I'm not saying anything else about it," Helen said. She shook her head.

"Okay, everyone. Well. Let's take a moment to reflect here, shall we?"

Beth was sitting quietly next to the professor. Her knuckles were clenched so hard you could almost make out the striations in the bones from across the room. Seamus understood immediately.

"I didn't write this poem about you, if that's what you're worried about," Seamus said.

"Don't talk to her," Ingrid said. "You don't get to talk to her."

"I'm sorry. What is this? I don't get to talk?"

"You can. Just not to people you've been violent toward," Garza said serenely.

"My poem isn't about her. Or her poem. It's not about any of you," he said. "I don't do social work."

Oliver flinched.

"Social work," Ingrid said with a careful nod. "All right then."

"Everyone, we are losing track of why we are here: *to witness*," the professor said, but Seamus was shaking. He stood up and set his annotated packet on the chair behind him.

"Yes, social work," he said. "Yes."

"And yet, somehow, Seamus, we're . . . in the same seminar? What does that make you?"

"Bored," he said sharply. "Fucking bored out of my mind."

"I suggest you de-escalate your tone," Linda said.

"Everyone—" the professor said.

"Or what? You'll have me expelled for *violence*?"

"Wow, is this what we are doing? Mocking survivors?"

"What?" Seamus said, whirling around. It was Beth speaking then. The edges of his vision had gone dark, and his eyes throbbed.

"Mocking survivors. Is that what we're doing? You say *violence* like you don't believe it exists."

"Of course violence exists," he said.

"No, that's not exactly what I mean. I just mean, you say it like you think it's some objective state and not . . . deeply personal and subjective."

"Something is either violent or it's not," he said, though he knew that this was untrue. He just hated to lose an argument. Beth's eyes grew wide. He could see this was costing her something, but it was also costing him something, and it was unfair. To her, to him, to everyone, and everything, it was all unfair.

"I'm sorry for what happened to you," she said quietly, and the room grew still and silent.

"What the fuck are you talking about?" he asked.

"Your poem," she said, and she took it out from her notebook and unfolded it. She read the whole thing to him and to the group, and as she read it, he felt numb. His ears filled with a loud drone that dampened her voice.

> *How vast your works, O Gorgon Head—*
> *the night, the century, the quiet, the cry.*
> *A solemn altar waits, the old God knows,*
> *how meager our repast, the small, the grand.*
> *Have you seen her waiting? Expecting?*
> *No, look there, beside the river on sheets of ice,*
> *she gives way, as time, as light, everything closed.*
> *I knew her once—long ago now, don't ask*
> *for then I would have to tell you it all,*
> *and this is no gift, only hush.*
> *The night, the century, the quiet, the cry—*
> *at last, she answers, speaks:*

"It's just a poem," he said when she was done, but she shook her head.

"It's not," she said. "It's not just a poem. I'm sorry for what happened to you."

"This is insanity," Seamus said with a loud laugh. "Nothing happened to me."

The professor had his finger pressed to his lips, and he was nodding as if he were listening to Beth's reading on delay.

"Let's discuss the poem, shall we? Not the person. The poem. Seamus, your seat, please."

Seamus lowered himself into his chair. Ingrid took out her notes. Oliver slid his foot against the back inside of Seamus's foot. It was a comforting gesture, but Seamus was too far away from himself to accept it. He grunted.

"It's obviously about unprocessed trauma," Noli said. "How it gets buried under traditional notions of masculinity and male pride. But is that new? Interesting?"

"I mean, the white male speaker of the poem is not sympathetic, and maybe that's what it's trying to do? I guess? Bend our sympathies?"

Seamus felt himself leave his body as they pulled apart the poem. A wet chill stuck to his lower back, and he realized that he was sweating. He watched Beth across the circle from him, watched her watch him, her expression placid and giving.

Ingrid said, "But do we believe him? Do we believe his pain? Is it real?"

"I mean, isn't that kind of like, rape culture?" Linda asked.

"That's an interesting critique," Ingrid said, nodding.

"The speaker clearly is struggling with their gender and sexuality, and how like, a body is signified by trauma and like, how that trauma encodes in the self—but like, how our society decodes and reads that trauma is in direct tension with the identity of the speaker. So, it's like, the trauma has, like, thwarted his masculinity."

"Astute," Helen said. Someone snapped and grunted in assent.

"And what to make of the form," the professor said. "A curious, almost classical form, yet it's clearly free verse. I admit, the scansion was . . . elementary. Almost as if a child wrote it."

"The innocence," Beth said. Seamus felt something acrid and warm at the base of his tongue.

"I wanted," he said.

"Seamus? Do you have a question?" the professor asked.

"No," Seamus said.

"Okay, let's redirect a little. Who do we believe the *she* is here?"

"Obviously his mother. There's clearly something damaged there, right?" someone said. "I mean, she's barely a body. She's some kind of maternal cipher."

"Maternal Cipher is my drag name," Noli said.

Linda laughed. Then Beth laughed. They all laughed, except for Oliver, who was still drawing circles. Seamus had not read any of the other poems in the packet. He had been too preoccupied with himself. He breathed out through his nose.

"Okay, okay," the professor said, laughing a little himself. "Maternal Cipher. The title?"

"An homage," Beth said bitterly.

"I think it's doing a lot of work, this title," the professor said. "The Gorgon, you know, is a woman who has the power to turn people to stone with just a gaze. And here, in this poem, there is a mysterious woman who is a keeper of some secret, right? And the speaker is recollecting an encounter with this . . . entity. Which seems to end in petrification. What do we make of it?"

"I think you're reaching, prof," Linda said.

"I think the poem strains toward meaning," Ingrid said. "I think the poem is trying very hard to grasp at something, but the title, I think, is ultimately just . . . empty intellectualism."

"I think it's like pop art," Helen said. "Right? Like, it plays with context. It plays with genre. It's meta. It references. I think it sticks."

"I don't," Ingrid said.

Seamus narrowed his eyes. He leaned forward and put his elbows on his knees. He was tired of watching them scrap over his poem. He felt less like he had gotten a trick over on them and more like he had tricked himself into doing something that he regretted. The poem was barely legible to him. He could barely understand it himself. He closed his eyes there briefly and remembered how the lines had come at last, after those three days, how good it had felt, and yet how inscrutable the lines had been. They felt right, but he could not pierce them, and that had felt like a betrayal of the whole project, and yet he'd been so proud of them, sure of them. They had felt right.

But as they tussled over his poem, he understood something he had not understood before. That the more right something felt to him, the less it truly did have to do with how it felt to others. He had been foolishly and childishly trying to convince the world that he was right, when it should have been enough for him to believe it himself. That was the fault of pride.

His stomach was sore. His arms were sore. He leaned back into his chair and he let them go. Their voices grew indistinct. Their chatter dull. Oliver put a hand on his thigh, and Seamus traced the line of the hand up the fingers to the wrist from the wrist to the arm from the arm to the shoulder to his face. Oliver was looking at him. Oliver smiled. Seamus shook his head, shrugged.

"I told you it would be great," Seamus said, as he turned to look back at his classmates. Linda and Ingrid were hot-faced. Beth looked on the verge of tears. It was the same sight every week.

He had the sense that he was in the middle of some great machine. They each were a widget that could be swapped in and out with hardly any trouble at all. He felt stupid for having cared so much about all this, for having been frustrated with Ingrid or with Beth. It had nothing to do with them or with him. Whether or not he submitted a poem, whether or not he wrote a poem, whether or not he could convince himself that any of this mattered at all, the world would go on. History would go on. They were all inconsequential.

Seamus crossed his legs and felt pins and needles in his feet. There was a faint rattle in his chest when he breathed. It would be all right, he knew. His shoulder ached. He put his thumb into his mouth and bit hard on the gristle at its edge. There was a sharp prick of pain, and then only dull heat. He could feel Oliver's hand steady on his thigh. No one seemed to care too much about it one way or another.

At the break, Seamus and Oliver went out into the cold to smoke. Oliver didn't usually smoke, but he was nervous, he said, about his poem. The smoke hung low around them. There were snowdrifts stacked up against the trunk of the cedar tree in the courtyard. Beth and Helen smoked nearby, watched Seamus from a distance.

"I hope it's all right," Oliver was saying.

"I bet it's fine," Seamus said, then regretted it immediately, as he'd revealed that he hadn't read the poem yet.

"Yeah," Oliver said. "You're right." But his voice was hurt, and his shoulders sank a little. "It's just my first time writing about, you know, this stuff."

"What stuff?" Seamus asked, his brows raising.

"About my mom's cancer—I . . . we talked about this."

"We did?" Seamus asked. Somewhere in the history of their friendship, this information glowed like a hot coal. Seamus could sense its heat. He knew it to be true, but the facts were hazy. "God, I'm sorry."

Oliver was quiet then. His expression closed off, turned cool. Seamus reached for his arm, but Oliver shifted subtly away from him.

"Yeah, anyway. We'll see how it goes," Oliver said.

Beth and Helen were walking by them just then, heading back inside. Beth looked at Seamus. She smiled at him, and then, seeming to think better of it, lowered her eyes.

"See you in there," she said. Helen just grunted. They were bundled in their scarves and coats. Seamus and Oliver were standing in the snow in their sweatshirts.

Oliver saluted them, and then dropped his half-smoked cigarette into the snow at their feet. "We better mosey," he said.

Seamus could feel the snow seeping into his sneakers. He could feel the whole, firm mass of the cold around him, like standing in the middle of the ocean. He closed his eyes and spread his arms and breathed deep. Smoke and snow and cedar sap, everything so clean and pure and true.

Seamus went into the hall after Oliver, and they kicked the snow off their boots. Their professor had just come back from the bathroom. He put a hand on Seamus's arm and said, "Great work, Seamus. It's a good poem."

"Was it?" Seamus asked. The professor's expression opened just slightly. Oliver patted Seamus on his lower back and returned to the seminar room. It was Seamus and the professor alone in the hall. Seamus could feel himself dripping cold water on the rug.

"Is that what you need? For someone to tell you that your work is good?"

Seamus flushed.

"I don't know what I need. I don't know what I'm doing. I feel like I'm wasting my time," he said.

"Oh, Seamus," the professor said, and Seamus looked at him.

"How do you know?" Seamus asked.

"How do you know what?" the professor retorted, his head jostling a little, like it was a game or a riddle.

"How do you know you're not just wasting your time?"

"If you don't know the answer to that, then I can't do anything for you," the professor said with a chastening laugh.

Seamus felt that he had been slapped on the nose and called childish. The world grew deep and saturated. It felt as if something vast and Godlike had peeled back the veil of his life and peered in at him. He had gone around giving away all his power, seeking certainty, approval. But that's what children did. Seamus had been a child, selfish and stubborn in his ways.

Oliver peeked his head out of the seminar room.

"Hurry up," he said. "You're late."

6

Let Us Sit Upon the Ground

The apartment filled with a cold, gray light—it was early spring. Noah and Bert were in bed, smoking, watching snow accumulate on the roof of the side porch. The house at the corner of Jefferson and Van Buren belonged to Bert, and Noah was renting one of the apartments on the second floor. That afternoon, though, they were in one of the empty units Bert was using for an office until he found a tenant.

They were stiff and musky from sex. The ridges of Bert's knuckles were chewed up from being pressed into the wall for leverage. Noah's thighs burned from the rasp of Bert's beard.

"The house ain't much to look at, but the land is good," Bert said.

"Oh—that's nice."

"It should go for a fair price."

"Does your old man know you're selling his place out from under him?"

"He's dying."

Noah took the cigarette from Bert's fingers. The filter was damp and tasted sour from Bert's beer. He sat up on the overly soft mattress and looked down at the mound of Bert's belly, the web of dark stretch marks, the cavern of his navel. He didn't look like anyone's first choice. Something flinty and desperate in his eyes, the balding, the thick glasses, the unironic trucker caps. Noah thought he looked like anyone anywhere.

"Well, that solves everything," Noah said, the smoke filling his throat.

Bert reached for the cigarette with his bruised, thick fingers. "It does. Don't feel sorry for him. Not a good man."

"In that case," Noah said. Bert had reached between his legs and was trying to make him hard again. His touch was fluent, searching, like a plea. Bert gripped him hard. The bed cried under them. The room was empty except for the bed and the dresser. The closet had some abandoned hangers, which made Noah's chest hurt when he looked at them.

"He wasn't good to us," Bert said. "My mom and me. He was a bad man, so don't think I'm being hard-hearted. He wasn't good."

Noah lay on his stomach so that he wouldn't have to push Bert's hand away. Bert settled a palm on the damp small of Noah's back. The room grew cold. The listless red of the cigarette's lit end drew an arc through the air when Bert talked. Noah watched it from the dark cradle of his arms.

"I'm not judging you," Noah said.

"He was a shitty father. I'm not glad he's dying. But I'm not sad either. He's old."

"Why do you feel so *attacked*?" Noah laughed.

"Because you don't know how bad it was then. You're what, twenty-three? You have no clue. Kids like you. You don't know."

"Is this a historical argument? I thought modern queers were ahistorical. Isn't that what PrEP is for?"

Bert flinched and pulled his hand away. He took a long hit off the cigarette.

"You know I hate that word," he said.

"It's a joke."

"People died," Bert said, "so we wouldn't have to hear that word anymore."

"People died in *Iowa*?"

Bert pushed up from the bed. He was big, both tall and wide, and his shadow covered Noah entirely. Noah watched him pull on a flannel and his jeans. Ash fell onto the bedsheet. His motions were hectic but slow, and Noah saw in their casual unfolding the signal that he was supposed to clear out. He sat up, too.

At the door, they did not kiss. Noah stepped into the cool hall. Light from the bathroom struck the wall and opened a small pool of golden light. Bert supported himself against the door frame.

"Well, goodbye," Noah said.

Bert did not say goodbye. He stood there silently a moment or two, and Noah waited for him to say something, and it was this waiting and withholding that gave the thing between them a shape. Noah went across the hall, and he heard Bert close the door behind him.

The bridge was scabbed with ice. Below them, the water churned gray and silver—the muted collisions of ice floes.

"I wasn't trying to provoke him."

"Oh, sure you weren't," Daw said. Gulls in winter white circled overhead. The industrial park issued tufts of clouds. "Totally."

"Leave me alone. Who asked you," Noah whined, but Daw only laughed at him.

They climbed the hill together. Daw had the gruff, square face of an Indiana farm kid, but he was from Connecticut and his parents were both professors—his father taught psychology and his mother taught business strategies. Both Daw and Noah were in the graduate dance program at Iowa. West Des Moines, Noah's hometown, was famous for gymnastics, and sometimes the other dancers in their cohort called him a *local*. The thin, dark trees pelted them with water as they crushed the soft snow underfoot. They were running late for class because Noah had overslept, and Daw had come to fetch him.

Noah's limbs were stiff, unreasonable. Climbing the hill sent random streaks of hot pain up his thighs and down his back. He could still feel Bert inside of him, and his eyes stung from the cigarette smoke even after his shower. He felt sweaty, and he suspected he had something like the flu.

"I swear to God, you always do this," Daw said.

"I don't, I don't."

"It's your own fault if you end up dissolved in lye and stuffed in a barrel behind some old house. You know that, right? Antagonizing a serial killer."

"He isn't a serial killer," Noah said, but he felt ambivalent about whether or not Bert actually possessed the capacity to murder him, or anyone for that matter. He just disagreed with Daw because it was fun to disagree with Daw. In truth, Bert had never been violent with him or loud with him. They didn't argue or shout or slap each other. If they were in love, or even in a relationship, it might have been different. But as it was, Bert was his landlord and sometimes they fucked, and whatever tension or anger or frustration that existed between them found vent when they were naked and climbing on top of each other, licking each other's pits, shoving each other's faces into pillows and mattresses. Sex with Bert wasn't hot or even satisfying. It was like yelling at the top of your lungs into a vast open field, how it left you panting and tired and in pain, but you felt that something had passed out of you and into the wider world. He was not attracted to Bert. He wasn't attracted to anyone, really. But Bert was as good as anyone else would have been, and sometimes he knocked eighty bucks off the rent, and that was as good a reason as he could have wanted. It wasn't love. It wasn't lust. It wasn't anything at all, and only in moments like this one did Noah feel a reflexive need to defend what it was that he and Bert did together.

"If you say so."

"And I didn't antagonize him."

"Then why did he kick you out?"

"I don't know," Noah said, but he *did* know.

"Oh, sure," Daw said. They were at the top of the hill near the Old Capitol Building. Behind them, on the other side of the river, where Daw lived, was the medical campus and arts complex, hidden behind a row of trees. The quad lay before them, blanketed in melting snow. The sun was low, but bright. The gray had burned off the world, and the shapes of the buildings emerged into sharp focus. Other students were milling around in anoraks and parkas. Daw pulled on the edge of Noah's jacket and said, "Come on, let's get a move on."

They jogged the rest of the way across campus, with Daw occasionally throwing his arms over his head to get his blood flowing. Noah felt resentful of his vigor. In the hall, they dropped their bags near the pile with everyone else's. They were not terribly late. The hall was still cold. In the large, open room, they sat on the floor with the five or so other dancers. The boards were cold, too, like a windowpane, a sudden, inhuman chill.

A few minutes later Fatima joined them, stretching her legs out on foam rollers. She had clear, dark eyes and a loud, raspy laugh. Daw looked away. He and Fatima did not get along—a rift that dated back to their first year in the program, when Daw had been standing around after a long rehearsal while people said some shitty things about Fatima always running late because of her job at the café, and Fatima had come around the corner and heard the whole thing and saw their faces. Daw tried to explain to her, but it all sounded like an excuse or a lie, and she had no reason to believe he wasn't like the others, judgmental and resentful of the fact that she worked and danced, as though she thought this made her a cut above.

People said the same thing about Daw and the physics classes he took. The dancers got to audit classes in other departments so long as the professors were willing to grade them pass-fail, and sometimes people took a language class or a lit seminar—the kind of banal intellectual self-improvement that was native to the middle class, so that by the time they were done and had paired and married and settled into cocktail parties and small errands in midsize cities or boroughs of New York, they might be equipped to summon up shards of half-read novels or partially digested critical theory. It was also something they did to make themselves feel better about studying dance, which they considered a rigorous intellectual pursuit while they were in studio or in class, but which seemed like a hobby, like yoga, when they were moving through the streets to the same circuit of bars and cafés they always frequented. But Daw was the only person Noah knew who took physics and math courses. Last year, he'd taken quantum mechanics. He wanted to go to medical school after he graduated, he said, and he wanted to make sure he'd be prepared. Noah always said it back to him with a little laugh—*prepared, yeah, me too*—but the lives they were each preparing for were as different as the lives that had brought them to this program in the first place.

They were all posturing all the time. Everything they did was a posture, defensive or offensive, meant to demonstrate something to the outside world, perhaps that they were worthy or good or all right, perhaps to imply that they were in on the joke, that they were nothing and all they had were these crude choreographies of the self.

At times like this when two people he liked very much did not like each other, Noah wondered what to make of the pernicious nature of loyalty. You couldn't be all things to all people, and any friendship contained such microbetrayals. This was the stuff of life. He leaned over and pinched Fatima on the thigh, which made her yelp and then slap his back. The sound of her palm striking him was like a bark from a startled dog, and the other people in the studio turned to look at them.

Troublemakers, their eyes said, *children*.

"Didn't hear from you last night," she said.

"I was busy," he said. Daw laughed.

"Busy—I see."

The instructor for class that day was Ólafur, who ran the modern subdiscipline. He was around fifty—lean and tall, with a meanness native to those who accept with bitterness a lesser, faded beauty later in life. He had come up in the Dutch National Ballet, but then he had spent the bulk of his career crafting agonized modern dances on themes of German aesthetics. He had a long nose and fair, graying hair.

Ólafur preferred the studio cold at first. *Warm it with your bodies, with your effort*, he said. *If you are cold, work harder.* The morning classes under Ólafur were difficult, both for the range of techniques he emphasized and also for the number of repetitions he demanded. No one wanted to see Ólafur first thing in the morning. In his first year, in the middle of his first session with Ólafur, Noah had vomited from the stress. Fatima worked under Ólafur directly, and sometimes she showed up to Noah's apartment after their sessions sore and drenched in sweat, shivering all over as though she'd seen the horrors of war.

The three of them lifted their eyes and watched Ólafur stretching at the front of the room, and they felt the threat in his easy flexibility.

He looked like he could still do *Apollo*.

"I love to start the day with torture," Noah said.

"I can't wait to revisit my breakfast," Daw said.

"This is the brand of optimism I need, boys."

Through the door came one and then two and then finally groups of other students from their program, until the room was filled with them, the rustle of their clothes, the smell of talc and resin. The girls sewed their shoes quickly. The boys snapped the elastic of their tights in anxious anticipation. Daw pummeled his thighs to wake them up. Noah's toes were numb. The floor was so cold and hard. Fatima was pinning her hair down, then stretching. She said she had a knot in her back. The bars were wheeled out and locked, and they aligned themselves, Fatima at Noah's back, Noah and Daw on opposite sides of the same bar facing each other. A smile, wry, vaguely competitive. They began.

There was an upright in the corner—Goran wasn't playing their class today, Noah saw with a little disappointment. The pianist was someone he didn't recognize. A strip of a young woman, with pin-straight light-blond hair. Her head was quite small, and her shoulders were narrow, but birdlike. She was warming up her fingers with scales, but she kept missing or flubbing. Noah hummed to warm the air in his sinuses, to get his face feeling more elastic. The tension in his shoulders abated. The pianist settled. Ólafur rose from a crouch and gave with a flick of his fingers the sign for the pianist to begin.

Bert's father owned a house on some decent land in the country. It was a two-story house, white with broad windows on the first floor and tall windows on the second. The land out behind the house rose and fell, so that from the front you could see the far fields but not the near fields. In the distance, there were dense trees that broke quite suddenly into open pasture. Noah understood the land at once.

He and his parents had lived in a similar house on a much smaller plot of land far out in the country. Noah had grown up driving tractors and climbing trees. That was where he discovered his natural flexibility and sense of balance, climbing and then leaping from increasingly higher branches until his mother spotted him and came screaming out of the house. They had neighbors who were also poor, and sometimes they exchanged vegetables or windbreakers or sweaters. They got by on his dad's salary in the factory, and his mom sometimes gave pottery lessons in the city, but mostly she spent her time smoking in the kitchen and making meals that were too salty or too hard. His father was Japanese but from Colorado, where his grandparents still lived and operated a laundromat, and his mother was white, from Iowa originally, going all the way back to the prairie days. Noah had been raised on Laura Ingalls Wilder and bad Chinese takeout. His dad smoked and drove a truck and wore denim jackets, and sometimes he'd swear and sometimes he'd pat the back of Noah's head and smile and say nothing. He and his dad had the same hair and the same crooked mouth. His dad had rough, blistered hands, and he could build anything at all, Noah thought, but the thing about his dad that perplexed Noah the most and sometimes kept him up at night was that when he told his parents he wanted to dance, it was his father who'd said sure and his mother who'd blinked as if stunned and said that it was no way to live and he should do something else. That first time Bert took him to the place in the country, Noah had experienced a weird feeling of recognition, and he'd wanted to cry, but he didn't.

It was about a week after their fight that Noah and Bert went back to the house in the country. Bert's old man was still dying, but Bert wanted help repairing some sheds and maybe building a place to store the firewood or other tools.

Back at the end of winter, Noah and Ivan had built sheds on the adjoining allotments. But this was on the main place, where Bert and his sister and three brothers had grown up. He thought he could understand Bert a little now, seeing the fields and how close the sky stooped in the distance. He understood the peculiar loneliness of such a place, the way that loneliness held fast to you, no matter how far away you ran. You grow up in a place like this, Noah thought, and it haunts your dreams until you die.

Anyway, he told Bert that Ivan had done most of the heavy lifting with the shed, but he could use a hammer and could hold things if Bert gave him directions. Bert laughed and said he wasn't looking for a foreman—what he had in mind was essentially what Noah had offered. Hold the boards, hit the nails, and so on.

The wind was the real killer. They were out in the fields unprotected. The yellow grass lay flat. The trees on the edge of the field swirled so hard that he thought they'd wrench free of the ground and blow away. Bert held a cigarette in the corner of his mouth while he nailed, and Noah held the boards as straight and flush as he could as they put walls back on the shed. Their hands were chapped and stiff by the time they had done even ten minutes of work. By the time they had finished one of the walls, Noah's hands were almost totally white and his knuckles hurt. Bert had banged the side of his thumb with the hammer, and now his nail was purple. They retreated to Noah's truck to wait out the wind.

Bert poured coffee out of a thermos into Styrofoam cups. They sipped it while the wind groaned against the windows. The sky was opaque and low.

"I was wondering," Noah said, "if you're planning to sell this place, why are we making repairs?" He said it as a kind of joke, and even meant to laugh, but his voice betrayed him, grew serious and quiet. Bert nodded, but then he shrugged.

"I don't know," he said. "I guess I just wanted to do something nice."

"For your dad?"

"No. I don't think so anyway. I wanted to do something. You know, he used to say I never did anything around here. I never cleaned up after myself or helped him in the field. He kept saying I was lazy, useless. That sort of thing. And I guess I just. I don't know. It felt important that I do *something*."

"That doesn't sound like you. Lazy, I mean."

"Well, it's different when you've got a business to run. And when you're an adult."

"Lots of kids are lazy. I was."

"My father wasn't the kind of person who believed that children should be excused from responsibility just because they were kids."

Bert's face was quite plump. He had shaved, but poorly, and there were patches of gray whiskers on his cheeks. Noah watched him as he spoke. He didn't grow pensive or thoughtful or anything like that, but there was a steadily growing sadness in his eyes as he looked out over the field at their patchwork job on the shed.

"I just wanted to do something."

"I'm sure he's grateful," Noah said, but Bert flinched as he said it.

"It's not for him—I'm not trying to prove anything to him. I am a grown man."

"I know that," Noah said.

"Fuck. Kids, fucking children."

Noah grunted and leaned back against his seat. He held the cup of coffee between his legs. His floorboard was full of papers and empty bottles. It smelled like old motor oil and gasoline. His father had signed the truck over to him when he turned sixteen, and Noah had driven it to out-of-state competitions and down to Iowa City when he started college. The truck had seen him through these last seven years, and it was not new or beautiful, but it kept going, and what else could he ask of it?

Bert had a bad knee and smoked menthols. Noah found it kind of nostalgic, like faded jeans and noisy windbreakers, white socks and sneakers. It reminded him of the nineties, all that VHS heartbreak and running around until his lungs ached, because in the nineties Noah had been, what, a toddler, born at the very end of that decade, barely squeaking into it, and so when he smelled menthols, he thought of his father and the truck and the trip back from the dance class, the city skyline receding in the rearview, and the encroaching darkness of the trees like a threat of rain, green bleeding black under the widening sky that canted and sank down. Anyway, it made a kind of sense to Noah that he would end up with a person like this, except, what did that mean anyway, *end up*, because he and Bert were just fucking—for the money, for the good time, for, what, for the laughs, to say that he had done it, fucked some soft-bellied white man, let himself be fucked by a soft-bellied white man who looked like he might have murdered someone? Some crazy-faced nobody? Some lonely little fucker out in the middle of nowhere who had missed AIDS only because it had swept over his tiny little crack in the world, except in the case of all those lonely dying men returning home from greater, vaster cities? Some lucky little nobody? Letting himself be taken? By some lesser colossus? Noah had no room to judge. Who was he? He'd grown up in West Des Moines, famous for gymnastics and other fag shit, and he had not left. No Juilliard for him, he of *almost prodigious talent*, he of *almost, almost good enough*, a shard of greater gifts, talented, but weren't there a million talented boys and no space for any of them? He was all right. He would make due. But who was he to judge Bert? Nobody. Nobody.

But still, Noah thought, that didn't mean he couldn't stand up for himself. Set the score right. Talk back.

"I am not a child," Noah said.

"You act like it sometimes. You think it's all acceptance and pride parades and easy psychology. You think it's easy to cut people out of your life when they treat you bad."

"I don't think that at all," Noah said. "You can't put that on me."

"You can't know how it was before. It was awful for us. Our people died."

"Let us sit upon the ground," Noah snapped, "and tell sad stories of the deaths of fags."

Bert turned toward him. Noah saw it from the corner of his vision. He sensed in that motion something bad. Something awful. But before he could do anything about it, he felt the coffee splash hot and urgent against the side of his face and his neck. He screamed as it soaked into his sweater and shirt. The coffee cooled almost immediately, but there was so much of it, and at first it was so hot that Noah couldn't feel his face. He shook, almost spilling his own coffee onto his lap. He tried to wipe the coffee away by pressing his face down against his shoulder, but he was wet and it wouldn't come off.

He couldn't breathe. He couldn't see. There was just the heat and the cry of the wind and the crackling as the plastic of his seat gave with his motion.

"I'm so sorry," Bert said almost immediately after he had done it. "Oh my God."

Noah could barely hear him. The coffee was in his ears. Everything had that muted, watery quality to it. Noah felt Bert press something to his face. It was only then that he could feel the distant, prickly surface of his body again. Not the sensation of touch exactly, but pressure, crude and insistent. Bert was blotting him off with his flannel. He could smell, sort of, his sweat and deodorant, and also whiskey.

"Stop, stop," Noah said, but Bert kept going, blotting and saying he was sorry, so sorry, he didn't mean it, wanted to take it back, and the wind cried on, and the trees went on beating their limbs against each other.

He was starting to peel along his neck and cheek. The skin was tender and pink. He had not been burned, only badly scalded, and though the coffee had raised welts for the first day or so, he was recovered enough to go back to his life. Outside, the cold had broken open. They were emerging from the brutal overhang of winter. True spring was on the horizon.

Noah had taken up the habit of going into the empty studio after the last rehearsal of the evening and working on a piece that he would use for auditions later in the spring. He was trying to find a place in New York or San Francisco or Portland. He was happy with any of those, and barring that, he would settle for Chicago or Atlanta. He wanted to leave the Midwest, and though he felt no particular allegiances to the coasts, he was ready to live in a proper city with hordes of anonymous people alongside whom he could vanish.

He had a couple of audition pieces he used for graduate school, but now he would need something more mature. He knew that one mistake he'd made before was not preparing a technical classical piece. Instead he'd gone in with mood and tone, some hastily prepared contemporary piece lacking narrative, lacking form. He'd made up for it with improvisation and the beauty of his line, but you couldn't fake the whole thing, and during the classical repertory phases of his grad school auditions, he'd made enough mistakes that he knew he wasn't getting into Yale or Brown, his first choices. Iowa had accepted him mainly because his undergraduate instructor was a faculty member and his audition piece had been crafted under her steady guidance.

This time would be different. Noah had danced *The Nutcracker* and one of Balanchine's neoclassical ballets during the fall and winter recitals. He took extra lessons alongside the skinny, terrifying girls who focused exclusively on classical, transplants from Bolshoi or Paris. They were not cold or clinical or precise. They laughed and joked like young girls anywhere. They had the awkward, shuffling step of dancers not in motion. And when he talked to them, they seemed much younger than they were. It made sense. They had sacrificed all the routes through life that did not terminate in a position at one of the world's leading companies. They had given up everything else to bet on this one chance, this one life.

In the evenings, Noah perfected his port de bras, his carriage. He tried to force his turnout a little wider. His fifth, which had never been good, became comfortable, easy. The sweat over the new skin stung and felt alien, like it was not a part of him, but he was so busy with the combinations that he soon forgot it.

He was grateful that Ivan came to watch, gave him advice on how he looked during a turn or a leap. Sometimes, Ivan would reach down and adjust his hip, push at the bend of his back, and Noah thought of the time in his truck out at Bert's place, when he and Ivan had sucked each other off out of boredom more than anything else.

"How's it going with Goran? And New York?" he asked one night. Ivan was stretching and cooling down in the corner. He didn't dance anymore, not really, not with his knee, but he liked to warm up and cool down just to remember how it used to be. Ivan leaned over and looked up at him, his body flat to the floor. Such perfect flexibility. Noah felt a twinge of envy. Some people got it all.

"New York is on," Ivan said with a slow grin.

"Yeah? You got it?"

Ivan laughed and pushed up. "Yeah, I got it. Interview was last week. I found out yesterday."

Noah slid across the floor to him, pulled Ivan into a bear hug.

"You didn't say shit! Come on! What are we doing here? We should be drunk right now. Are you joking?"

"No, this is important. I want you to kill this audition."

"No! We are getting drunk and then high immediately," Noah said. Ivan leaned back on his hands. He flushed bright red under the studio lights. He couldn't stop from smiling. But then his eyes welled up, and his laughter turned to a hiccupping cry.

"I'm so happy," he said. "I'm so fucking happy. And it *terrifies me*."

Ivan was choking, sobbing and choking and smiling and wiping tears. Noah hugged him. Then kissed him, as if he could steal a little of that happiness and a little of that terror for himself. They kissed, and then Noah stood and pulled Ivan up.

Noah bought them a six-pack at John's and they went back up to

216 | BRANDON TAYLOR

his apartment, where they drank and got high, and they laughed and they cried and Noah said, "Your life is going to be so fucking beautiful. You don't even know. It's going to be incredible."

"I've been so afraid to tell Goran," Ivan said. "The last time, he just. I'm so scared."

"Fuck Goran," Noah said. "Fuck him. This is for you."

"Easy for you to say, fuck Goran. I mean."

"Listen. If he wants to be with you, he will go with you. If he doesn't, I mean, hey, so what. There are plenty of dicks in the sea."

"Ha-ha," Ivan said.

"No, not ha-ha. Listen. Do you know what I would give to be in your position. I mean. Fuck. I'm about to go on these auditions, to be looked over like chattel. And if I have too much fat in my ass or my turnout is five degrees off, it's like, sorry, get a new life. It's miserable. But you have something. Like, come on! It's brilliant. You got your ticket out. How is that not worth celebrating."

"I'm happy. I'm just afraid."

"Hello, he slut-shamed you. For doing what you had to do. He is codependent! And toxic!"

"He's your friend too. You don't have to lean on him to lift me up, Noah."

"Okay, yes, I was talking shit, okay, yeah. But come on. This is for you. Cheers. To motherfucking Ivan the Terrible. The rest will take care of itself."

They toasted, and then they got high, and they toasted, and then they got high, and when Noah's apartment got too dark to move in, they fell asleep where they were.

On one of the nights when he was practicing, Noah looked up to see Ólafur enter the studio from the side door. Their eyes met in the mirror, and Noah thought he saw a brief smile.

"It's midnight," he said.

The studio was warm. Outside, rain tapped the high window. The studio had been a gymnasium, converted after the Second World War. There was a legend that people had learned bayonet technique here, the perfect way to spear a person.

"I know," Noah said.

"You're not supposed to be here."

"Just practicing," Noah said.

Ólafur sat next to Noah's things and rested his back against the mirror. He smelled like fresh coffee. His gaze was warm, playful. It was entirely unlike him.

"Your turnout is better," he said.

"Thank you."

"So this is why you don't puke in class anymore."

"I puked one time."

"You're not fat, either."

Noah rested his hands on the barre and stretched backward until he heard the satisfying pop of his back, the slight shift in his sacral bones.

"You are doing well—but your face, what happened?"

"Oh, this? Must be the weather," Noah said. When he righted himself, Ólafur was still watching him, not amused by Noah's little joke. "It's nothing."

"Come here," Ólafur said, waving to a spot on the floor in front of him.

"It's fine."

Ólafur ceased his waving and pointed instead in a clean, perfect line. He would not talk again until he was *obeyed*, Noah knew from class and from Fatima. Ólafur wielded his silence like a gravitational field. Noah sat. He could smell his own sweat and the stink of his tights. Ólafur came close, and his fingertips were cool. They smelled of cigarette smoke and something more acidic, bright, like vinegar. He had a mole on his left cheek, flat and dark brown like a fleck of rust. His touch was firm, as if he were correcting bad posture or a lazy hip, when he touched Noah's face. His jaw at first, shifting it so that Noah's head tilted upward. Noah felt the subtle strain of his muscles, the opening of his shoulders. His body moved out of a reflex to please. Ólafur touched the boundary between the new and old skin, which had started to flake and fall away.

"Something very hot did this," Ólafur said.

"Clumsy," Noah said.

"That I believe."

Noah laughed, but Ólafur had begun to stroke his cheek. The motion revealed to Noah all the fine hairs on his own face, which caught on the surface of Ólafur's thumb. It was like a second skin, a raised barrier that existed just a few microns out from the surface of his actual body, as if they were touching without touching, a pressure before pressure. Noah looked away. He couldn't stand the intense focus in Ólafur's eyes. It made him feel small and transparent, like some kind of eel or baby lizard.

"San Francisco is out of your league, Noah. You should focus on your Portland audition," he said.

Noah nodded tightly. Ólafur withdrew his hand, but they remained sitting there together in the warm studio.

"You have a chance," Ólafur said. "A real one. It's not true for everybody."

"Sure, I know," Noah said.

Ólafur scratched his jaw. The rasp of his nails through the bristle of his beard filled the studio. More rain against the high windows. Their reflections were a little warped by the dimples near the bottom of the mirror where the panels had been joined. A hole in the floor filled with grit and dust. Noah watched Ólafur lift his hand again, watched its slow, downward dive, like a bird, and he knew before it touched him where it would land. It moved from the light of the studio into the warm, dark hollow between Noah's legs, and when the pressure came over him, cupping him through the tights, Noah sighed because it was a relief to have been right.

Fatima stood under the café overhang smoking when Noah arrived, slightly out of breath.

"Took you long enough," she said with a practiced boredom, looking for a moment like a teenager faking cool. Noah bowed with a flourish. The rain was cold and sharp. Across the street, the gravel pit filled with a grayish sludge.

"I see you already found a smoke."

Fatima nodded, puffing her cheeks. "So I did."

Noah dropped into the chair next to her. He peeled out of his anorak. His arms and back were sore. His thighs hummed, stray muscles twitching, jerking to life like startled horses. There were sodden, sad feeder boxes clinging to the railing.

"I want to die," he said, putting his head on the cold table, some cheap aluminum thing.

Fatima unfurled her arm and flicked ashes into the rain. Through the café window, he could hear the music: Chopin? Satie? No, it occurred to him suddenly, it was neoclassical, electro-influenced.

"Don't whine."

"You sound like Ólafur."

Fatima grunted.

"Can I have another?"

Noah took the cigarettes from his inside pocket, and Fatima drew one from the miraculously dry pack. The aroma was deep and pungent, sweet. She closed her eyes.

"What's with all the huff and puff," Noah asked.

"I'm pregnant," she said. The smoke rose swiftly and then was obliterated by the rain. Fatima shook her head as if to clear a thought. "Not for the first time, but still."

"Oh," Noah said.

"Don't get histrionic. Life goes on."

"It's . . . Are you all right?"

Fatima shrugged, shook her head again. Her eyes were clear and sharp. The rain struck the overhang with the insistent *tat-tat-tat* of pretend gunfire. She was still wearing her barista apron. It was her lunch break. She picked at the underside of her fingernails, the cigarette held skillfully in place at the corner of her mouth.

"Do you need anything?"

"Time, money, an abortion—the usual."

"Fatima."

"No, I'm fine. It's fine, I don't know. It'll be fine."

"Okay, sure," Noah said. To give his hands something to do, he took out the novel he'd been reading at home when Fatima had texted him that she needed a smoke, *stat*. He lay it facedown on the table and flattened its spine. It was a novel by Mauriac, but now he wished he'd brought along something lighter, like Colette. Noah had aspired to muster the kind of sturdy patience necessary to get through Mauriac's work, which was elegant and precise but tedious and upright. But now he felt exhausted by the demands of Mauriac's moral vision, which was like a long channel from which several streams were drawn simultaneously. Mauriac's work was dominated by mercy and reason. There was an astringent, Jesuit pragmatism to the novel Noah was reading. It made him anxious for something to grasp on to—fury, pain, destruction. Instead, the novel felt like a cool, flat sheet of ice into which he had wedged the dull, inadequate blade of his attention. He tried to read, but the text swam under his eyes.

Fatima joined him at the table and rested her head against his shoulder. The smoke burned his eyes, but he didn't complain. There were things in the world worse and harder than secondhand smoke. He turned so that his face was in Fatima's hair. He kissed her head and looped an arm around her so that he could rub her arm. She didn't say that she cared or that she enjoyed it, but she moved closer to him somehow in that moment, and they watched for a while as the rain plummeted like a dying species.

Bert was still sorry about the coffee. Now, when they had sex, he was gentle and slow in a way that made the sex *less* enjoyable for Noah. He tried to explain to Bert that he didn't need such *consideration*, but Bert could only feel remorse, which to Noah seemed like carefully calculated self-pity. Sometimes, when he touched the place on Noah's neck and cheek where the skin was still faintly lighter, he was so overwhelmed with emotion that he couldn't even get hard. Then Noah would kneel for fifteen minutes between Bert's fleshy thighs, sucking on him, trying with all of his might to urge him into *ardor*, into *life*, but no give, no heat, no pulse, only the gray slab of flesh. Like trying to bleed a stone except the stone was a sponge, he said to Daw, to Fatima, to Ólafur.

It would have been one thing if the coffee had erased their argument along with a portion of Noah's skin. But it did not. They still fought about the same, vague thing: That Noah couldn't understand how bad it had been for *him*, for *them*—meaning, Noah assumed, the whole line of homosexuals in the greater Midwest in the late midcentury. How could he, when Noah had learned to fuck via the internet and other digital caves of affirmation, enclaves where no one called anyone else faggot except as a sign of brotherhood, of love? It was, Noah knew, ridiculous. Sentiment pulled inside out and turned to spite.

Noah suspected that their arguments were a kind of penance. Residual generational guilt. Bert felt he had to pay something for pleasure, for joy, for forgetting for just a moment that he was, if not free, at least unburdened, that the world no longer required of him his constant vigil: the sending up of flesh-and-blood atonement. That he was relieved of his duty, that his watch had ended.

That thing you said," Bert drawled. "What was that from?"

They were in the empty upstairs apartment again. There was still no tenant. Smoke hung over them.

"What thing?" Noah asked.

"That sit-on-the-ground thing."

"*Richard II.*"

"That's a person."

"A play. About a person. Or a version of a person, anyway."

"It made me nuts."

"It's kind of about self-pity," Noah said, turning over. He put his head under the pillow, where it was cool and smelled like sweat, like their bodies, like detergent.

"Is that who I am to you?"

"I'm nobody, who are you?"

"What?"

Noah laughed.

"I can't hear you," Bert said. His hand was on the small of Noah's back, and then there was more of him suddenly, coming closer. The whole hot weight of his body pressing into Noah. He sank into the mattress. The pillow went taut, and Noah could no longer lift his head. The pillow pressed close and hot. He couldn't breathe, really. It felt as though his neck would snap if he tried to sit up. So much pressure, tension. "I can't hear you," Bert said. His voice was muffled, far away: "Speak up, speak up, speak up."

The auditions went as well as Noah could have hoped. San Francisco wasn't looking for his *particular set of strengths* at the moment but would keep him in mind for future openings, and Portland liked his overall package and liked that his advisers called him team-oriented and a hard worker. Minneapolis said yes, but they wouldn't have a spot for him until the following winter. Oklahoma City was interested but had to wait on their funding to be approved to know what and when they could offer officially. Dallas was out. Memphis was out. Joffrey had laughed, but they said they'd keep an eye out for visiting roles he might slot into. Miami was thrilled he had auditioned but cool afterward, so that was likely a no, too. Noah had spent three or four weeks flying to various cities, burning through his travel stipend from the department, landing and dancing and hoping, depositing in each city a tiny fleck of his self-worth and value, and what he felt after that long stretch of travel apart from a sleep deficit and permanently bruised ankles and knees from knocking into strange bedside tables was a sense of having ended a part of his life forever.

He might never dance again, he knew, and even if he did, he might not ever dance the way he had wanted to years and years ago, as a kid, when it wasn't a job or a prospect but just something he did. He had known this for a while, but it had never occurred to him in just those terms, not until he got off the plane from his last audition, the one in Portland, and stood silently weeping in the Cedar Rapids airport. It was over. It was over. It was over.

When Noah told Ólafur about the auditions in totality, Ólafur nodded.

"I knew it. Yes. I knew it. See, it's fine," he said with the calm of someone placating an anxious child. They were in Noah's bed again. Ólafur's partner worked in the medical school and the hospital as an instructor and surgeon, although Ólafur said he preferred the teaching to surgery. Ólafur sat cross-legged, reading the email on Noah's phone. The room felt close and musky. Above them, stray footsteps, the sound of something banging. The summer tenants had come early. Noah thought of Bert out in the country, in the house with his dying father. He hadn't heard from him in a week or so—it had been hectic with the travel, with the auditions, with life. Bert alone in the rural darkness, staring out the window, seeing stars, the glint of lights in the homes of their distant neighbors, listening to the beep of the machines, a dying father reduced to a husk of flesh and an assortment of cables and whirring pumps.

"Maybe I won't do any of it," Noah said. "Maybe I'll just drift. Or get a real job."

"Is that what your parents want for you? A *real job*?"

Noah laughed at that, a little alarmed at the prospect of his parents intruding into his life. He hadn't spoken to his mother in years. It wasn't bad with them. They just didn't have anything to say to each other on the phone.

"No," he said. "No, not like that. I think they want me to be happy."

"How American," Ólafur said with a sneer, his voice a little cold. "Happiness."

"You dance for a living."

"Ah, yes, but who said happiness had anything to do with it?"

"I guess that's true."

"Dancing is not about happiness. It's about sacrifice."

"Ah, yes, ritual bloodletting. How could I forget?"

Ólafur dropped the phone onto Noah's stomach. Noah jumped— it didn't hurt, but there was a terrifying, hollow thump. He hadn't been expecting it, hadn't hardened himself to the impact.

"You don't know anything," Ólafur said, sounding in his own way like Bert.

"No, I don't," Noah said. He put his arm across his eyes. "I don't know anything at all." There was a resinous, burning taste in Noah's mouth, and he wondered if it was from the semen or the cigarette or the pepper on the trout at dinner. Or if it was something else entirely, some part of himself sloughed off and dissolving. His nose filled with a sulfurous smell. Ólafur's weight shifted on the bed, and Noah sat up to watch him get dressed. He was going home to his partner and their house, which was filled with the shrapnel of their lives, and for a moment, just a moment, Noah was overwhelmed with the idea of the totality of those things, all those many artifacts that he would never see or touch or know, and this was sad to him, that after all this time of knowing Ólafur and having experienced particular and intense arrangements of their bodies, there remained more about him that he did not know. He did not love Ólafur. He did not want to be in his life, really, nothing like that. No, it was the sudden, brilliant awareness of how small this was between them, how little it meant, and how his life had become the assembly of such small, inconsequential things.

Ólafur leaned back across the bed and kissed Noah hard, and Noah wound his fingers through Ólafur's hair, then gripped at his shoulders and back. He pulled at him, but Ólafur was stronger, sturdier, and he shoved Noah away—and back he went, off the side of the bed, and his head hit the corner of his dresser with a quick, hard rap.

"Oh God," Ólafur said, but Noah just closed his eyes. The world vibrated and pulsed. His breath was heavy and slow. Ólafur crouched, and Noah smiled then laughed—his vision swam and there was something like a dark stain spreading beneath his field of sight.

"Well done," Noah said.

Daw stayed with Noah—the doctor was not sure if it was a real concussion or *something like* a concussion.

"You can't be a *little concussed*," Daw said. But Noah shrugged. He was noncommittal on it, but Daw stayed with him for a week. Noah taught him how to make miso. They played cards in the dim room, and Daw read him the end of the Mauriac novel and then later, because Noah begged for it, Daw read him some Proust. Toward the end of the week they watched a movie, and when Noah couldn't look at the screen because of the splitting pain behind his eyes, Daw lay a cool cloth over his face and massaged Noah's feet. They laughed and shuffled through the gossip of their lives—Daw had taken a practice MCAT and planned to do a gap year. He was done dancing for one lifetime, he said. Fatima came over on the weekend and lay on her back on Noah's bed with a water bottle on her stomach. She and Daw didn't fight or ignore each other. They talked, too, about plans made and then undone. She was going back East.

"This is it, boys. The start of our lives," she said.

Daw was the first one to laugh at that, then Noah, then Fatima.

"You make it sound so optimistic," he said.

"This year has been hell," Noah said.

"But we survived it."

"Barely," Daw said sternly, and with an emotion that Noah couldn't penetrate.

"How are your boyfriends taking the news of your departure?" Fatima asked, and a bolt of panic lanced its way through Noah, because it was not clear to him until that very moment that Fatima knew about Ólafur.

"Oh, well," Noah said, looking away, out the window, where the trees swirled in dark circles.

"Ólafur will be fine," Daw said.

"Who even told you?"

"It was obvious."

"How was it obvious?"

"Don't be naive," Fatima said sharply. Her eyes flashed with anger, but she settled back onto her elbows. "It's fine. Take what you can get."

"It wasn't like that."

"It's always like that," Fatima said. "It's always always always like that. You just pretend it isn't. You go banging around through life, and then you're surprised when you end up with a concussion."

"That is an unfortunate extended metaphor," he said.

"We all knew. It's no big deal. Don't act so surprised," Daw said.

"You should be more worried about the serial killer."

"He isn't a serial killer."

"The more you insist he isn't," Fatima said, "the more I feel compelled to point out that . . . he did in fact try to *suffocate you*."

"It wasn't like that," Noah said before he could stop himself. Fatima's laughter filled the room, and Daw could only shake his head.

Bert's father died in the middle of May. There was no funeral because Bert said it was a pointless expense. Noah rode out to the house to see him. A cold snap had frozen the water in the soil, so the ground had a hollow, crunching quality to it. Noah leaned back against his truck door in the front yard. Bert stood up on the porch, looking down at him.

"Good to see you," Noah said.

"You've been a ghost."

"I was busy."

"I bet," Bert said. "Do you want to come in?"

"No, no. I just came to see how you are."

"Well, here I am."

"You look okay," Noah said. Bert was thinner and paler. His hair had a tawny sheen to it. He looked delicate. His eyes were raw and red. His cap was threadbare. The door was open behind him, dark like a mouth.

"Do I?" Bert asked in genuine curiosity. "I don't feel it."

"I'm sorry."

"Don't you start that, too," Bert said. "Sorry for what?"

"I don't know," Noah said. "I guess, I just feel like, I'm sorry you're in pain. For your loss. For whatever lack of peace you have about it all."

"You don't know anything about it," Bert said, knocking his knuckles against the banister.

"I do," Noah said. "I do know about it."

"What do you know?"

"My dad died, too, you know. While ago, but he died. I know about it."

"You didn't say anything."

"I imagine you can understand now why not," Noah said laughing, but his throat was hot and his eyes were burning. "You get it now."

"Suppose I do."

"I'm leaving in the summer."

"I figured."

"I'm going to Portland."

Bert nodded stiffly. Noah sucked in the cold, clean air. He looked at the sparse grass of the yard, the peach tree that flowered prematurely and now was frozen. The rolling fields, the houses sitting like animals in wait.

"Wish you'd said something before," Bert said.

"About?"

"The lease. It'll be hard to fill your apartment."

Noah smiled. He put his hand on the latch of his truck door. "Not in the summer, it won't."

He popped the door, and there was the familiar whine of the interior. Bert raised his hand slowly and gave a jerk of a wave.

Noah lifted his hand back, waving in counterrhythm.

It was a little like a dance, he thought later as he drove the road home, away from that place. He hated the feeling of relief that moved through him when he realized he'd never do it again.

7

Sussex, Essex, Wessex, Northumbria

On weekends, in the rec center pool on Burlington, Bea gave swimming lessons to small, poor children and led a group of old people through water-resistance exercises. The money was not very good. She was paid out of a small grant funded by the university and the community, which had established the program for the worst schools on the boundary of Iowa City and Coralville.

The university and the community might have used the money for a food bank or for new textbooks. She couldn't understand what swimming lessons were supposed to do for a bunch of hungry, tired kids, but she was grateful either way for the small pay and the opportunity to use the pool.

The kids didn't ask her anything. They mostly just wanted to jump into the pool and splash each other. She had made an effort to teach them the strokes. She stretched out on the cool tile beside the pool and mimed the motions for them, but when she looked up from her spot, she saw that the children were regarding her with a cool cruelty, as if they were about to bash her head in.

She resolved to let them do what they wanted so long as no one drowned, and the on-duty lifeguard mostly spent her time on her phone anyway, or policing the lanes to make sure people were sharing properly. The old people reminded her of her father, except that they were overly solicitous where he was hard and mean, and so she didn't know how to respond when they called her *dear* or patted her shoulder and said she'd done a fine job as she helped them out of the pool or into the pool or gave them towels. Sometimes, in the middle of their slow-motion exercise, she caught them gazing at her like she was an illusion or a mermaid, and she felt pretty, until she realized that they were staring because they could barely make her out. She chastised herself.

Bea taught the lessons and the class because the girls on the swim team didn't want to do it. They were fearsome, tall girls with taut skin and broad shoulders. When Bea showered after being in the pool, she could hear them changing for their weekend practice. They had to use the regular women's locker room because the building had been built during a time when women's sports facilities weren't deemed a necessity. This meant that on the days they practiced in the pool, there was an overlap between this curious, alien race of women and the rest of their mushy human selves. They talked like girls anywhere: about the randomness of moles or freckles, about the weird flexibility of a thumb joint, about bad food from the night before, about their boyfriends, their girlfriends, the dumb videos of their pets their lonely parents had sent them, about assignments, professors, coaches, kisses, the slow sweep of a hand coming to rest against their back, the loneliness of mornings, the brutality of their work. Bea felt close to them then, the water striking her sternum as she listened as keenly as she could to what they talked about, and she felt that in another life, she might have been one of them, and though this was not true, in the moments when Bea was kindest to herself, she let the thought last a little longer than she should have.

One afternoon, after the children had been returned to the care of their chaperone and herded like a pack of wet and yowling sheep onto their bus, Bea sat on the edge of the pool, slowly kicking her legs. The old people would not be coming because there was a nasty infection circulating in one of the homes, and it was thought best for everyone's sake that they be kept indoors. This meant she had the rest of a Saturday afternoon to herself, which was unusual, and she thought she might go home and clean her apartment. It was one of those empty afternoons that reveals after a long period of solitude just how much your life has turned inward on itself. There was no one to call and nothing to do. No one required her. No one needed her to do anything. She did not feel freedom or sadness—instead, it was as if she'd been soaked through with cold water. The feeling was all that remained.

She watched the girls from the swim team on the other side of the pool. They were rolling out mats and lying down to stretch. The girls were impossibly flexible, pushing on one another's legs to a degree that looked dangerous and painful. Then they would trade off and offer themselves up to be bent and twisted. Their chatter was a low hum that skipped across the water. The last of the civilians were climbing out of the pool and wrapping themselves in towels, trooping off to the showers. The lifeguard climbed down from her perch, gave herself a sharp twist, and looked directly at and through Bea.

"Better mosey," she said, and Bea nodded, but she went on sitting there, unable to look away from the girls even when their coach—tall, hairy, voice dark and low—came through the back hall. He stood over them with his hands on his hips. He had scraggly, curly dark hair.

"Okay, okay, drills," he said. And the girls leaped backward into the water, not elegant or graceful, but like a flock of anxious, laughing children. Then they climbed out and shook the water from their limbs. She knew it immediately: acclimation. The coach looked at her, and Bea went cool and clammy all over. He squinted and made to come around the pool toward her, so Bea gave him a quick wave and stood. The floor was slick under her and she had to catch herself to stay upright. She collected her towel, and at the open doorway she looked back over her shoulder and watched just a moment longer, the girls leaping into the water and climbing out, getting accustomed to the coldness and the depth and the smell of chlorine.

Bea lived alone in Iowa City. She spent a lot of time at her desk looking out the window down into the yard. She had a view of the pine tree, its spreading branches and the birds rooting around. She was on the second floor, in an old house that had been split up into three apartments. The couple on the floor below were mostly quiet. One of them went to work very early. One left later in the afternoon. On weekends and sometimes on weekdays, the dancer in the apartment next door threw loud parties, but Bea didn't mind, because hearing other lives going on in parallel to her own made it like she wasn't totally alone.

Bea had been an only child most of her childhood, except for one slim, dark year when she had not been.

On her desk was a small cardboard box in which she had constructed a diorama. The walls of the box were painted matte black, and she had made little furniture from strips of medium-density fiberboard. The color differential between the pale furniture and the matte backdrop was such that the fiberboard seemed to glow or vibrate. The edges of the furniture bled a little into the air, so that there was a kind of doubling effect. It was hard to look into the black void of the box, to see the furniture, and so one did not know quite what they were looking at. Bea called the piece *Domestic Disturbance.*

She had created several such boxes filled with furniture and sometimes with tiny humans, whom she constructed with varying levels of detail. Some of them looked like people. Some were just crude stick figures, others futuristic geometric blobs. There was a kind of tumble and turbulence to light when she looked into her dioramas, and it was that coarse texture of reality that matched her own experience of the world. But that was how everyone felt when they looked back at something they had made—every creation was just a silly, slightly deformed inward reflection.

That day, after the pool, Bea took up her knife and a thin strip of MDF and carved a flat human finger. Then she carved another and another, until she had on the table in front of her thirty or so fingers—some bent, some straight, some quite lined and detailed with folds of skin, others cartoonish, blocky. Some were the length of actual fingers, others about a third or more the size, and some as fine and small as a fingernail. But they were all thin, two-dimensional renderings of human fingers. Forefingers, ring fingers, pinkie fingers, thumbs, middle fingers. She carved fingers she had seen and known, some of which she had put into her mouth or had put inside of her. Fingers from her own hand, fingers from the hands of those she had loved or hated. Some fingers she had never seen before.

Carving the fingers required a tight, almost angry control over the blade of the knife, and the strip of MDF was coarse against her arm, shivering like a fearful animal as she cut into it. Her forearms were scraped, and they bled from the irritation. Her knuckles ached from holding on so hard, which she knew better than to do. And for what—these fingers were of no use to her, just something to make with her hands to get her mind settled. And now her palms were raw and her arms hurt. Her eyes were stiff and scratchy from loose particles of MDF, the dust from wicking and chipping away. She had better stop, she thought. But she kept on anyway, because she'd found a rhythm to this useless, simple activity, and it was a shame to throw away a thing as beautiful as a good rhythm.

Summer in Iowa was thick and lush. Her apartment had one window unit in the hall by the kitchen. She couldn't feel the cool air at her desk, and she had grown sweaty. Bits of the MDF stuck to her, and her thighs grew tacky on the chair. She wanted to dip herself back into the pool, but it was closed for the practice, and it wouldn't open later that evening, as it did during the week. She might get in her car and drive up to Lake Macbride or try her luck at the local Y. There were options, choices, things she could do to alleviate her suffering, but she did none of them. She went on making the fingers until the evening was upon her, and it was that part of the day where the light goes vertical and blue, and everything takes on a spectral quality. For about half an hour, it's like living in a movie. Everything attains a quality of luminosity and importance, and everyone is beautiful and languid.

When the first blue shadow fell across her desk, Bea stood up and went into the hall where the window unit sputtered. She leaned down so that the cold air hit her chest and then her face, and she closed her eyes and stood there suspended in a slot of cold darkness. Her nail beds were sore. She could feel her pulse in her fingers. She braced herself against the top of the pane, which was quite warm from the sun, stood there for a moment longer, then lifted her head so that she could see through the window and down into the yard. She could see her neighbor, Noah, and some of his friends reclining in lawn chairs, lifting glasses from a crate used for a table. They balanced plates on their knees and wore sunglasses. Bea had spoken to Noah only in passing—downstairs at the mail slot or briefly holding the door open as someone ambled in with grocery bags from the co-op. He was a little taller than she was, and a dancer, and his body vibrated with health and vitality even though she saw him smoking at least once or twice a day, including at that very moment. The window was smeary, and now and then it was fogged up by a contrail of cold. Spiderwebs and dust clung to the outside of the glass, and it was like looking down through lace, through a haze of time into the blue world beyond. She saw them, though, those shining, happy people with their quickly made dinner and their patchwork glamour. She wanted to slap the glass so that they'd look up and see her, too, so that the perfect awful tension of their lives would shatter and something like relief would rush in. Her palms on the glass felt heavy and hot. She could feel the impact, that prickly smack, though it hadn't yet happened. She might break the glass, send it plummeting down into the garden. She might do anything at all, and it was the array of what she might do that kept her from doing anything.

Bea withdrew.

Downtown at the Ped Mall, Bea stood under the shadow of one of the dying ash trees. She had bought some plums from the Bread

Garden, thinking they would cool her off, but when she lifted them from the chilly mist of the fruit stand, she found them warm to the touch, almost feverish. They were fresh from the back of whatever truck had brought them in, and she thought momentarily about leaving them behind, but she was a little hungry, and so she'd bought the plums anyway. Now she was back to regretting it. The actual flesh was pale and lusterless. It had a mealy, fetid quality about it, as if it were already in a state of decomposition. The meat of the plum was translucent, like her filthy window, and she could see the dark pit at its core. Eating the plum was like chewing up her own body.

A level below her, in a strip of thick, burning sunlight, a group of children ran across wet, dark stones through a water feature. The jets of water had a hard, chemical smell, and they struck the ground with a sputtering sound like urine into a bowl. Heavy water. The children screamed in delight as the lukewarm water wet their shirts and hair. A small girl with a splotchy face and limp pigtails lowered herself to the ground and licked at the stones with a slurping sound. Another girl lifted her sundress and pissed into the small hole, through which the stream would erupt a moment later in a terrible reverse osmosis. But none of the parents noticed or cared. They sat on benches scattered around the playground. Other children flung themselves from the multitiered play castle and landed on their backs on the spongy turf. They picked themselves up and climbed again so that they could leap and fall. Parents went on talking and reading, shielding their eyes from the sun, turning to one another and placing hands on thighs, on shoulders, on backs, this choreography of love and life, and their children went on screaming and destroying and tearing at the seams of the world.

Bea sucked on her plums until her eyes were sore. She pricked her gums with the pointed ends of a plum pit, then flung it back into the feeder box. Thick clouds, tall and white like bluffs, moved in and out of the eastern part of the sky. The clouds were dark, and the river had risen swiftly into a churning gray froth. Some years before, there had been a terrible flood, so bad that the sitting president had come down to visit. There were pictures of him standing on piles of people's ruined possessions, his shirt so crisp that it was almost fluorescent against the grainy darkness of the rest of the photo. But that was years ago, and the river was only *mildly* threatening to flood, which the veterans of that earlier catastrophic year told Bea was good news.

There was a bit of a breeze, but her hair was too heavy, like a pelt on her neck and shoulders. Gnats whined near her, attracted by the sticky plum juice on her fingers. She climbed onto the low stone railing and tightroped along the perimeter of the feeder boxes, stopping sometimes to read the placards nailed to the trees, which designated them as infected and dying. It gave her a darkly giddy thrill to imagine herself indifferent to the plights of the trees. Here they stood rotting from the inside out, their bark crumbling and shattering on the bricks of downtown while hundreds of people passed below them unmoved, unnoticing—it was a reversal in the natural order of things.

When Bea was much younger, she had lived on a sturgeon farm in North Carolina with her father and mother. Her mother had died ten years ago, when Bea was twenty-five, and as she stepped out of the hospital and stood under the pine trees at the corner of the medical campus, she'd thought it was unfair that these trees could go on being when her mother, a real and true and good person, had gone out of the world. It was ugly, a sign of the hardness of things, that the world had no way of accounting for the size and scale of her personal loss. But then she had gone on, Bea had, gone on and lived, and here she was ten years later, hundreds of miles away from home, a different person than she had been then. Her father sold the sturgeon farm that year to pay off the medical bills. It was to be the first year the sturgeon produced caviar. Sturgeon were oddly like people in this way: It took years for them to pay back what they owed you for all the love and care you had paid into them, all that food tossed into their great, growling tanks of cold water. It took a decade for a sturgeon to show its worth. But it had gone belly-up, their small family operation. Sometimes Bea wondered what her father had been thinking, growing sturgeon in North Carolina. Of all things. He might have grown anything. He might have fished anything. But sturgeon.

A foolish, reckless bet for a man with a family.

One of the children screeched, and Bea hopped down from the feeder box. She stood in front of a jewelry store: Ten Thousand Villages. The child went on screaming until it was all Bea could hear. The scream was not an even sound. It rose and fell in pitch, sometimes splitting open entirely, a jagged procession of hiccupped notes, shrieks, and belts. One scream turned to two to three, and then there was a chorus of screams rising off the playground. Bea turned the corner and found that one of the children had thrown himself from the play castle and landed on the boundary between the pavement and the Play Safe Turf. There was an ugly cut on his face. Lots of blood, and his arms shook. None of the parents had risen from their seats yet. They were frozen in place, a pantomime. The child sat alone screaming as other children cried and gestured toward him. The parents sat just a few feet away. Nothing changed. Nothing moved. No one did anything. Bea had to look away. She walked quickly by the child, who reached desperately toward her, and when she reached the corner of the street, she swore she could feel the sticky wet heat of a bloody thumbprint on the back of her leg. But when she looked, she was clean except for the shimmer of her own sweat, and when she looked back to the playground, there was no bloody child at all.

Bea dipped herself into the perfectly cold water of her tub. She sank as low as she could. Her feet rested on the corner near the nozzle. Her body was a murky dark shape under the surface.

Her father used to say: *Sussex, Wessex, Essex—no sex for you, young lady.* It was his favorite joke after she turned thirteen and grew leggy and tall for her age. The years before she grew coarse and thick from the work around the sturgeon farm. *No sex.* Bea had lost her virginity her second year in college to a knock-kneed boy, a lacrosse player from Vermont. They called him Tex for reasons Bea could no longer remember. That was how it was in college, she thought. You lived so far outside the context of your life that names stuck to you in a way that they would not have otherwise. There was a weird sleep logic to college life, associative, random, lacking strict connection. Tex was awkward and had a leathery smell. When he put it inside Bea, he'd spasmed so forcefully that she thought he would break in half. Bea didn't sleep with another man after that.

No sex was certainly one phrase to describe the way she had lived. She didn't know what to do with herself when there was another body involved. She could only understand bodies stripped of their context. She could understand the lower backs of the girls on the swim team, their shoulders, their smiles, the taut lines of the insides of their thighs.

Bea closed her eyes and pressed her knees together. She summoned in the dark pool of her mind the girls from the swim team, the broad, blunt ends of their fingers. She imagined the chlorine-hardened texture of their palms, the sudden flexibility of their knuckles. Those fingers she had lovingly and slowly carved from the MDF. The water in the tub sloshed quietly. The distant hum of the window unit went on. Bea felt herself open, the inner heat of her body, the animal warmth. The water moved between her legs, the pressure of her own palm, the girls from the team. Her knees slipped past each other, and she squeezed her thighs tighter, slipped lower into the water, and it rose over her face, and Bea was submerged.

There wasn't a *Nosex*. The name of that petty kingdom was Northumbria.

Sussex, Wessex, Essex, Northumbria. She had told her father that, after she finally got tired of his little joke, and he'd looked at her with a sneer and told her no one wanted a frigid bitch.

His other favorite joke was to pinch her breasts quite hard and make a sound like a goose. If she dropped the feed pail, he pinched her. If she was slow with the hoses, he pinched her. If she was scared to climb the ladder and look down into the tanks, he pinched her. If she talked back, he pinched her. Some days, her chest hurt so bad she could hardly stand it. And she'd peel off her shirt and lie face-down in their pond. When her mother got sick, Bea returned to them to help. She fed her mother, cleaned up after her—vomit, shit, crusted dishes, drool, spoiled food. Bea did it all, and one evening, when she'd cleared away the dishes and helped her mother onto their front porch, she asked her as directly as she could why her mother had let him do that to her.

"Do what, dear?" her mother asked.

"Pinch me that way, hard on my chest, here," Bea said, pressing her hand flat to her chest, where she could still feel his fingers gripping, twisting. Her mother's eyes were dark and milky. She looked out over the trees, over their vast yard to the lower fields where the tanks were kept. She smelled coppery in those days. Her body was like a deflated balloon.

"Oh, he was just playing with you, honey."

"It hurt. It hurt so bad, and you didn't do anything," she said.

"What was there to do? You lived, didn't you?" her mother asked, and she gave a sharp cough. She reached for Bea's hands, and Bea let herself be held.

Yes, she had lived. She had survived it.

During the months when she nursed her mother, her father did not touch her. He moved apart from them, going to and from the sheds where the sturgeon slept and grew. Sometimes, he came in smelling like pond water. Bea cut her hair and wore it short. She found herself doing her old chores, clomping around through the barn in shorts and a denim shirt, pliers in her back pocket, some tacks in a small bag in her shirt pocket. It was her only way to get out of the house, away from her mother. She didn't want her mother to die feeling resented, but resentment was all Bea could feel. For all she hadn't done to stop him.

Her father was tall, aloof, and hard. But to their animals, he was tender. She had watched him feed baby calves and cry when they didn't make it. She had seen him carry around baby chicks in the pockets of his chore coat. He sometimes read to the sturgeon. She would get up in the middle of the night and walk among the tanks of slumbering fish and find him there, leaning against the tank and reading to them from old hardbacks he'd found in the barn. He loved them in a way he didn't love Bea and her mother. Or else he was just better at showing it with the animals.

Her mother died, and Bea moved away, and she didn't talk to him except for monthly calls, when he talked about his health. His lipids. His enzymes. His decreasing muscle tone. She saw him one time in the last year, and it was true, he looked ruined, like an old operation stripped for parts and of limited utility. He didn't pity himself, which made her want to pity him, but he wouldn't have it. At the ends of their phone calls, there was always a space the size of *I love you*, and then nothing, not even a dial tone.

Bea could feel the grit on the bottom of the tub. Filth from her own body. All that sweat. She pulled the plunger and it drifted upward, the cool chain brushing her ankle. Gray water glugged down the drain, and she sat on the rim of the tub watching. Sandy dregs, a crescent of dirt and skin. An impression of herself. A silhouette of a sort.

Bea was alone in the yard. She liked to come down and leave a small bowl of formulated oat feed along the back fence for the deer, who certainly didn't need her help, but it kept them from eating the heads off the hydrangeas and stripping the shrubs. She retreated to the lawn chairs left behind by Noah and his friends, and she sat in the cool dark. Gnats and mosquitoes bit her legs and thighs, but she sat perfectly still, staring into the side hedgerow that abutted the house next door. She had poor night vision. Everything was gray shapes. There were lights across the street and an ovular pool of light from Noah's window on the grass between her and the back fence. The deer never entered the light. They lurked in the darkness like a stray, half-formed thought or a memory on the edge of consciousness. But she knew when the deer were in the yard. She could feel them. Something in her tightened.

Three deer tonight, long and frightfully elegant, close to the wall, their hooves combing the grass and weeds. A shadow in the pool of light. Bea looked back over her shoulder and saw Noah in his window, for just a moment before the light went out. The outline of the light remained, an inverted negative imprint, and in its center, a glowing angry blob, vaguely Noah-shaped. It burned in the center of her field of vision like a stain or a scar, but then it receded slowly.

She did not know the deer from one another. She had not named them. Her sentimentality was small and deformed, manifesting as it did in curious, random whims like feeding the deer or helping the children into and out of the pool, a hand to their slippery backs as they squealed and tried to backflip off the stairs into the water. She felt their limbs twist in her hands, and she feared sometimes that they would snap or come out of the socket, and she'd want to scream at them to stop trying to destroy themselves, to be good, to get out of the water because their time was over, hating in those moments that she had allowed herself to care, to trust and to care. The rustle of eating. She could hear their fur brush the inside of the metal bowl, the tinkle of the feed, the way the grass squeaked as the deer rocked the bowl with their snouts.

The largest deer lifted its head and peered directly at Bea. She could feel the weight of its animal intelligence, refined through the millennia, and she felt the great waste of it used on her. Her throat ran dry. The other two deer lifted their heads, too. Their ears flicked. Their hooves moved through the grass. They left the yard as they had come, quietly, with great purpose, and were gone. Bea felt she could breathe again.

The light from Noah's room returned, and it lay upon the grass like a tablecloth. She looked back and saw him at the window. He had never left, she knew now. He had stood there all along watching the deer. He had stood there and she had sat there, and they had been together in the dark looking at the animals. They were together in a vast collection of darkness like an ocean, looking, watching. The deer had known it. They had known and they had permitted themselves to be looked at and had taken the food as payment, as tribute. Of course she hadn't been alone, Bea realized. Of course not, of course not, there were always eyes in the dark, even when she couldn't see them.

Someone was always watching.

During the week, she tutored the children of university professors in math and science in the library on the Ped Mall. She was in her midthirties, but she looked younger and could pass for a college student, though she had not been one in over a decade. The parents of the kids she tutored sometimes squinted at her and asked what she was studying, and Bea could only smile and shrug and hope this came across as harmless idiosyncrasy.

On Monday, she tutored a slightly chubby boy named Shelby, who preferred to be called Bee, though his mother, a professor of women's studies, called him Shelly in her emails and at drop-off. He was surly but diligent.

"My name is Bea, too," she said.

"What's your real name?"

"Bea."

"That's stupid."

"Maybe so," she said, laughing, a little shocked at the sound of her own voice. She realized, somewhat foolishly, that she hadn't spoken since Saturday in the pool with the children from her lessons. It could be like that. Days without speaking to another person, her voice going cool and raspy with mucus, like a membrane reknitting itself after a trauma. Bee squinted at her and took out his work-sheets. They were smooth and glossy, like the pages of a magazine. She rubbed the corner of a page between her fingers. Bee had the cramped, irregular handwriting of a child who had been given a cell phone far too early.

"If you have four balls and two are yellow—" Bea read.

"Half," Bee grumbled, writing a top-heavy numeral two over the top half of the box and a four on the bottom.

"Right. Okay, so if you were to add that to—"

"Do you have a boyfriend?" Bee asked.

"Pardon?"

"Do you have a boyfriend?"

"No. I live alone," she said. Bee looked at her with bright brown eyes that were widely spaced. He had thick eyelashes and a delicate mouth. He studied her.

"Your life must really suck," he said.

"Sometimes."

"If you killed yourself, would anyone feel sad?"

"How about we focus on fractions?" she asked in return, and smoothed the sheet flat to the table. Her neck burned. She could hear the electricity in the lights overhead crying out. Bee pressed his pencil hard to the sheet, so hard that a small pile of graphite shrap-nel was left behind when he wrote his numbers.

"I think fractions are stupid."

"Me, too," she said. "But if you learn fractions, you can do anything."

Bee squinted at her. He also had the perfect incredulity of a child who had been given a cell phone far too early.

"That's stupid."

"Is everything stupid to you?"

"No, some things are okay."

"Like what?"

Bee's eyes glinted, flashed. He took out his phone, swiped it open, and showed her a looping ten-second video of a soldier flinging puppies from a mountainside. Bea felt something rigid and bitter move through her throat. She stood up sharply.

"Why don't you work on the sheet for a little while longer," she said.

"Whatever," he said with a shrug. "Whatever you say."

In the bathroom, Bea washed her face. She ran the water over her hands until the water became hot. It was painful and then it was not. Her breathing echoed. She thought about not returning. But the money was decent, good, necessary. She needed it to live. She saw, in her mind's eye, the grainy footage of the man picking up the puppies, small, yowling little things, and flinging them into an abyss. Swirling green on pale brown, dizzy with motion. She had seen that footage years ago. When the war was not new but not as old as it was now. She remembered the public outrage. She remembered the fury of recognition, that they could no longer deny the ugliness of it all. How awful. And now it was a thing children shared on their little devices.

Bea washed her face again. She calmed her breathing. She went back out into the library's main room and sat next to Bee. He had finished half the sheet. He didn't need her help.

"Good work," she said quietly, resting her palm against the back of his head. "Good job."

He stiffened under her touch, startled like an animal, and she could feel the quivering, beating alive thing inside of him. She could feel it, the part of him that was not human but real and alive. It was fear, she thought. Fear that she'd hold his head down and wouldn't let it up again. A reflex.

He finished the sheet and turned to the next. She felt the muscles in his body relax—relief.

At the Ped Mall, they had taken the last of the dead trees and replaced them with younger, fresher varietals. Something hardy. She didn't recognize the kind of tree. The air was heavy with the scent of manure and fertilizer. They'd dug up the planter boxes, and the soil had come up dark and fragrant. It reminded her of pine forests. Home. The woods. She stood in the burning strip of sun and tried to get over the curiously uncanny sensation of smelling trees where there were none, not really. Kids screaming, running. Bars down on the corner blasting music. Televisions flashing with sports. A whole little world going on without her. Her phone rang.

It was her father's monthly call.

He opened abruptly, "The sturgeon are dying."

"The whole planet is dying. Haven't you heard?"

"You're so crass. Mannish. Like your mother."

"At least I come by it honest."

"Irony is a bad habit."

"Maybe in the nineteenth century," she said. Her father went quiet, eerily quiet, and Bea wondered for a moment if she had gone too far, been too rough with him. "How are your lipids?"

"Not that you care, but they're fine. My doctor says I'm in *robust* health."

"Maybe you'll outlive the sturgeon."

"That isn't funny."

"We don't even own the farm anymore," she said. "Why do you care about what happens to the fish?"

"They're yours," he said. "I care about them because they're yours."

"Not anymore. Hey, Dad, I have to go," she said.

There was a pause. A space. And then he was gone.

Bea breathed deeply. She saw, across the street, Noah walking briskly. He turned, as if drawn by her gaze, and saw her. He was in the bright, scorching light of day. She was in the shadow of the trees. He raised his hand. She waved back. There was a smile, small, fleeting, and Bea felt her place in the world's great, calculating machine shift slightly. She was set apart. Of all the people who had ever lived, in that moment she was set apart, because she had been seen. Noted.

She looked overhead, and there were geese, more than twenty of them, in smooth gray formation, rising higher and higher, headed for somewhere else.

It is enough, she thought.

8

Local Economies

Fatima works in a downtown café frequented by graduate students, professors, and a certain amalgam of townies that she sometimes calls the *un-landed gentry*.

The other dancers argue about money in terms so abstract and moral that it isn't even really money they're arguing about so much as *economic systems*. They are for the most part blandly socialist—the seizure and redistribution of wealth, the proliferation of welfare systems, a general softness to the analytic frameworks of the world. Fatima thinks about money in the real-time, concrete way: as in, how is she going to pay her tuition, feed herself, launder her tights, pay for afternoon movies, pay for electricity, for internet, for heat. Money is like an animal, changeful and anxious, ready to flee or bite. There is never enough of it.

She makes espresso and sandwiches. She cuts her fingers and burns her arms. She mops the floors and sweeps the patio. She refills napkin dispensers and makes sure there are enough straws. She adjusts the bolts behind the dishwasher and stacks the glasses on the shelf under the counter, cuts the banana bread when it's still warm from the oven and greases the muffin tins into which she pours the white, goopy batter.

At the end of her shift, Fatima leaves through the door in the alley and walks across campus to the building where the dance classes take place. In the cavernous basement, she changes out of her work clothes into her tights. The hair at the nape of her neck is still damp and limp. She dances with burns on her fingertips, with splinters in her palms. She dances with nicks and cuts and scrapes on her elbows and arms. Sometimes batter sticks to the ends of her hair and she finds it hours later, hardened like exoskeleton. Her life is a series of minor translations between these two modes—the café and the studio.

"But this is the *real work*," one of her classmates says to her one evening after they have just warmed up and are about to begin rehearsal in earnest.

"I don't know what you mean," Fatima says. "It's all work, you know. Work, work, work."

"Yeah, but this is the *real work*," he says with an expression so earnest it pains Fatima to look at him directly. He is skinny and blond, with taut muscles and quite curly hair. He looks like a little doll, perfect and beautiful. His name is Cheney.

"Yes," she says, nodding. "Of course."

Cheney beams at her, and then, as if in confidence, he leans over and whispers, "Honestly, I think it's cool that you, like, have a job. The *dedication*—but I know you know that this is the real deal. *This.*" He motions with his arms to the studio, to the other students stretching, making ready. Fatima follows the sweep of his arms. Sees the tarnished floors, the filthy mirrors. The stench of their sweat and a dozen different shampoos, lotions, body sprays, deodorants, and ointments. The scent of rosin. The slightly irritating resonance of the piano—the room is too narrow and too small for a piano, and so the music has a braying, abrasive quality to it. She hates it all. She resents the stiffness in her muscles. The reluctance of her body toward movement. The creeping water stain on the ceiling above them. The windows, which have been cracked open but still allow too little air flow. The air-conditioning is always too slow, too stingy, always on the brink of breaking. She hates it all.

But *this*, she thinks, *this*.

Fatima and Cheney are in a section of modern led by Ólafur. They are a dozen total, but only five, including Fatima, are his direct advisees. Ólafur supervises their modern section closely. They are working their way through *Bestial*, Ólafur's response to and meditation upon Martha Graham's seminal work *Lamentation*. *Bestial* requires them all to lie flat on their backs for five minutes in perfect silence, moving only when they sense motion from the person to their immediate right. In this way, the piece is at once choreographed and totally spontaneous. Each person has a series of movements from which they can select at random and in any sequence. But once a movement is selected, it can't be repeated until the entire series has been cycled through. Freedom via restriction, improvisations tapping into the deep rhythms of the universe where everything is ordained and set and utterly free.

Ólafur's work is pretentious and derivative, but when Fatima performs his pieces, she feels as though she is giving herself over to something larger. No, not *larger*, which denotes a kind of magnitude. It is *deeper* in her. She feels she is giving herself over to something inevitable, like gravity or the sheer forces of ice sheets sliding past each other down a mountain. Something ringing in the column of the world, passing like electricity, raw, feral light.

She hates this feeling, because she knows it would be better just to ignore him. He is a man, after all. It would be simpler to call him a quack, bluster, noise, and heat. But when she lies on the floor and breathes and waits for the first pulse of motion on her periphery, she can feel it beating in her like a cosmic clock.

Fatima has been dancing her whole life. First to Janet and Deniece Williams in her parents' living room in North Carolina. It always makes her laugh to think of how she came to dancing as an act of joy, kinetic fizz, swing and hitch, and yet her reward for a natural sense of rhythm and balance is to dance these somber pieces, steeped in pseudo-religious order.

Some people think that modern can be lazy, that there is no discipline to it. This is the genius of Ólafur's piece. It grapples with the very nature of modern dance, the improvised spontaneity of it deriving from a series of mastered, disciplined steps. Freedom through restraint, through revision. That is the thing about truly great dance. It has the look of being totally natural, easy, but it is in fact the result of many hours of work and dedication to the understanding and articulation of the smallest possible units of motion. It is abstract and analytical. It is emotional. Ólafur understands this about dance, and she resents him for the clarity of his insight. And still it makes Fatima laugh, the more she learns, because it's funny that she has ended up here, doing *this*. Funny in the way all random things are, because nothing that is right ever really makes sense.

The piece begins, and Fatima feels it come over her, and she gives herself over to it, dipping into the cool, white relief of dance.

After rehearsals, some of the dancers go downtown to the poet bar, which is better than the bar where the fiction writers congregate.

The fiction writers are always going around projecting a self onto the world. Their bar is dark and anxious, and even though they play pool and laugh and run the jukebox in the back of the room, there remains some kind of static in the air. Like a pack of passionless cats, all itchy hatred and suspicion. The poets, though, are raucous and tingly. They rub up against one another and pound the tables. As the dancers enter this evening, the poets are crammed into some tables in the very back and the low string lights over the top of the bar give the place a kind of dull glow.

Fatima, Cheney, Noah, Daw, Alina, Moira, Eve, and Sayaka. They're sweaty and alive, and they carry the scent of the outdoors—gravel, cigarettes, juniper, and jacaranda. The room is too warm. There's a fan set up by the bar at the front door pumping in tepid air. Noah unwinds his arm from Fatima's waist and frowns.

"It's a fucking sauna in here," he says.

"Don't whine," she says. "It's ugly when you whine."

There's a booth in the back, which suits them fine. They pile in after each other. Daw and Moira go up for the drinks. The rest of them stretch and mewl. The next booth over vibrates with raw poet energy. A few of them tucked on the end of the table peer around at the dancers, and Fatima suppresses the urge to laugh. Alina is a streak of a girl. She has that look of stunted adolescence that some dancers have because they either starve themselves or exercise until their periods dry up. Eve is rectangular, boxy, broad-shouldered, and midwestern. She looks like she accidentally stumbled into a dance studio and never found her way out. There's a clumsy grace to her. She looks too nice, too guileless to be a dancer, and yet here she is with the rest of them. Sayaka is from Tucson, and she has a loud, brash laugh. Sometimes, during rehearsal or warm-ups, you can hear her bones cracking from the other side of the studio. She's a jangle of noise. She teases Noah about not knowing anything about being Japanese. Noah receives Sayaka's chiding with a passive, amused roll of the shoulders. Tonight, he's restless and irritated because of the heat. He snaps at Sayaka, who shifts, and sure enough there's a muted cracking sound from her wrists and shoulders.

Eve looks over the tops of the poets' heads into the back wall, which is lined with lacquered photos of famous writers who had blown through town at one point or another. Cheney waves his hand in front of her face to draw her attention, but it's no use. She's out of here. Fatima knows the feeling all too well. The heat lies on them, musky and humid. There is an AC in the back, and it's rattling, struggling for all it's worth, but it is inadequate. She wants to put her hand on its side as if it were a weary horse and say, *There, there now, you've done your best.*

The drinks come—water, whiskey, seltzer, cans of cheap beer. They slide, shift, make room for Daw and Moira. Truthfully, there are too many of them in this booth. It would make sense for one or two of them to grab chairs and sit at the end of the table the way the poets have, but by now they're so accustomed to one another's bodies, being in one another's space, that it's akin to Ólafur's piece. They fit together, arm under arm, leg over leg, the shifting of their knees and thighs. They anticipate one another, moving out of the way just enough so that someone can drink, someone can lift their can and toast. Their eyes and mouths swivel, take in snatches of conversation, parts of one another's faces, voices. The conversation is formless, fragmenting again and again like a segmented worm. Fatima occasionally finds herself in different channels at different times: Daw and Noah talking about—what? Noah's boyfriend, the old guy

who looks like a murderer, Bert. Moira and Eve talking about Ólafur, his hands on their thighs, their backs, his touchy adjustments,
the brutality of his gaze. Sayaka and Cheney chattering amiably
about nothing, so trivial that they might as well be speaking lorem
ipsum. Alina checking her phone, Noah checking his, laughter from
the poets.

A sore spot between Fatima's shoulders, some damp, throbbing
hurt. She can feel it when she leans against the wood of the booth.
It grows more pronounced when she flares her shoulders. Weird
little bother. She frowns. Seltzer and lime. She's drinking it slowly,
letting the bubbles dissipate across her lips, letting it cool her down.

"You're quiet tonight," Daw says.

"I'm *ruminating*."

"How *august*," Noah chirps.

"Leave her alone," Alina says.

"I'm fine."

"Suit yourself," says Moira, who is on the edge of the booth, sitting next to Fatima. She shrugs, brushing Fatima's arm, which
makes the sore spot between her shoulders hurt.

"I will."

"No, but seriously, what's up?" Noah asks.

"Nothing. I'll live."

"Well, yeah, it's not like you're scaling the International Space
Station," Eve says.

"No, I'm not."

"I bet it's the dishes," Cheney cuts in. "You know, you spend all
day doing dishes at the café and then you dance, and it's just, probably very taxing."

"I don't do dishes," she says laconically, but it's true that she does sometimes do dishes, but more often she carries them from the front area in plastic bins to be washed in the back, and sometimes, like on days when the café floods with undergrads with exams for which they are hurriedly and belatedly preparing, there are so many dishes and the bins are so heavy.

"Sure," Noah says.

"I think it's hard—that's why people in the arts only come from like, wealthy families, you know? Because it's hard to be as dedicated as you need to be to the art itself while also like, supporting yourself," says Eve with the rapid, smooth cadence of an NPR host.

"Or people get loans," Moira says. "I mean, God. The loans."

"Barriers to entry."

"I was reading this really excellent piece in *Salon* or like, online at the *Times* or something, about this very fucking thing, and it's so unfair," Cheney says. "But also, like, I think it's important to have gates. I know, I know." He bats his palms at them as if to fend off a horde of protests.

"But hear me out—like, gates make it harder to enter, right? That is the very function of a gate. But that means that the people who get by the gates are—for a variety of reasons, some just, some not, I give you that—those who can do this with longevity, those who really have something to contribute."

"That is such an asinine argument," Fatima says. "That is so stupid. I cannot believe you wasted my time by saying that out loud with your human mouth. God."

"No, no, listen," he says, dropping his hand to her forearm. "I think that, yes, it's not morally okay? You know? I get that. But you have to admit, for the betterment of *the art*, we need practitioners who can give this fucking thing their all, who can be in it for the long haul, and you know, I'm not saying it's right, but some people just . . . can't. And we have to acknowledge that."

There is a beat or two of silence at the table. The music overhead changes. Country-inflected trap music, which in a bar populated by poets and dancers feels like a joke. Fatima closes her eyes against the heat spreading behind her face. She is not ashamed. She is not humiliated. No. She's angry. Irritated at the facility of the argument, its shallowness of thought. Here is mere posture, bravado, bluster. She wants to reach into Cheney's mouth and pull his wet tongue until it snaps and rolls back like a measuring tape.

Alina gives a nervous laugh. The phantom pain of rehearsal moves through Fatima as though her body is signing in slow language some message for her to understand.

"How about that," Noah says. When Fatima opens her eyes, she can see Cheney's glistening forehead, the brightness of his cheeks. The others are cool, distant, aloof.

"That's classist bullshit," Daw says. "And you know it."

"I'm not saying it's right," Cheney says. "I'm just saying it's a thing that's true. The truth isn't always morally right. Like, with racism."

"I am not drunk enough to hear you talk about racism," Fatima says. "I will never be drunk enough for that."

"No, I just mean, like racism is bad, right? It's shitty, awful. But it's there, in the world. And we acknowledge it, you know?"

"Do we?" Fatima asks. "Is that a fact? We acknowledge racism?"

"We don't go around pretending racism isn't real. It's there, I mean, hey, there's only a few people of color in our program, and like, that's not okay—"

"Except," she says, "you think it means that those of us who've managed to get here deserve it, right? Like, we're the ones, the chosen few?"

"Yeah, something like that," Cheney says.

"God," Noah barks.

"But come on, you all think it, right? Like, in your core?"

"Engage your core," Moira says in a shockingly accurate imitation of Ólafur's voice.

"Core is truth. Core is beauty," Sayaka adds.

The poets stand and leave, shuffle out into the evening. They're a gleaming, chattering procession in denim and nylon and leather. They glance at the dancers, and the dancers glance back. There is, briefly, a charged unity as their groups slip into uneasy occupation of the same space, and then it is gone.

"Don't you just know they're all sleeping with their teachers and writing shitty poems about it?" Eve whispers.

"You think?"

"Oh, definitely. Are you even allowed to be a poet without *ache*, without *pain*, without *inappropriate and misguided attachments to authority figures*?"

Fatima laughs at that and catches Noah looking at her, not exactly in a plaintive fashion but not *not* plaintively either. She's gotten too close to something. To someone. Ólafur, whom she saw leaving Noah's apartment one night just after midnight when she was on her way to borrow some weed.

Fascinating, she says to herself then. Everyone knows. Still, it's funny to see Noah so tingly about it.

"Bunch of walking trust funds," Daw says.

"So say we all," Noah retorts obliquely.

"Like I said," Cheney resumes. "I'm not saying it's right. But goddamn, it's true."

After the bar, they go their separate ways. Fatima loops arms with Noah, but they find it too warm and separate. They live over the bridge, or at least they will until Noah leaves them all for Portland. The program is ending. They are at the end of their time. Fatima is going back east for a while. Her parents were thrilled to hear it. They don't know what a person does in Iowa. They find the concept of dance abstract and morally dubious—dance to them is something you do when you make dinner or something you do when you're looking for sex, for attention, for men. Dance isn't how you build a life. Her mother would prefer her to go to business school or to become a lawyer. Her father would just like her to find a good, stable husband.

What Fatima wants from life changes daily—sometimes what she thinks is that she'd like nothing from life except to be free to change her mind at any moment. She'd like freedom from having to feed herself or buy clothes or pay bills, material freedom. But she does not have that. So she is returning to her parents, where she will work at a corner store and save up money to move to New York. The commonness is so maddening to her. Everyone moves to New York. Everyone saves and scrimps just to suffer and struggle so that they can say that they lived, that they tried. How stupid. How stupid. How stupid.

The river is swollen, high and greasy. A string of squat, stone buildings along the bank projects gold light out onto water. Noah and Fatima take the stone path at the end of the bridge and wander among these buildings and peer into their broad windows at the exhibits there. They're in the constellation of facilities that orbit Art Building West and the Visual Arts Building. The first is an elegant modernist construction set close to a sheer hillside with a protruding second level, and the other is a metallic Gehry confabulation, all twisted planes of metal and dissolving vanishing points. They're an odd pair. The galleries are brutalist, somber, but in the thick evening air with their soft gold lights, they feel intimate, quiet, a little melancholy.

Noah takes out a cigarette and lights it. His smoke is sluggish in the air. Birds, quick dark shapes, flit by, roost overhead. There is the constant, murmuring chatter of the water under the bridge.

"You *were* quiet tonight, though," Noah says. He brushes something from his mouth with his fingertips, still holding his cigarette. He has a habit of pressing his thumb to the space on his upper lip where there is a pale, knit scar from a cleft lip correction.

"Well," she says. "Well, well."

"Suit yourself," he grouses. Sucks down on the filter. The crackle of the shaft burning. Her nose stings. Above them, the trees shift, wind through the branches.

"I don't know what's wrong with me," she says, shrugging. "I just feel weird. I don't know what to do with myself."

"Does anyone?"

"I mean, no, probably not. But it feels particularly fucking pressing, at the moment anyway," she says. How to explain how she feels to this person, her friend.

"You regret it?"

"Regret what?"

Noah pauses under one of the dark, knotted trees. He hums the opening notes of the accompaniment to *Bestial*, and Fatima feels somewhere far away inside of her contract, as if in anticipation. He sighs, flicks his ash. He looks up. Fatima sees the muscles in his neck, the hard column of his throat, tension at the corner of his mouth.

"I don't really . . . I mean, how should I . . ."

"Oh, the abortion," she says quickly, dumbly, as though she were talking about someone else's body and not her own. "It's an abortion. You can say it." The tension in the air goes slack, sour.

"Okay, then. Do you regret the abortion?"

"No," she says. "I do not."

"All right, then."

"You didn't tell anyone, did you?"

"No," he says, shrugging, but the gesture is too stiff, too awkward to be entirely sincere. "I wouldn't do that."

"Regret isn't the word."

"Then—?" A flourish of the cigarette, his eyebrows lifting, spreading.

"I don't know," she says, because it's the truth. The ambivalence of her feeling stings like a betrayal. Too little and too cold.

"All right. You don't have to know. That's okay," he says, and the kindness of these words makes her eyes water.

"Shut up," she says. "Shut up and give me one of those." She extends a hand, palm down, and Noah gives her his pack and his lighter. The first taste is bitter, burning, but she breathes through it. There is pleasure in this, if nothing else. Pleasure and heat.

. . .

The next morning, Fatima is late for her shift. She's on opening. There's still an ache between her shoulders. Her body is stiff and difficult to make limber. She wipes the tables down, peels away the webby plastic from the muffins and pastries. The bitter acid of processed sugar. Fills with long, glugging pours the canisters of cold cream, of half-and-half, of 2 percent. Replenishes the beans, fills the register, folding out damp, green bills like dealing cards. On come the lights, slow and flickering to life.

The café is filled with art from local painters. Two hundred dollars for something that looks like a Lisa Frank/Hello Kitty collaboration. Three hundred for a painting of a buckle. These local economies. Everything so much more expensive near its source. How else to explain the five-dollar eggs in the co-op, the ten-dollars-a-pound meat from happy cows, farm raised in your hometown, the fifteen dollars for organic chicken breast, the thirty-dollar brews of local wheat. Food on the industrial scale is so much cheaper, the cost of production borne by the gaseous corpus of large business, but in the local economy the cost is borne by the consumer. The ten-dollar crumbs of ten-dollar muffins she wipes away from the counter.

The fucking piety of it all.

Already they mass near the front door, waiting to be let in. Fatima sighs. Straightens. She is supposed to have help in the mornings, but here she is, alone. She twists the lock and the people stream in, claiming their usual tables and chairs near the available outlets. She sets the playlist to a soothing, quiet classical. A gurgle of static lifts in the back of her mind.

She receives their orders. She makes their coffee. They smile at her and wait. A line grows. She glances up from below the counter where she's reaching into the back of the fridge for soy, for almond milk, for oat milk. She strains to remember who wants what and where and how and in what quantities. Cappuccinos, espressos, pour-over, seltzer, juice, fresh squeezed please, no, I wanted a double, no dry, no wet, no a latte, no sugar, please sugar, no, that one, no *that one*, over there, behind, does this have gluten, does this have albumin, does this have protein, avocado toast, tomato on rye, sourdough please, why don't you guys have, please give me that one, no, please, please, please.

What never ceases to amaze Fatima is how people conceal their rudeness and the hungry desperation of their demands with polite words like *please* and *thank you*. There is something menacing and biting about those words, as though the very language itself dares her to refuse it. She sighs. Dabs sweat from her forehead. She can taste the nicotine from last night still in her gums. She should quit smoking. More customers, *guests*, sidle up. Young with shaggy hair and tattoos, like cast members from a rougher, modern production of *Oliver!*

No rehearsal or class today. The sky is opalescent cloud cover, through which she can sense something vast and threatening.

Fatima's on the café patio, smoking. Noah and Daw hang over the railings. It's her first break of the day. She's taking a longish one. Her help never showed for his morning shift, and when he finally did blow in, he was red-faced and apologetic. *Sorry sorry sorry*, he'd said. He thought he had switched out with someone but hadn't, sorry sorry sorry.

Daw's reading something on his phone that looks like a foreign language—he's studying for a calculus exam. He is irritatingly prepared and on task. She hates him. Noah is studying a scab on his knuckles. He says he scraped it on his popcorn ceiling when he was changing a light bulb. Fatima does not believe him, but she doesn't have the space to deal with the truth if it's something grisly. She lets it ride.

"Daw's doing his MCATs soon," Noah says.

"Oh, is he?" Fatima asks. She flicks ash onto the concrete. The world has that dim, prestorm energy about it that makes everything lush and vibrant.

"Am," he says.

"Well, good luck, I guess."

"Thanks."

"Don't be surly," Noah says, knocking hips with Daw. He almost drops his phone.

"Don't be such a child," Daw says, slapping at the back of Noah's neck. Fatima feels too warm.

"Okay, boys, that's enough."

"Sure, Mom," Noah says. Fatima feels a sharp prick of hurt. She almost gasps at the casual, thoughtless cruelty. She presses her lips together to stay quiet, to tamp down the sudden, rising pressure in her throat.

"Shit," Noah says.

"All right, then."

"What?" Daw asks, squinting at the pair of them. Fatima leans over and puts her hands across his eyes and tries to laugh.

"Nothing, you nerd." She feels Daw's long eyelashes lick her palm. She withdraws. Noah looks at her as though he were the one stricken. She will forgive him. Only a minor calamity. Only a stupid joke. Only only only.

The smallness of the world gives her vertigo sometimes. That is all. A wild, rushing inversion.

Overhead, a loud crack of thunder that shakes the glass and the table. It reverberates through her and through them, and for that moment everything is united, vibrating like one great plucked string.

Weeks ago," is what she says to Cheney when he asks her about the abortion.

"My God. You didn't say anything."

"There was nothing to say," she says. "There was absolutely nothing to say."

"That's a lie, and you know it," he says. "You could have told me. You could have said *something*."

Fatima sighs. They're in one of the empty rehearsal rooms. They have been working through the chain combinations of *Bestial.* She kept messing up the transition from the floor to her feet, snagging on some tenuous beat of music she couldn't hear or feel, lingering just a little too long in the comforting oceanic hum of her fetal position. Cheney kept saying, *What's up with you, what's up with you, why are you messing this up? Is it the café? Is it your job? This is so much more important than slinging coffee, God, you have to be more dedicated, you have to try, try, try.*

He kept going on and on about trying and so she'd just let it slip out, *It's not that, it's not, I'm just in a weird space since the abortion, I'm just in a weird moment.*

Cheney is sweating, pacing. The room is too hot. She wants to crack a door. But he keeps shutting it every time she pulls it open.

"What the fuck is the matter with you?" he gasps. "Why aren't you talking about this? An *abortion*?"

Fatima almost laughs. There is a man shouting at her in a dance room about an abortion. There is a literal human man screaming at her because she terminated a pregnancy. In Iowa. It seems like the kind of thing people write Facebook posts about, eliciting sympathy, eliciting collective rage. The sort of story that unspools in a thread on Twitter or a long caption under a teary photo of her face on Instagram. Imagistic, scrubbed of all human particularity and specificity—it's a kind of story, a kind of thing that happens to people, but that exists primarily as anecdote ready for consumption. Another kind of local economy.

"I don't owe you anything. I wish I hadn't said a word. Let's get back to work," she says, but he grips her arm in a tight, hot band. And she jerks back, but he holds fast.

"What is the matter with you? You just aborted a child and you act like nothing is wrong? You don't say anything? You go around like everything is all right, and a child is *dead*, Fatima. A child is dead, and there are people in this world, people who so want a child or whose child is suffering, and you just flush yours? God," he says. Not frothing. Not consumed in rage. That's what irritates her about this. Because Cheney is talking with the same breathless bafflement with which he talks about her job at the café or barriers to entry, his whole scroll of irritations and frustrations with the contemporary world. To use his words, what he is experiencing is *aesthetic anger*, not *material anger*. Aesthetic because it is a posture. Aesthetic because it has nothing to do with the world in which they reside.

Nothing to do with the constraints of her body and her circumstances, her options, her goals, her dreams—Cheney is angry, but not at her, not at what she has done. He is angry because of what it *says*, how it operates. Aesthetic feeling.

She watches his pupils narrow, his mouth close and part like a little fish. She pulls her arm away from him, sweat slicked. His fists knot. He is larger than she is. Taller. But she is not afraid of him, no, not really. Only the threat of his body. What it means. Aesthetic fear. Attitudinal caution.

"Do not touch me again," she says. "You don't have a right to my body."

"Whose was it?" he asks.

"That's none of your business."

He raises his fist, holds it to his temple. Sweat along his hairline. His pores are clogged.

"Whose?" he asks again.

Fatima steps away, turns. She won't engage. Their shadows are on the floor. She pulls the door open, but he slams it shut. He presses her face to the door's mirrored back, gets up close on her. She can feel the wet animal heat of his body. The weighted pressure. The glass is slippery, grimy. She feels the filth of her own skin, her own sweat. She pushes with her palms at the mirror but gains no purchase, slips flatter.

"Get away from me, Cheney," she says. "Right now."

"You are such a fucking little slut," he says. His hand on her hip. His nails dig in at the start of her tights. "I bet you don't even know."

She breathes deep. The calculation—if she resists, if she fights, if she protects herself, what will it cost her? People always say *I would have kicked his ass, I would have fought*, but they are only ever thinking of that moment, the instant of the accost, of the assault. They don't think about all the minutes after, the hours of a life spent waiting for retaliation. There is always retaliation for black women. They are never safe.

But here, in this moment, not knowing if Cheney will leave her or if he will do something worse, she thinks she must try. She must do what she can. She closes her eyes. He's pressing himself against her. The stink of his breath now. She kicks back quickly, hard. She feels as if he is too late, too slow to close his legs and protect himself. He drops. She turns. There he is, laid out beneath her. There he is, vulnerable, clutching himself, as if in the first pose of *Bestial*.

What Ólafur says when Fatima reports Cheney is that it was a misunderstanding.

"He says you two were having an argument and he got a little hot. Signals, you know. They cross."

"It was unambiguous," Fatima says. "He forced himself on me. He attacked me."

"*Attack* is a violent word," Ólafur says. They are in his office on the third floor of the dance building. It's small, cramped, but there are black-and-white snaps of him in his roles through the years. She watches the beautiful veins of his arms, the graceful gestures with which he is dismissing her report.

"It *was* violent. That's what it is," she says.

"Yes, but he is the one who had to go to student health. He is quite bruised down there. Frankly, he's very upset that you misinterpreted his actions this way."

"Well, I am upset that he tried to have sex with me against my will. So I guess we both have that to deal with, don't we?"

"He says that he didn't. I have to take both of you at your word, but he is the one who is hurt, darling."

Fatima bristles. Involuntarily she remembers the texture of Ólafur's palm on the nape of her neck, the tight fit of his hand between her thighs. A frisson of unwanted pleasure, undesirous recollection. He rises from behind the desk and moves to sit in front of her on its edge.

"Look," he says. "Okay, so, say it got out of hand. That's okay. You can change your mind. No harm, no foul. How about that?"

"He assaulted me," she says.

"Getting close to someone is not assault," Ólafur says, looking down at her. She grunts, slides back in her chair and crosses her legs. She is late. Her shift is starting in fifteen minutes, and she hasn't showered or prepared. She has to go. Ólafur leans forward, puts his hands on the arms of her chair. She can smell his aftershave, can see the tender pinkness of his eyes—long night. "I don't want trouble amongst my duckies, okay? Just make up and play nice."

"Sure," she says. "Sure, sure, sure. May I leave now?"

There is a momentary silence. She is not sure that he will say yes. She is not sure that he won't touch her. There is a moment in which everything is possible. The air between them heats, tingles with electricity. It feels as though something remarkable and irrevocable is about to occur, as if the molten blue hand of the divine is about to reach through the void of the world and touch them, mark them out in strange, awful ways. And perhaps that is what happens. Perhaps that is what you call it when you appeal to the world about something that has happened to you and the world answers back that it's fine if you leave, as though you were nothing but an irritating child being sent on your way.

She learns something about herself and Ólafur in that moment. It is something that she only suspected before but now she knows with great certainty: she must leave this place and never return.

"If that's what you want," he says. "You may go."

It's on her way to the café that she spots overhead a flock of geese. They are going in the opposite direction as Fatima, back toward the river. They seem so peaceful. So free. They move as part of the same formation, but each is different, each has a role to play. Spontaneous unity. The choreography of flocks and herds. She stands on the corner waiting for the light to change as the geese pass her and dip down low beneath the buildings to land on the river.

Fatima crosses the street. The heat of the day has grown unruly, angry. It burns her skin. The prick of sunlight. She's walking as quickly as she can.

At the café, she takes up vegetable chopping duty. Celery, carrots, bell peppers. She cuts loose heads of broccoli and watches them roll across the plastic cutting board. She's in the back room, sweating through her thin shirt, feeling the straps of her apron cut against her shoulders. At the next station, Hal the dishwasher is rinsing the cups, putting them on a drying rack. He looks at her, smiles, goes back to his dishes. Fatima is relieved when he tucks his gaze away, relieved that he isn't asking anything of her.

After a while, she bins the loose scraps of vegetables into the compost bucket under the sink. She rinses her hands and takes from the cooler some fat from the ham she cut for the sandwiches out front. She puts it on a little dish and takes it through the side door, into the alley. She sets the dish down and waits, looking for the one or two stray cats who people this strip of walkway. They come along quietly, stealing out of the shadows, and they situate themselves near the dumpster, watching her, waiting to see if she will leave them to their work. She rises from her crouch, wipes her hands on her apron, and steps away. The cats are small and white, with black ears and swishing tails. They descend upon the ham fat, eating at it with jerking chomps. A weary satisfaction at watching them consume.

Her manager said they shouldn't feed the cats because it makes them want to depend on people, makes them more likely to hang around, which isn't good. But her manager isn't here and the cats are.

Back in the café, she washes her hands in the boiling-hot water that shoots from the spigot. Industrial soap. The skin around her nails peels, flakes away. She hears her name from out front, and she goes to see who has *beckoned* her.

It's Daw and Noah.

"What's up?" she asks down the counter where they put drinks and plates that are ready. There's no business at the moment. The café is quiet. Everyone is satisfied.

"We heard," Noah says.

"Fuck that guy."

"Oh," she says, embarrassed. "Oh, it's fine."

"It's not," Noah says, flaring. "It's not okay."

"It's the end of the world soon anyway," Fatima says, shrugging. "Graduation. It's not worth the hassle."

"Did you report him?"

Fatima nods, already tired by the prospect of having to recount it all again. "And suffice it to say, it achieved nothing."

"I'm so sorry," Daw says.

"Hey, me too." She leans on the counter, though she has been instructed not to. There's a large group across the street. She can see them coming. A little flurry of activity, just what she needs.

The other cashier is sipping a smoothie. Furtively.

"It's not right."

"Did you come all the way here to tell me that?"

"What?"

Noah looks flustered. Daw steps back a bit.

"Did you come all the way here so that you could tell me it's not right? So that you can be on the record as having said that it's not acceptable to treat me this way?"

"Fatima," Noah says.

"No, I mean it. I know it's not right. You know it's not right. The whole world knows. But why did you come here to tell me this? To my workplace?"

"I just wanted to help," Noah says.

"Oh, I see. Well, thank you. Very much. Help received."

Noah's gaze is flat and dark. Daw sighs and puts a hand on Noah's shoulder, pulls at him.

"Come on," he says. "Let's go. Everyone is okay. Let's go."

Noah shakes his head, is drawn away.

"Double cap, no foam," the other cashier says, sliding the receipt down the counter at Fatima. She feels bad now. She feels awful for having said that to Noah. She reaches out quickly before he's completely out of her reach, and she grips his fingers, squeezes.

"I'm sorry," she says.

"I'm sorry," he answers.

She makes the cappuccinos and then accompanying lattes and rooibos chai. She sets them out, calls the name attached, waits for them to be collected. Sighs to herself when it's all done. Her shoulders sore, her back drenched in sweat.

She hears Noah's voice again. *I'm sorry.*

Fatima stretches her neck until it pops, and she takes a seat in the back room again. She's on her phone reading stray articles about crisis after crisis, moral and environmental.

A pulse races through her phone, and she sees at the top of the screen a message from Cheney:

No hard feelings

9.

Altruism, Empathy, Passion, and Pain

They caravaned in two cars across two days from Iowa to the Adirondacks, and when they arrived, they climbed the stairs into the house and fell into stiff, uneven sleep. All of them except Daw, who could not sleep in that house and who stayed awake as if he were a guard dog set to keep watch over their bodies.

In the morning, they took their coffee and tea to the patio, where they looked down into the cedar forest and squinted in the distance for the lake. The air was cool and full of a luminous mist that was momentarily so beautiful to them—now that they'd left the hard, starved landscape of the Midwest—that they were stunned into silence and a few nervous laughs. The mist intensified throughout the morning, until it was a soft rain, and still they did not try to escape it. But Daw walked over to a small crank near the sliding door and turned it, unfurling in a series of juddering creaks a large covering for the patio. It opened like a slow, arthritic wing, and they were safe, but bewildered that the rain had enough substance to leave them damp and cold. It had seemed nothing at all, they kept saying, they hadn't noticed how much of it there was until they were no longer in the stream of rain. Daw went into the warm darkness of the house, seeking out a towel and spare clothes, already regretting having brought them here.

There were six of them, including Daw: Noah, Fatima, Ivan, Goran, and Stafford.

They were all scattering after graduate school. Noah was going to Portland. Fatima to North Carolina and eventually, she said, she hoped, New York. Ivan and Goran were also going to New York, together, but to separate apartments. Stafford was going to Vermont for a fellowship. And Daw was going to spend a year in rural Quebec, helping out at small clinics. Noah had been insistent that they take this trip together and spend one last bit of time together before they went out into the world and became their real selves, and it had so moved Daw to think of this as a meaningful plank spanning two periods of his life, that he'd stupidly mentioned the lake house to Noah. And Noah had kept on him until Daw agreed to ask his parents if he might use it for a week or so, and they'd said yes, themselves baffled by the request because Daw so seldom asked them for anything, and they themselves rarely visited the lake house.

The house was on Lake Placid, though in fact it was about a half mile or so from the lake itself. When he was very young, four or so, his parents would bring him and his sister, Celia, up in the summer and on weekends in the fall. They were happy here.

But one fall day, deep in October, his sister had been taken from the road on her way home from the library. She was eight. She was happy and smart. Sometimes Daw could not remember her voice or her face. Sometimes, he could remember only pictures of her and recordings he had heard. He remembered remembering her, and it was this tough, artificial memory that had grafted deep inside him, so that it was only in small, quiet moments that his mind touched the real flesh of her memory and he was torn anew. There was no body. She had been snatched into the air and never returned.

Daw found the towels in the laundry room. His mother had come up a few days before to prepare the house for them. He thought he could feel residual warmth in the cotton. But it wasn't true. The towels were cool and stiff. He carried them to the others on the patio.

They were all leaning against the railing, sticking their palms out into the rain. They were laughing and jostling one another. Noah had lifted himself up and leaned out the farthest, teetering over the trees below in a moment of foolish hubris.

"Get down," Daw said at once, "get the fuck down from there."

His face flushed. He dropped the towels onto his empty chair. Noah turned back to look at him, smiling.

"Relax, Dad," he said.

Daw's chest hurt. The others had turned to look at him, too, and he felt awful, like they were all on one side and he was on the other. And he couldn't blame them. He didn't blame them.

He wished they'd all slip and fall, because then at least they'd know.

In the early afternoon, Daw and Noah drove to the grocery store in his parents' old station wagon. The seats had cracked. The back was filled with buckets and fishing tackle and dry-rotted towels. Noah pulled a faded paperback novel from under the seat. He read from its opening pages.

"Jesus, where did you get that?" Daw asked. The car was sluggish and heavy. The brakes gave a weary whine at the Stop sign at the end of the driveway. He drove with his shoulders quite hunched.

"I didn't figure you for a fantasy nerd," Noah said, thumbing the pages. Daw stiffened.

"I wasn't."

"Oh, sure." Noah laughed and fanned him with the novel. Daw slapped at his hand, coasting out onto the street.

"I mean it," he said, and Noah leaned back into the seat with the novel. He read from more of the pages, and Daw leaned down to turn on the radio so that he couldn't hear Noah's voice. The radio scraped the airwaves, searching for purchase, and bits of songs and news reports flared in and out of reception. He glanced up to keep an eye on the road, then back down, fiddling with the knobs, not really remembering what the stations were that played whatever kind of music, literally anything so that he couldn't hear Noah. But Noah kept on reading, and the car drifted slightly to the shoulder of the road, and it was hard, so hard, for Daw to do all those things at one time, twisting the dusty knobs, steering the car, listening to Noah, trying not to listen to Noah, and all the while, his heart beating harder and faster because the novel was not his, and he had never seen it before, and what he was afraid of, more than anything, was that it had belonged to his sister.

"Do the radio," he said at last, and he sat up. His brow was damp. There was a knot of tension between his eyes. Noah studied him carefully, and then he complied. With an easiness that Daw resented, Noah found the station right away, and John Cougar Mellencamp filled the car. The road was smooth, and the station wagon had an easy gait once it was going.

Noah slouched lower and put his heels up on the seat. The pages whispered as he turned them. Daw put his turn signal on. They coasted along, not speaking. The radio was too loud. Daw had twisted the dial way up, but now Noah was quiet, and the windows rattled. He switched the radio off.

"So what's the deal?" Noah asked.

"I think beef flank is on sale."

"Oh, that's nice."

"Might make a stew."

"Love a stew."

"Mmm," Daw hummed. Noah closed the book around his thumb and shifted so that he was looking directly at Daw. Four-way stop. The car jerked a little when Daw pressed the brakes. He checked both ways. Nothing, nobody, nowhere.

"You didn't have to agree. You could have said no," Noah said.

"About what?"

"This week. You didn't have to let us use the house. If you—"

"Oh, shut up," Daw said. They had reached the grocery store. It was yellow and faded, longer than it was wide, with a decaying blue trim and failing roof.

"I mean, all right, but if this is going to be your attitude all week."

"I don't have an attitude."

"You do. You definitely do, and like, okay, I get it, but you definitely do."

Daw squeezed the wheel's leather casing as tight as he could. The windshield was lousy with leaves and twigs and other dying plant matter wedged under the wipers. He had learned to drive in this car in his parents' backyard in Connecticut, doing circles out by the trees. The leather casing had softened and hardened from the sun. He ran his thumb around its rim.

"All right," he said, like that settled it, and pushed the door open. "Let's go."

The store was cool and dim and smelled like mildew. The doors on the upright coolers were so worn that there was hardly any resistance at all when Daw pulled at them. They pushed a small cart with a squeaking wheel around. Filled it with fish and beef flank, with cheap white bread, with butter, with jam, with more coffee. They bought a lemon popsicle and snapped it in half to share. They circled their mouths with it as they nudged their rusty cart among the aisles. The produce was sad and soft. But they bought carrots and peas. Noah kept picking up snap peas to sample, biting them raw and chewing with a dissatisfied frown. They bought fruit, too. Cereal, granola, oatmeal.

"Do you remember if there was soap? Did you bring any?" Daw asked.

Noah was crouching, inspecting a low shelf that contained tampons, condoms, and exactly three boxed perms.

"I don't remember," he said. "Did you?"

"No," Daw said, frowning. He held a large bottle of shampoo that weighed as much as a small child. "Should we?"

Noah shrugged. "Maybe, right? Do you think anyone else did?"

"I just kind of thought there would be soap here. But I have no idea if my mom left any when she was up here getting things turned on."

"Huh," Noah said. He put his finger to his chin and stood up.

"This costs ten dollars," Daw said. "It's so expensive. And it's not even . . . it's a cheap shampoo."

Noah laughed.

"You think they'd be okay with bar soap?"

"Like, a bar per person? Can you imagine? They'd leave it all around the tub."

"Carve their initials in it."

"Until it got wet and faded," Daw said, sighing. "I guess we should probably get this. Just in case."

"It's a lot for a week."

"There are six of us."

"True, probably."

Daw put the enormous bottle of shampoo and another of shower gel into the cart and shoved off. Noah lingered in the aisle, kicking at the low shelf with his foot.

"Coming?"

"You go ahead."

"Are you going to perm your hair or something?" Daw asked.

"No, I was thinking. Uh, never mind."

"You didn't bring condoms."

"No, I didn't," Noah said with a tight laugh.

"Planning something?"

Noah squinted at him, not quite a scowl.

"Mind your business," Noah snapped, but then, more tenderly, "No. I'm not. But the best-laid plans, you know, et cetera."

And he did know, at least he thought he did. The randomness of want. The changing tide of desire. Sex, as random as a bolt of lightning out of the blue sky. Noah didn't seek sex out so much as it came up to him like an anxious dog in need of affection. Daw suspected that Noah had slept with Goran, Ivan, and Stafford. He was uncertain because it might have just been the tension in the air. It could be that way with men. There was always something there, something burning and in danger of combusting. Daw nodded.

"Sure," Daw said. "I know. Get them, if you want."

Noah sighed in obvious relief. Daw suspected that Noah really did feel uncertain about Daw's commitment to the week, to their friendship. Buying the condoms, a small blue box much lighter than it might have been, represented—what? a proposal, a plan, a concrete suggestion of what might happen if not between them then at least among all of them, including Fatima. Noah tossed the condoms into the cart and kissed Daw briefly, wetly on the mouth. Daw felt desire, but more than that, he felt at peace. He put his arms around Noah's waist, drew him close, and they kissed again—it was so innocent and chaste that it might have been a family kiss, a loving kiss, a kiss that said *I accept you for all that you are*, a kiss that said *I hope you're all right*. Noah grinned at him, then patted his cheek, and they were back to pushing the cart along the aisle, eating the popsicle that they had not paid for.

Fatima was the only one on the patio when they returned. The others had decided that they would walk down into the village. She was tired, she said, from the drive. She had brought along a bag of very large Missouri peaches, pale and firm, too firm to eat, but she was hungry, so she sat on the table with her feet in the chair, eating the peaches, when they arrived.

Noah hugged her as though they had been separated for years and years rather than the hour it had taken to visit the grocery store. He joined her on the table and sat with his head on her shoulder. They extended their hands to Daw to join them, and he stood on the edge of the doorway, thinking he should join them, but also feeling a sick, downward sweep in him that told him not to.

"No," he said. "Dinner won't make itself."

"That's hours away," Fatima said, pulling on the air as if that might make Daw more amenable to their demands.

"And who will make it if not me!" Daw pushed from the doorway and onto the patio. Noah closed his eyes. They dropped their arms.

"Are you all right?" Fatima asked. "Really?" The question was soft, gentle. Exploratory more than accusatory.

"Aren't we all?"

"No. No, we're not."

"That's a shame," Daw said. The sky was still overcast, and there was an almost metallic sheen to the cloud cover. "They're going to get soaked if they don't get back soon."

"They're big boys," Fatima said, letting his deflection stand as its own answer.

"Every man for himself."

"Something like that," Noah said, yawning. Fatima gave him the peach and he bit into it. Daw's palms grew hot and clammy.

"I'll help you," she said, rising from the table.

"No, don't," Noah and Daw both said. Noah wrapped his arm around her tighter.

"Don't be a brat," she said, slapping Noah's forehead. To Daw, she said nothing else. She brushed by him through the door. Daw shrugged. Noah lay flat on his back on the table eating the peach, shielding his eyes with his forearm. A strip of skin showed when his sweatshirt rode up. There was a breeze, dark and damp, coming in out of the trees. It smelled of cedar.

In the kitchen, Daw and Fatima washed the vegetables. There were mixed greens and turnips and small, bruised tomatoes. There were also carrots. And the snaps. The sink was a broad, deep basin, room enough for the two of them, with two spigots. They rinsed and set the greens on the counter, where water collected and ran sideways, dripping onto Daw's feet, which grew grimy from the dust on the floor.

Fatima carried the large kale as if it were a bouquet, to lay out the leaves on the patio. Daw soaked the swordfish steaks in lukewarm water and let them float.

"Tasty," she said, looking over his shoulder. "Isn't Stafford a vegetarian?"

"We have vegetables."

Fatima laughed.

"Should I make an eggplant then? Would that be weird?"

"He'll live," she said.

"Now I feel bad." Daw lifted the large metal bowl out of the sink and onto the counter. The floor was quite spectacularly wet now. He almost slipped.

"Every man for himself," she said. Daw laughed. Fatima laughed.

"Ah, yes, altruism is the first thing out the window."

"Altruism, empathy, passion, and pain," she said. "In that order."

Daw filled a glass with water. "Those last three are Ólafur's virtues, aren't they?"

"They are indeed."

"Why is pain last?"

"Because with pain," she said, "you can always find your way back to the other two."

"He is so ridiculous."

"But not always wrong," she said with a note of sad resignation in her voice.

Ólafur was tall, severe, prone to philosophical nonsense. On their first meeting, he had stood in front of the room asking them what were the most important traits for a dancer to cultivate, what were the beatitudes that turned dance into *art*. Daw could remember thinking, flexibility, musicality, strength, stamina. He could remember thinking in terms of technical mastery and physical limits, the concrete reality of a dancer's body, how there were only so many times you could plié or leap and land safely. There was only so much life in the joints, only so much a person could give. Daw had been thinking of his limits, the boundaries of his life in dance, what had brought him as far as it had. But then Ólafur had turned from them and stood with his hands on the barre, shaking his head. He declared them all hopeless and said, *Empathy, passion, and pain. Above everything else, you aren't an artist if you don't have empathy, passion, and pain. You must seek it out. Find it. Make it your own.*

"That's stupid," he said. The water was hard. He poured the rest down the sink.

"I always thought so, too, but then, I don't know, there's something to it, I guess."

"What a bunch of mumbo jumbo."

"Are you sad about giving up dance?"

The question startled him.

"A little," Daw said. "I guess I hadn't phrased it as such."

"Goran says that Ivan is still sad about it."

"Oh, but surely that's different. He had no choice."

"You're right," she said. "He didn't. And you do. So there's agency, I guess. But, it's still a big change."

"It wasn't a random decision."

"I didn't say it was. I just mean, it must be difficult. Right? To give it up, to quit."

"Maybe you're the one who should go to medical school," he said. "You'd make a good shrink."

"I'm just trying to help."

"I don't need it."

He washed the carrots again, though they were clean, and Fatima let it drop. But he was restless and irritated, so he said, "Ivan is going to be an investment banker. What's he got to feel busted up about?"

"People have their own hurts," Fatima said blandly. She was slicing the tomatoes and setting them on a tray to roast them. The salt sounded like hail as it struck the pan.

"I think I will go out and get that eggplant," he said.

"I didn't mean any harm," she said.

Daw smiled at her and said, "No hard feelings." She blanched. She withdrew. She shook her head.

"You're such an asshole sometimes," she said. "It's too much."

She went down to the lake with the others. Daw stayed in the kitchen, drying.

Daw regretted saying it the moment he stepped out of the house onto the gravel walkway. *No hard feelings* was what Cheney had texted Fatima after he'd harassed her in a private rehearsal. After Fatima had reported him. *No hard feelings* meant that there were hard feelings. It had been petty and cruel to throw it back in her face.

He thought again that it was a mistake to have brought people to this house. It was a mistake to have thought that they would have a good time here.

Daw sat on the last step from the back of the house and put his head against his knees. He tried to breathe. The wind smelled like coming rain and something burning. Like coal and lighter fluid. When he felt sufficiently annoyed at his bad mood, Daw stood up. He passed the car and stepped onto the dirt driveway that wound down through the forest to the village and the lake. He would go to the smaller market there, get some eggplant, come back when he learned how to be a human being again.

At the corner of the yard, just before the tree line, there was a plastic playhouse where he used to play as a kid, before wasps built a nest there and stung him badly. That was the last full summer they'd spent in this house, two years after his sister had gone missing. It amazed him to think back on that time now, because it seemed that they'd stopped coming to the lake house immediately after her disappearance, but in fact they'd persisted for two entire years. His parents' thinking was opaque to him, mysterious and arcane.

Those two years were on the very edge of his memory. He had few specific details, beyond the fact of the playhouse and the smell of the car. Everything else was gray and vague, subject mainly to the intensity of his attention. But he could remember the year they stopped coming regularly. Could remember the awfulness of those wasp stings on his arms and back. He remembered his mother putting cool cloths on them, and how she held him tightly as he cried. Even recalled the sound of the late afternoon rain, and his father in the garden picking cucumbers for a salad, the heaviness of his step in the house, so deeply quiet and strange. But he couldn't remember now, stopping to put his hand on the roof of the playhouse, its brittle, worn plastic, why they had continued to come, how they had continued to come.

The others were already on their way back by the time Daw made it halfway through the trees. They were wet and shivering. Ivan had his arm around Stafford's neck. They were shirtless under unzipped lightweight shell jackets and Lycra shorts. They looked like any leggy, shaggy adolescent swim team. Goran's long, hitching step marked him out. His glasses were fogged. Stafford was compact and blond between the two of them.

"Here you are," Daw said.

"Here we are," Stafford returned. They paused with a large, exposed root dividing them on one side from Daw on the other.

"I was just on my way to get an eggplant for your dinner."

"Oh," Stafford exclaimed, "it's totally no problem, don't worry about it."

"No, it's absolutely fine," Daw said. "I'm just going to the stand down the road."

"It's fine."

"No, let me."

Ivan unhooked his arm from Stafford's shoulders and hopped over the root. Goran followed. Stafford braced his foot against its thick bulk.

"I'm totally fine having what the others are having."

"It's swordfish."

"I eat fish."

"You don't have to—"

"He said it's fine," Goran said. "I think you should let him decide what he can handle."

Stafford reached out and put his arm against Daw's shoulder and pushed down, kicking up and over the root. He landed with a laugh and gave a little shimmy in triumph.

"See, I'm perfectly self-sufficient."

"The water was choppy," Goran said. They were walking back through the trees. Their steps scraped over the loose stones and compact earth. Stafford put an arm around Daw's back. Their jackets crinkled as they went, dripping water, smelling pungent like the lake. Stafford felt cold, densely cold from the water. His skin was puckered and deeply hued, like a bruise. He pressed his damp face down in Daw's shoulder, and the depth of the cold made Daw ache.

"I'm feeling better about my choices," Daw said.

"It wasn't so bad," Ivan said. "It was nice. Exhilarating."

"Maybe you're a sadist," Daw said. Ivan laughed. "Are you ready for the big move? Do you have an apartment yet?" Daw asked.

Ivan nodded without looking up. Goran shook his head.

"I'm not too worried about it. One of my friends has a spot," Goran said.

"You mean your parents," Ivan said.

"Why aren't you two staying together?" Daw asked. "You could split rent. Make it easier on yourselves."

"Ivan wants to be in Midtown like a psychopath. My parents' place is near Dimes Square."

"Hell's Kitchen. I'm staying in Hell's Kitchen."

"Ritzy," Stafford said.

"Not very—it's a rent-control thing. I got it from this old drag queen who has been there since the nineties."

"How'd you swing that?" Stafford leaned forward.

"Someone I know from ABT knew someone who knew someone who knew this guy wanted a sublet for a little while. He's going to be in Palm Springs with his husband."

"Well, how lucky," Stafford said.

"It'll be nice to have our own places," Ivan said. "Our own lives in the city. After being on top of each other in Iowa. It'll be good for us."

Goran snorted like he didn't believe that. Stafford laughed.

"Are you excited for Vermont?" Daw asked.

"It's a short fellowship. I'm probably going to wash up in New York after. I'll come find you," he said to Goran, reaching out and slapping the cords of his jacket.

Ivan tensed. "Yeah, he'll come find you."

Goran didn't look at Ivan or at Stafford. He was squinting up through the trees.

"But what about you, Betty Crocker? Do you even speak French?"

"My parents sent me to French day school," he said.

The others snorted and said *of course*, and Daw felt self-conscious the way he did sometimes when other people made him aware of his parents' wealth and class. They pointed it out to him in the Midwest, where it was obvious, but back home it hadn't seemed that interesting or remarkable. All the kids he'd known in high school he'd also known in French day school. They'd grown up together in the same circle of blond-haired people. They'd played in the same parks, had taken the same swimming lessons. He could barely remember their names now or their faces, and though he sometimes did feel a keen loyalty to them, that made him feel traitorous among his real friends. Those kids were just memories, parts of his life that had ceased to mean anything at all.

Stafford dug his fingers into the nape of Daw's neck and he shivered.

"What?" he asked, and Stafford just shook his head and smiled.

"I'm going to draw you."

"Oh, why?"

"Because you look like you need to be drawn," he said.

They trooped up the steps just as the rain returned in earnest, a gray screen falling behind them. Goran stayed inside the door at the base of the inside stairs, looking out through the back door into the trees and the downward slope of the yard. The others shed their shoes and clomped up to the first floor. Goran's face was lit by the silvery light of the rain, and in the shadows by the stairs he looked beautiful and melancholy, like an actor in one of those quiet and slightly too long films in which people use their real names and act out versions of real conflict. Daw left him there after a few moments because looking at him was too sad or too wonderful, and besides, there was the fish to cook.

On the patio, Noah had primed the grill. Daw lay the swordfish steaks upon it, the beautiful dark meat. Fatima asked if he had forgotten the eggplant, but Stafford interrupted, saying he didn't mind, that he wasn't really a vegan or a vegetarian, not a real one. And Daw wondered if this was true or if it was a defense mechanism, to give people what you thought they wanted so that they wouldn't resent you. It was a mechanism he himself understood quite well.

They ate their dinner on the patio despite the rain and the cold. Daw had found a space heater in a back closet, and it gave them a little heat. The steaks were cooked well, but mainly because Ivan had taken over for him when the first one had come out too blackened. Ivan had stood at the grill carefully monitoring everything.

"The key," he said, "is leaving it alone. You can't keep touching it."

"I'm sorry it's raining," Daw said. "We spent two days getting here, and it's raining all the time."

"Are you kidding? This is beautiful. It's perfect," Fatima said.

"Yeah, man, relax," Stafford said. He was sitting quite close to Daw, and Daw kept looking at him out of the corner of his eye. The salad was good, rich. Fatima had added slices of peach and apricot. She'd improvised a kind of vinaigrette that was acidic and sweet. There was a polenta, too, made from a potentially ancient box in the back of the cabinet. This had been Goran's contribution. The polenta was good with the tomatoes and the steaks. The meal itself was a little bland, but everything was so warm and good in the rain. They ate and laughed, talked, told stories.

Goran started in on a long anecdote about boys from his school.

"I had a friend when I was younger, like ten or so, anyway, he used to wear a helmet to school. And sometimes the other kids would pick on him. And it was just me and him, sitting by ourselves on the playground, and that was okay. That was fine. That was okay, you know? It was all right, just us, sitting there, drawing with our stupid chalk—anyway, there were other kids, bigger than us, they looked like they'd been held back seven grades or something, and one day they come to us and they just say, 'What are you faggots over here doing? This isn't art class. It's gym.' And one of these little fucking turds pulls down his pants and just pisses on our drawing. And the kid with the helmet, just sits there waiting, and waiting. And I get up and I'm like 'Gross, oh my God,' and the kid just keeps pissing, the longest piss I have ever seen. It was horrible, and his little friends start to get nervous too, because it's going on for *so long*, and it is a truly absurd piss, but then he finishes and shakes off, and then the helmet just gets down in a crouch, covered in this kid's piss, and just barrels into him, just cuts through him like he's paper, right? Into the nuts, gets right there, packs this guy's lunch, and it's just chaos after that. We're fighting, we're screaming, we're just brawling out there, and the whole time, the helmet is perfectly quiet, so calm, like he didn't just impact this kid's urethra."

Goran stood up to enact the crouch, the impact, the piss, and then he righted himself, his face glowing, his eyes streaked with moisture. "It was amazing," he said, breathless. "So fucking amazing."

Fatima clapped and said, "Good for him. Kids are such monsters."

"It's no wonder," Stafford said. "I mean, look at us. We're just walking damage from our parents."

"My parents were fine," Ivan said. "They gave me so much. They gave me everything. They're fine. Wonderful parents. I love them. I don't feel *damaged*."

"Oh, so your parents would be fine if you'd stayed a dancer and not become a banker sellout?"

Ivan's face tightened. A vein in his neck thickened. This conversation was going to all the wrong places. There was clear animosity between the two of them, having to do with Goran, but also to do with Ivan's chosen vocation. Daw didn't see what was so terrible about investment banking. Well, that was not true. He knew it to be an insidious and dark art. The propagation of money for money's sake. More money than any one person or family would ever need. Wealth generated for the sake of more wealth, simply to say that you had it. And yet, there he sat in his parents' second home, with these people he knew only because he had money enough for school, for college, for food, for clothing, for knowledge acquisition. It was hypocritical. It was a moral posture and stance, an attitude one adopted at parties and in conversation, a disavowal of one's attachment to the material wealth of one's station. You had to be willing to give it all away. Or to pretend you didn't have it. But he could understand Stafford's frustration. Ivan stared back at Stafford with a directness that made Daw's blood freeze.

"I stopped dancing because of my tendons. I didn't stop because my parents made me."

"Right, but it worked out for you."

"Worked out for me? You think I wouldn't have wanted it the other way? You know how hard I fought for it?" Ivan had stepped closer to Stafford. His knuckles were white, like he meant serious harm. "I got injections. I did the rehab. The acupuncture. I danced on ruptured tendons for *weeks*. I wanted it more than I've wanted anything my whole fucking life."

"But you didn't die for it," Stafford said. Then, laughing like he'd made a terrific joke, "Like, you could have *died* for it. And now you're going to make more than the rest of us combined," Stafford said.

"Speak for yourself," Noah said. "I plan to become *quite wealthy*."

"As wealthy as a middle-class white person, anyway," Fatima said.

"My parents are middle-class white people," Goran said.

"If you're middle class, then Daw is middle class."

"Truly," Noah said. Goran frowned and tapped the edge of his fork against his plate.

"That's not nice," Daw said. "Let's not talk about money."

"*Let's not talk about money*," Fatima said. "That's my cue, boys. I'm going to clear the plates."

"No, Fatima. Don't," Daw said. "I can."

Fatima bowed and said, "But it is my profession."

Daw blushed. The other boys at the table looked away in embarrassment, even Goran. Daw knew what this was, payback for what he'd said earlier, and he deserved it.

"I'm sorry," he said. "I should have kept my mouth shut."

She kissed his forehead and took his plate away and said, quietly into his ear, "It's nothing to worry about. We're okay."

Noah helped Fatima with the plates. Goran migrated into the house, where he found the upright piano. The tuning wasn't bad, he said, but it wasn't *great*. He sat down at it, and Ivan, watching him, smiled. Goran began to play, saying randomly, "My first teacher made me play Bach, and he had really bad breath, so I try not to play Bach as a rule, because it reminds me of him."

Instead of Bach, he played the first bit of a Rachmaninoff piece that Daw recognized because he'd danced one of his first-year spring revue pieces to it. Goran had been his accompanist, playing from just offstage in the big auditorium, where the first-year dancers went on in succession for their short solos so that their progress could be evaluated. Goran had been recommended to him by Noah, who seemed to know everyone, then and now. He felt a tingle of recognition in his lower back and in his knees, the body giving way to an older version of itself.

The Rachmaninoff piece gave way to something soft and tender, gentle almost.

"This is Ravel," Goran said, playing with the kind of delicate precision that made his usual manner of wild, slicing play seem all the more remarkable. The piano was out of tune, so that the piece was not quite itself but some sort of improvised echo, as Goran reached for the themes and constructed them out of what was at hand. Just listening to him from the couch, Daw knew that he was gifted—and not just that he was gifted, but that he loved music and loved playing. The piece hardened in the middle, pensive and aloof.

Stafford sat in the lofted window seat, and Ivan sat with his back against the piano bench. From the other room came the sound of water flowing into the sink. Then dishes. Things clattering. The whisper of Noah's and Fatima's voices. The whine of the space heater. They grew quiet. The music lifted over them.

It was a moment of peace. They had all put down their weapons. Their sharp and pointed ideas about one another and themselves and the world. Ivan and Stafford were both looking at Goran as he played. Goran was oblivious to their attention. He was in the throes of his music, which he seemed to offer with generosity. It was not given in hopes of extracting anything from them. Not really. It was so rare in the world that anything was given as freely as Goran was giving them this music in this moment.

Daw felt himself drifting off, his eyes growing heavy. Rain outdoors, striking the patio roof. He tried to remember if he had shut all the windows in the house. He was responsible.

In the morning, he woke before everyone else. He made espresso and drank it on the patio. A strong wind had come through in the night. More rain. The furniture was damp because he hadn't thought to bring it in. His parents would be annoyed, irritated, if they ever returned to the house anyway. Anytime soon.

He put his head on his knee. The espresso was hot, steaming in the morning haze. The trees were dark and beautiful, whooshing down below.

"You're up so early," Stafford said from the doorway.

"It's not so early," he said.

"For us, it is."

"How did you sleep?"

"I'm up early, aren't I?"

"That could mean good or bad," Daw said.

"I think it means both."

Stafford sat in the chair next to Daw, but he jumped up when he felt how wet it was. But then he sat down again with a cranky expression and took Daw's espresso for himself.

"This house really is amazing," Stafford said.

"It is," he said.

"But you don't come here, you said. Right? You don't spend a lot of time here."

"Not if I can help it," Daw said.

"Can I ask why?"

"You can," Daw said, "but it doesn't mean I'll say. Or that there is anything to say."

"Why?"

Daw took his espresso back. He drank what was left, feeling his jaw and shoulders lock up from the heat, from the pungent smell of it, from the kick and bite in his throat. He shook himself.

"My sister was kidnapped here. Not *here*, but down the street. She was walking home from the library."

"Fuck. What. When?"

"I was six," he said. "She was eight."

"Jesus Christ—what happened?"

Daw smiled because he didn't know what else to do. He looked up at Stafford. His damp blond eyelashes. His bright eyes. Daw kissed him, and when their lips parted, he said, "Nothing happened. Nothing ever happens."

They went back through the house, quietly. Daw was sleeping in the master. He pulled off his shirt and then pulled open the shorts that Stafford had been sleeping in. He was musky. Uncircumcised and quite pale. His body was solid and smooth. Daw took Stafford into his mouth, and Stafford sighed, gripped at Daw's shoulders for balance.

Daw wondered about Goran. Wondered if this was about pity or about making Goran jealous. But then, he thought, Stafford could make his own choices. He could decide his own reasons for doing the things he did. Daw didn't mind too much. And Stafford seemed willing, interested. He had no reason to stop. No reason to change his mind. No reason to say *What about Goran? Aren't you in love with him?* But that was love and this was sex, or about to be sex, so they really had nothing to do with each other.

Stafford grew hard. Then a little soft. He was giggling nervously. Daw looked up.

"You all right?" he asked.

"I'm just. Is this where your parents sleep?"

"No one sleeps here," Daw said. "No one comes here."

"Oh," Stafford said. The room was large, but spare. There was a dresser on which there were old photos and a stack of novels. The room had a dusty, unaired smell to it. And in the night, Daw had thought he felt spiderwebs or something thin and itchy. Stafford was looking around the room, so Daw went back to sucking him, and then Stafford groaned and pushed Daw back so that he could reciprocate. The heat of Stafford's mouth, the hard, bumpy ridges of his palate, and sometimes the stray cut of his molars, were concretizing.

Daw could feel more in his body that way. The boundaries of his particular human self.

"I can top, if you'll let me bottom later," Stafford said.

"Later? Are you suggesting we're going to do this again?"

"Yes," Stafford said with a laugh. "I am."

Daw hadn't bottomed in a long time. He hadn't had sex in a year. He hadn't wanted to, not really. It was not unpleasant, but not really worth it to him, because in his mind it was always reduced to frictive rubbing. But he lay on his back and pulled his knees to his chest and breathed deeply. Stafford entered him, and it was awful at first because it was always awful, but then the tension broke, and Stafford slid deeper, and Daw could breathe, and it was pleasant and warm, and Stafford moved gently at first, letting his rhythm build a head of steam. Daw wound his legs around Stafford's waist and pulled him closer, and they were kissing and groaning, and it was no longer two bodies, but one body, sliding through itself.

They took a shower together afterward, getting warm and soapy. Stafford kept shyly looking away, and Daw kept wanting to grab his cheeks and hold his gaze. But he didn't have it in him to look at Stafford head-on. He didn't have it in him to look at anyone head-on. He had a feeling of being looked at, though, and it wasn't Stafford who was doing the looking. It was as if there were a pair of eyes gazing at him through the shower wall, through the bulk of the house, through the trees, on the other side of the lake and beyond that, too, farther still, across the Adirondacks, across the ocean, across sky, far and beyond, vaster and vaster. He felt that these eyes could see everything he did.

"Where are you?" Stafford asked. The shower was striking the back of Daw's skull. He could hardly hear the words. "Where are you?"

"I'm here," he said. "Right here."

Stafford put his arms around Daw and kissed his chest and said, as if greeting him at the end of a long journey, "You're here. Thank God, you're here."

The rain had stopped, so they went as a group through the trees together.

Goran hummed the Ravel from the night before. Ivan joined him. They were holding hands. Daw felt less guilty about Stafford and the shower. And besides, Noah had fucked almost everyone on this trip. He'd probably slept with Fatima, too. Daw saw Noah and Stafford playfully shoving each other as they went. Goran's gaze was fixed on them. But then Ivan whispered something in his ear, and he laughed, and they seemed okay. Like they were going to make it. Good for them, Daw thought. Good for them, and for Noah and for Stafford. Good for all of them, these people he knew, his friends. Jealousy was so pointless. No one ever belonged to anyone. Not really.

Fatima looped her arm through Daw's. The trees were quiet, but they moved in the breeze. It would rain again later that day, surely. He could tell in the clouds, their slow, unfolding language.

"You seem better," Fatima said.

"I didn't know I was bad."

"You weren't. But you do seem better."

"I'm sorry," he said.

"It's your house. You don't have to apologize for being weird. It must be strange. Two houses. I can't imagine."

"We didn't come here much, after a while," he said, his throat thick. He inhaled. "It's not strange."

"My family lived in a trailer," she said, laughing. "A house with stairs is strange to me."

"People are happy here," he said.

"I think it's spooky," she said. "All these white people in one place."

"That's true," he agreed with a sense of rising awkwardness, a desire to deflect, to defend, to obfuscate.

"Are you happy here?" she asked.

He wondered if he was. Happiness. What was happiness? He looked out ahead of them at their friends. Climbing over the large roots. Pushing one another, pulling one another, falling apart, coming together, kissing, hugging, laughing. The low sky, beautiful and heavy and gray. The trees. The rich, dark colors of the woods. The smell of the lake. Of people's homes. The wet earth. What was happiness if not this moment, if not then, right then, the group of them, together for maybe the last time, coming together for this moment, for this very instant, what were they if not happy? Noah climbed onto Stafford's back and squeezed his knees and said *Go, go*. Their damp jackets, spotted with rain, the wind kicking up. Fatima pulled her hood. Above them the sky opened, and the water came, gray and fast, filling the whole world until the rain touched everything and everything touched the rain.

Daw could feel them inside of him then. He could feel each of them in him, their happiness, their kindness, their love. Before they began to run back to the house, up the slippery, muddy slope, he turned to Fatima. ✦

Acknowledgments

This novel was possible only because I had the support, patience, and tremendous brilliance of trusted friends, readers, and collaborators. They believed in this project and these characters even when I was lost in the wilds of doubt and fear. Thank you for all the conversations, the pep talks, the long walks, the museum strolls, the laughter, and, most important, for your belief.

In no particular order, my thanks to: Meredith Kaffel Simonoff, Dana Bryan, Nora Gonzalez, Calvert Morgan, Catalina Trigo, Claire McGinnis, Jynne Dilling Martin, Hal Fessenden, Derrick Austin, Natasha Oladokun, The Slacc, Adam Dalva, C Pam Zhang, Jeremy O. Harris, and a special thanks to Lee Pace for a life-altering conversation that saved this book.

WINNER OF THE STORY PRIZE

An astute chronicler of our times

In each of his award-winning books, Brandon Taylor shows he is "an extraordinary cartographer" (*Esquire*) of contemporary life. In prose that's elegant, involving, and at times hilarious, he explores the lives of his all-too-human characters with care and insight, peeling away their fondest hopes and deepest fears, their hidden desires and their unspoken pain. The results are books that probe our humanity as they show us who we really are.

"A powerhouse." —***Newsweek***

"A brilliant writer." —**Garth Greenwell**

"One of the most exciting young writers working today." —***GQ***

© Haolun Xu

A hotly charged, deeply satisfying work that mines the depths of desire, violence, and human connection— from the Booker Prize–shortlisted author of *Real Life*

Psychologically taut and quietly devastating, Brandon Taylor's *Filthy Animals* paints a tender portrait of the fierce longing for intimacy, the lingering presence of pain, and the desire for love in a world that often seems bent on withholding it. Whether scrambling through the woods at night, stretching their bodies in the clean, mirrored light of a ballet studio, or waiting in the warm hum of a car ride back home, Taylor's characters navigate relationships jagged and treacherous in their search for moments of understanding.

"Sumptuous, melancholic portraits of characters overwhelmed . . . Taylor has a talent for taking the dull hum of quotidian life and converting it into lyrics. . . . A perfect companion piece for our nervous era."
—**John Paul Brammer, *The New York Times Book Review***

"If Brandon Taylor isn't on your radar, change that immediately. The Booker-nominated novelist is one of the most exciting young writers working today." —*GQ*

"A brilliantly inventive storyteller, and one whose beautifully drawn characters have that rare ability to really make you care." —*Vogue*

A Finalist for: The Booker Prize • The National Book Critics Circle
John Leonard Prize • The VCU Cabell First Novelist Prize •
The Lambda Literary Award • The NYPL Young Lions Award •
The Edmund White Debut Fiction Award

A Best Book of the Year: *The New York Times* • *The Washington Post* •
New York Public Library • *Vanity Fair* • *Elle* • NPR • *The Guardian* •
BBC • *The Paris Review* • *Harper's Bazaar* • *Financial Times* • *HuffPost* •
Shondaland • Barnes & Noble • *Vulture* • *Thrillist* • *Vice* • *Self*

A work of startling intimacy, violence, and mercy that introduced readers to the voice of Brandon Taylor, "one of our finest chroniclers of intimacy and loneliness" (*Esquire*)

In this widely acclaimed novel, Brandon Taylor peels back the layers of hostility, desire, and pain in a young man's life, asking if it's ever really possible to overcome our private wounds, and at what cost. An introverted young man from Alabama, black and queer, Wallace navigates a series of messy social interactions over the course of a late-summer weekend, fracturing his defenses while raising difficult questions about the constricting roles we play, our deepest understandings of hurt, and what comes after.

"A keen observer of the psychology of not just trauma, but its repercussions."
                                            —Jeremy O. Harris, *The New York Times Book Review*

"Equal parts captivating, erotic, smart, and vivid . . . [rendered] with tenderness and complexity, from the first gorgeous sentence of his book to its very last."   **—*Time***

"Brandon Taylor emerges as a powerhouse."   **—*Newsweek***